DIAMOND BOY

Also by Michael Williams,
and published by Tamarind Books

Now Is the Time for Running

DIAMOND BOY

MICHAEL WILLIAMS

Tamarind

DIAMOND BOY
A TAMARIND BOOK 978 1 848 53143 7

First published in the USA in 2014 by Little, Brown and Company
Part of the Hachette Book Group

First published in Great Britain by Tamarind Books,
an imprint of Random House Children's Publishers UK
A Penguin Random House Company

Penguin
Random House
UK

This edition published 2015

1 3 5 7 9 10 8 6 4 2

Copyright © Michael Williams, 2014
Map illustration by Edel Rodriguez
Cover design by Janene Spencer
Silhouetted images on cover © Shutterstock

The right of Michael Williams to be identified as the author of this work has been asserted
in accordance with the Copyright, Designs and Patents Act 1988.

Penguin Random House is committed to a sustainable future for our business, our readers
and our planet. This book is made from Forest Stewardship Council® certified paper.

MIX
Paper from
responsible sources
FSC® C016897

Tamarind Books are published by Random House Children's Publishers UK,
61–63 Uxbridge Road, London W5 5SA

www.**tamarindbooks**.co.uk
www.**totallyrandombooks**.co.uk
www.**randomhouse**.co.uk

Addresses for companies within The Random House Group Limited can be found at:
www.randomhouse.co.uk/offices.htm

THE RANDOM HOUSE GROUP Limited Reg. No. 954009

A CIP catalogue record for this book is available from the British Library.

Printed and bound in Great Britain by CPI Group (UK), Croydon, CR0 4YY

For Amy Kaplan, *lector benevole*,
and our thirty-year-old friendship

MARANGE DIAMOND FIELDS

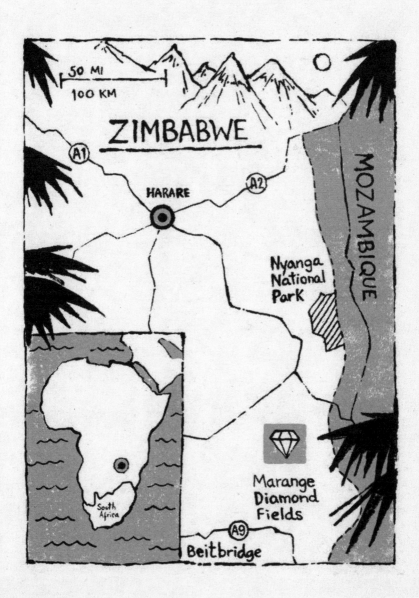

How did you get here, Patson?

Sometimes the simple questions are the hardest to answer.

My tongue lay like a chisel in my mouth; my eyes leaden. I was swimming from a place of no feeling, moving steadily upward into a world of sensation to the dark, throbbing pain that lived in my leg. My old companion had not left me in this new place, waiting for me as I drifted to the surface, sharpening its teeth.

"Patson, how did you get here?"

Could it be the voice of my *baba*? I still feel his hand resting on my arm; hear his answer to a question, always far longer than it needed to be. Arguing with my father was futile. He would talk until your head spun with new ideas. Then, just when you were exhausted from the journey of his words, the answer you needed would surface, like a small cut diamond, sparkling with clarity.

The room had too many shades of white. The bed too high off the floor, the sheets starch-stiff, and the pillows too big. But I was grateful for everything, grateful to be alive. I rested my head against the oversized pillow and turned to the window. The enormous flat-topped mountain loomed over the city. A huge cloud rode the faraway cliffs, racing down the gray rock face as if being chased, whipped and driven by an invisible force.

"Where's Jesus?" I mumbled. "Is he here? And Grace? I must look to Grace." I struggled to rise but I was too weak. My head was far heavier than I remembered. My body pressed down into the bed.

"You're safe, Patson."

Can't it be any easier, Baba? Isn't there a shortcut I can take?

You have to tell everything, son. You have to tell it all. The story you tell makes you who you are.

"Shhh. Rest now. We'll speak again later."

Yes, rest now, son. That's the most sensible thing to do in these circumstances. The body needs time to recover. You will be strong again, but first you must rest.

You're right, Baba. You were always right.

◆◆◆

JOURNEY

1

"Wake up, Patson," Grace whispered into my ear. "The diamond fields are close now. Just over that elephant-head mountain." My eyelids were gently prised open, and my sister's face came into focus. For a brief moment, I saw hints of my mother in her eyes. But then it was all Grace, poking my cheek with her finger, her breath warm and soft on my skin. "You've been sleeping too long, big brother."

My disorientation ended when my head bumped painfully against the window as the driver swerved to avoid one pothole only to hit another. Here in Zimbabwe everyone says that if a man drives a straight line down a road, he must be drunk. Outside, the sun rested above the thorn trees and the air filled with amber dust. I must have been asleep for a couple of hours. I remembered closing my eyes and wishing we had never left home, angry with my father for having no money, hating the Wife for the power she had over him. Even my perky sister's positive nature had irritated me. We had been driving for fourteen hours across the dry plains of Matabeleland, over the Runde and Munyati rivers and through the hills of Masvingo Province, and I longed to get out of this cramped car and go for a heart-pumping run.

My father says that a journey should always change your life in some way. Well, when you have nothing, I suppose a journey promises everything. As long as we arrived at a place better than the one we had left, I would be happy. I had known for some time that my family was heading downhill and something had to change. I could see it in the drawn, worried face of my father as yet another day passed and there was no food in the house. I could hear it in the shrill, hysterical voice of the Wife, who ranted and wept as she hid from the neighbors out of shame. And I could feel it when I hugged my little sister, with her bones now so fragile in my embrace. I knew we were poor but what I couldn't understand was why, after every month that passed, our situation only got worse.

My father leaned over from the front seat and handed me a water bottle. "Grace is right, son. We're almost at Marange."

Before I had a chance to drink, though, the Wife snatched the bottle away. "I'm thirsty," she said. "Joseph, ask the driver how much longer before we get there. My legs are stiff and my back is in a knot. I want to pee. Tell the driver to stop. Tell him to stop right now."

"Yes, Sylvia, but I don't think—"

"I mean it, Joseph. Tell him to stop now."

The driver looked at my father's wife in the rearview mirror and shook his head. "We can't stop here. In another thirty minutes we stop."

"You stop now. Or I mess in your car."

The driver was no match for the Wife. He was about to protest, but my father turned to him and shrugged his shoulders. The driver understood.

"Two minutes. Okay? Just two minutes. It's dangerous here," he warned, checking the road behind him before pulling off the highway. "The police check every car that stops on the side of the road."

The Wife insisted he open the trunk of the car.

"Joseph, I asked you to pack toilet paper," she berated my father, her hands on her hips. "Did you pack it? I should have done the packing myself. I can't trust you to do anything. This bag is a mess."

Because you're not looking, I wanted to say, and you do nothing but complain. Instead, I got out of the car and left them to fuss over the Wife and her toilet.

"I'll help you, Amai. I know where it is."

As always, Grace came to the rescue. My sister seemed to have a built-in early-warning system when it came to the Wife's moods. She would appear, sometimes magically, when the Wife was about to lose her temper, to smooth out an awkward moment or distract her from turning on my father. Somehow

Grace was always able to restore the peace. As she did now by pulling out a small bag from the back of the car, quickly finding the toilet paper, handing it to the Wife with a smile. The driver, meanwhile, swore under his breath, anxiously glancing up and down the road, while my father fussed and fretted, doing the Sylvia-dance to keep his wife happy.

Grace's elephant-head mountain was really only a mass of boulders that rose above the distant flat-topped fever trees and towered over the surrounding smaller hills. I imagined myself running to the top to look out over the bush, east to Mozambique, at South Africa to the south, and back toward Bulawayo in the west. Inviting wisps of cool clouds hung below its highest point.

Something moved in the grass on the other side of the road. At first I thought it might be shy impala darting through the bush, but three boys cautiously emerged. They stared straight through me. Had they been there the whole time, watching? Perhaps it was the trick of the fading light, but their legs and arms, and even their faces, appeared to be dusted a light gray. We stared silently at each other, the tarred ribbon of the road between us. Then one of the boys lifted both his hands and slowly moved them together until his index fingers and thumbs met to form a diamond shape in front of his face.

Was he signaling me? I could not read his expression framed by the tight space between his fingers. Did he want me to do something? I shrugged and lifted my arms, not knowing what to say. He nodded abruptly at the space he had shaped with his fingers. Then the boy to his right pulled something out of his pocket. He was offering it to me, as he gently tapped his outstretched palm with two fingers of his other hand. The third boy stepped back a little, glancing furtively around. His eyes seemed to be pleading, as if I was his last hope.

"Where did those boys come from, Patson?" Grace was at my side, her hand slipped into mine.

"I don't know."

"Why are they so gray?"

"I've got no idea." I stepped forward to speak to them.

"No! Get back in the car. Now!" The driver grabbed my arm, pushed me back to the car, shoved me into the backseat, and slammed the door. He scooted Grace back to her seat and shouted at the boys across the road, but they had gone, disappearing into the tall yellow grass.

"Who are they?" I asked as the driver started the car and pulled away in a cloud of dust, gunning down the highway.

"They are *mailashas*—smugglers—signing their death warrants by sticking their necks out like that. They'll be dead in a week. This road is littered with their bones." He drove fast, straight over the potholes, fleeing this place of gray ghost-boys.

"What did they want from me?"

"Money. Money for diamonds." He lifted his hands from the wheel to make the diamond shape with his thumbs and index fingers pressed together. "Now is the safest time of day for them to sell their stones, when army patrols are blinded by the setting sun."

"But they were just boys," said my father.

The driver nodded. "*Gwejana*. Children diamond miners trying to sell their stones. They are gambling with their lives by becoming thieves and smugglers."

"I didn't see anything. Why doesn't anyone ever tell me what's going on?" complained Sylvia. "What are you talking about?"

I opened the window and the Wife's words were lost as I leaned out to study the bush flitting past. The orange glow in the sky sank slowly behind the distant hills but I could no longer see the boys. The driver was talking quickly, strangling the steering wheel.

"The closer we get to the mining fields, the purer the stones become and the more we are in danger," he said. "Those *mailashas* take the diamonds they find and try to sell them outside of their syndicate. They think they can fool the members and take the money for themselves. But there are spies everywhere and if those boys are reported to the syndicate bosses or the police catch them selling diamonds...well, let's just say that I've heard some terrible things."

"My brother, James, says there are diamonds for everyone," said the Wife. "And he runs the best mine in Marange, so he should know. I'm sure you are exaggerating."

"James Banda hates *mailashas*," muttered the driver, glaring at me in his rearview mirror. "You don't talk to these boys. Ever. You understand?"

2

Diamonds for everyone. Those were the exact words that had drip-dripped like a leaking tap into my father's ear at breakfast, after school, even late at night when the lights were out and I could hear the Wife's needling voice through the thin walls: "Why must I suffer here with a man who cannot provide for his family? Should I be poor the rest of my life? I could have had any man in my village and all I got was you. A poor, useless teacher. There is money to be made in Marange, Joseph. People all over the country are traveling to the diamond fields to make their fortunes. And we sit here with no money, no food, and no proper job. James says that in Marange there are diamonds for everyone."

I had never met Uncle James, but I knew I wouldn't like him. He was the one who told the Wife, "There is money to be made in Marange and all you have to do is pick it up off the ground. You don't need to stay a poor teacher's wife. If your husband were more of a man, he could become a rich Marange diamond miner."

My father did have a proper job. He was one of the best teachers in Bulawayo and had won the Outstanding Teacher Award at Milton High School for four years running. The Wife claimed it was not a real job because he made no money. That wasn't true either. He did make money. Suitcases full. Millions and millions of Zimbabwean dollars.

It was not his fault that the money was worthless.

I remembered him coming back from the government office, after being promised three months' back pay, and placing a large suitcase on the kitchen table. He opened the case and we all stared at the thick elastic-wrapped bricks of Zim dollars stacked in neat rows.

The Wife glared at the contents of the suitcase. "And what are we supposed to do with all this money? Eat it? Do you want me to make soup from this? What do you think this will buy us, Joseph? Nothing. Do you hear me? Nothing," she shouted, digging her hands into the suitcase and throwing the stacks of money at my father. "This is not worth more than two American dollars. Three months of back pay and they give you this? And you are mad enough to gratefully accept it?"

My father just sat at the table, cleaning his glasses, as Grace built a small house with the bricks of cash. The Wife ranted on about how ashamed she was to beg for food from the neighbors, how she hated wearing two-year-old clothes, how there was hardly enough money for even her cell phone. "I thought that when I married a teacher I would be someone important, but every year we become poorer and poorer and people stare at me and feel sorry for me. I would have done better marrying a beggar." Then, looking at Grace, she added, "That's all your back-pay money is good for, Joseph Moyo—child's play."

"There will come a day when our economy will recover," my father replied. "When Mugabe dies, things will be better. We just have to be patient."

"Patients in a madhouse, you mean," retorted the Wife. "And how are things going to get better when the old man dies? You're still going to be a teacher earning no money, and I'm going to be laughed at as the-girl-who-married-a-poor-simple-teacher."

My father always met every problem with thoughtful composure. He lived in a world of books, and was at peace with the life he had chosen. This inward contentment often infuriated the Wife, who, if she wasn't afraid of the power of his beloved books, would have thrown every single one of them at him. I watched how he gracefully bore his young wife's taunting, and how he smiled at his friends who teased him about who wore the pants in his house. And he never, not once in the three years they were married, ever said anything bad about the Wife to Grace or me. But there was one subject that even his pretty wife knew was sacred, and that was his occupation as a teacher.

"Teaching is not a job, son," he said to me once. "It is a calling. When you are born with a gift, God instructs you to use it carefully. You have been given a gift, too, Patson, and you may not allow it to lie fallow. Even though you don't know what your gift is yet, when you find it, you must nurture it, let it grow inside you, and let it become your life's work."

Sometimes my father sounded like he was reading from the Bible, like it was his way of tuning out his worries and the Wife. He said he loved her but surely no ordinary man could bear the tongue-lashings he endured.

So, without telling any of us, he phoned the inspector of education in the Chiadzwa district outside Marange, and offered his services as a teacher of mathematics and English. Two days later he proudly announced that he had received a fax from Mr. Ngoko, the headmaster of Marange's rural Junction Gate High School, and that there was an opening. And best of all, that he should come at the beginning of the next term.

"And did he say how many trillions of Zim dollars they would pay you at this Junction Gate High School?" the Wife asked scornfully.

"We will sort that out when we get there," my father replied, and quietly retreated to the sanctuary of his desk.

"You might have plenty of brains, Joseph, but you've got no sense," she called after him, and rolled her eyes at us. "You see what I have to deal with?"

I hated the way she turned us into her accomplices. We were expected to agree with her and sometimes it was hard not to. I wished my father would do something to make me proud of him. He might be a good teacher but it counted for nothing in Zimbabwe. If only he would stand up against the Wife and tell her not to shout at him. He always told me not to raise my voice, but rather improve my argument, but the problem was that as much as I was loath to admit it, there was a part of me that agreed with the Wife. My father could be very impractical. Junction Gate High School? What kind of name was that for a school?

"We are going to Marange. You got what you wanted," said my father, opening a book and closing the conversation with the Wife, who merely glared at him and stormed out of the house, slamming the front door.

"Shall I ask her if she wants some tea?" Grace said in the silence that followed the Wife's departure.

"That's a good idea, Grace," said my father, cupping her cheek. "I'm sure she'd appreciate that."

Grace and I exchanged glances as she left: Even when the Wife got her way she still wasn't happy.

"But can there really be enough for everyone?" I asked once I was alone with my father. He looked up from his book, puzzled. "People are going to Marange for the diamonds, Baba. At school, everyone knows someone who has packed up and left for the diamond fields. I read in the paper how the government is inviting people to come. How can there be enough for everyone? It just doesn't seem possible."

Though my father was a slight man with the hands of a piano player, his long straight neck gave the impression of him being taller than he really was. This was useful in the classroom, where he towered over his pupils, particularly those who, in the way of students, thought they could get the better of him. He was the owner of a formidable voice, capable of every nuance required from a teacher. He could bellow instructions across a soccer pitch, but also gently console a disheartened eighth grader.

"Patson, we are not going for the diamonds, son. We are going to start a new life. We are going to be part of Sylvia's family."

"So we're leaving because *she* doesn't like our family here in Bulawayo? Why do we have to listen to that—"

"Patson, I won't have you speaking badly of Sylvia. Remember, you must always keep your words soft and sweet..."

"Just in case you have to eat them," I said, finishing the old Shona proverb he was fond of quoting. "I know, Baba, but sometimes, well, she irritates me," I said, and immediately regretted how petulant I sounded.

"When your mother died, Patson, I knew I had to find another wife. I had hoped that you would like Sylvia, that she would be a friend to you and a good mother to Grace. But what you have to understand is when you marry your partner, you are also marrying a whole new family. We have to think of the Bandas as our new family, Patson. They will look after us and help us to settle into our new lives in Marange. You will meet your cousin Jamu. He's your own age, and you'll probably be classmates at school. And despite what Sylvia says, I'm not going to Marange to become a diamond miner. I am a teacher. I will always be a teacher, only now at a different school. The change will be good for us all."

I hated the faraway look in my father's eyes when he struggled to explain why we were so poor. This was not the future he had planned for himself when he was a young graduate fresh out of the University of Zimbabwe at Harare, and he was puzzled at how the mundane practicalities of food, money, and rent seemed so unattainable. It was one of those rare moments when my father gave me his complete attention. It was also the perfect opportunity to ask him why, of all the women he could have chosen, why he chose her. Did he truly love her? Didn't he see how she made him less of a man than what I knew him to be? But I let the moment pass.

For a while, there was peace in the house as we packed up our things, selling what would not fit in the trunk of the car Uncle James organized for us. Then, at the end of the term, we said our good-byes to our neighbors, and drove east for fourteen hours toward our new lives.

We sped past a donkey-cart clattering along the side of the road, a sign that read MARANGE 20 KILOMETRES, a burned-out shop advertising Coca-Cola, and an old woman selling pecan nuts from under a grass hut. On the road ahead, soldiers in olive-green fatigues jogged in formation, bearing down on us until the driver had no choice but to pull off the road to avoid plowing through them. They were singing a Chimurenga war song and the beating rhythm from the throats and feet of fifty men filled our car—until it faded away when we returned to the road heading toward the hump I had named Elephant Skull.

I reached for my mobile. There were two messages from Sheena:

> How far are u? ☺ Running this afternoon. Wish u were here. ☹☹ I hate to do Uggy's Hill alone.

And:

> Back from my run. What's up?? How many bars u got!? Wanna Mxit!!

I was disappointed, and a bit relieved that she didn't mention what had happened between us in her bedroom a few days before I left Bulawayo. If she wasn't going to talk about it, then neither would I. I had kissed my best friend, and although a part of me wished I hadn't, another part wanted to kiss her again. I had known Sheena since primary school, and she was my running partner on the Milton High cross-country team. After we kissed, though, it suddenly felt as if we were strangers, embarrassed to be alone with each other. I knew if we could go for a good, long run up Uggy's Hill, we would sort out the huge question mark that hung between us. During the last few days of term Sheena and I had circled each other, making sure that we were never alone and always in the comfort of a crowd. And then term ended and I left without really sorting anything out. My thumbs flew over the keypad but the reception was patchy and the message didn't go through. I groaned. If connectivity in Marange was bad, I would be stranded in off-line oblivion. Sheena would not be happy; she had to know everything.

Around the next bend the driver swore at the sight of a police checkpoint in the middle of the highway.

"Nobody say anything." He slowed down as a policeman stepped out onto the road and stopped us.

"I have my letter of appointment," my father reassured the driver, reaching inside his jacket pocket.

"What use will that be? Let him do the talking, Joseph," the Wife snapped. "He knows what he's doing. Remember what my brother said about the security around Marange? We will be fine if we do what the driver says."

The Wife took out a mirror from her handbag and refreshed her hibiscus-red lipstick. She grinned at herself, dabbed a tissue in the corner of her mouth, and polished her teeth with her finger. The policeman peered into the car, taking in my father in the front seat, Grace sitting in the middle of the backseat, me, and the Wife, who straightened her back, fluttered her eyelashes, and gave him her most radiant smile. The policeman stared longer than needed at the curvy outline of the Wife's breasts, before turning away.

Our driver spoke politely; the policeman officially. My father started cleaning his glasses with his handkerchief—a sure sign that he was worried. The policeman ordered the driver to open the trunk. He turned off the engine and together they walked around to the back of the car.

On the other side of the road, policemen were searching

three women whose arms were lifted above their heads while the men ran their hands over their breasts, down their backs, and between their legs. One of the women caught me staring as an officer half her age snapped her bra strap and made a crude joke about where else she might be hiding her jewels. I quickly looked away, embarrassed by her humiliation. All around the checkpoint were the stains of police at work: cigarette butts, empty whisky bottles, bullet casings, and the scorched earth from cooking fires.

The trunk was slammed shut. The policeman walked slowly around the car, to peer one more time at the Wife's breasts.

Then he turned to the driver. "Kill yourself," he said, "before I kill you."

The driver nodded up and down. "Okay, okay. No problem," he said, climbing back into the car. "This is not good, not good at all. We must pay him."

"He's going to kill us?" I asked my father, bewildered at how calmly he had reacted to the policeman's statement.

"It's a code, Patson," he reassured me. "He wants to be bribed but cannot say it out loud. Instead he is asking the driver to make him an offer to let us continue to Marange."

My father's dollars quickly went from his hand to the driver's and disappeared into the policeman's pocket.

Once again we were speeding down the highway. "The police have begun Operation End to Illegal Panning," the driver explained. "There are too many people going to Marange to look for diamonds. They are trying to stop them from coming to this area. We were lucky to find one who could be bribed." He angrily punched a number into his phone, and then spoke so rapidly I couldn't understand anything of what he said.

"This is not good," he muttered again, stuffing the phone into his shirt pocket. "You will have to walk. I can't take you all the way. It's too dangerous."

Suddenly we were off the highway, bumping and jostling along a dirt track heading deep into the bush. The Wife shouted at him to slow down, while my father attempted to find out what the policeman had told him and who he had phoned. Grace squeezed my hand tightly.

"I think there's a problem, and no one wants to talk about it," she said.

"We'll be okay, Grace," I whispered. "I'm sure we're almost there."

Twenty minutes later we stopped beneath an enormous baobab tree, its rootlike branches reaching toward the sky. When I was a child my father told me a story about Father Baobab, the Goddess Mai, and how the moon found its way into the sky, but I couldn't remember the details. Under the enormous baobab's outstretched limbs a group of men sat on their haunches upon mats laid out on the ground.

"Who are those people?" asked my father.

"They are diamond dealers. This is the Baobab Diamond Exchange," the driver replied, stopping the car and shouting a greeting to the men through his open window. Two of the dealers hurriedly rolled up their mats and trotted off into the forest. "Diamond dealers are always nervous of strangers. Wait here." He got out of the car and walked quickly over to the rest of them, talking rapidly and pointing back to us. Whatever he said had no effect, as all but one of them rolled up their mats and disappeared into the forest.

"Joseph, do something," demanded the Wife as she got out of the car.

"The driver knows what he is doing," my father soothed.

"Don't just sit there!"

By now the driver had returned, opened the trunk, and was dumping our bags onto the ground.

"Now, wait just a moment." My father got out of the car and watched helplessly as the driver emptied the trunk.

"The highway is too dangerous. There are too many road-blocks. It's safer for you to go through the bush."

"You can't just leave us here! We're in the middle of nowhere! James paid you to take us to Marange. I'm going to phone him immediately—"

"That man knows the way," the driver interrupted the Wife. "You can trust him." He slammed the trunk shut.

"Now, listen to me," said my father firmly, as if addressing a naughty schoolboy who was paying him no attention at all. "The arrangement was that you would take us all the way to Marange."

The driver shook his head and opened my door. "Out, out! Quickly," he instructed Grace and me. We tumbled out as my father continued upbraiding the driver, who got back into the car and slammed his door.

"It is not far from here." The driver cut off my father's protests. "You'll go east, toward that mountain, and the diamond fields are just on the other side. Maybe half an hour's walk. You will be there well before dark."

The engine roared to life and he drove away, leaving us in a cloud of dust.

"Joseph, how could you let him drive away? What sort of man are you? There's no reception out here. I can't get hold of James. What are we going to do with all these bags? You are useless! A useless man!" shouted the Wife, her voice becoming harsher at each unanswered question.

My father arranged the pile of luggage in neat rows, dismissing her words as if they were no more than flies buzzing around his head. Grace looked up at me and sighed. We both knew that there were too many bags for us to carry any distance at all.

"Walking won't be so bad," said Grace. "We've been in the car for hours. I think we should go and ask that man to help us."

Grace held out her hand to me, and together we walked over to the man standing at the foot of a massive baobab tree. As the dust settled, the orange glow slipped behind the faraway hills, leaving us with maybe two hours before dark. The baobab towered over the forest, its limbs glowing in the dying light of day, and the man watched our approach with as much interest as a buffalo showed a pair of tiny ox-peckers.

"He looks a bit scary."

"Keep smiling, Grace, and let me do the talking."

The man was tall, with broad shoulders and muscular arms. His head was bald and he had black eyes, a little hooded. His face seemed chiseled out of hardwood by someone with little talent, and his nose was bent completely out of shape. He wore a sleeveless maroon T-shirt and a white tie around his neck, neatly knotted and patterned with squiggly black lines. He was chewing slowly. The corners of his mouth were stained with the telltale flecks of red beetle-nut juice. He spat out a long stream of bloodred saliva and put another nut into his mouth. The closer we got to him, the smaller and more insignificant I felt. He was the ugliest man I had ever seen.

"I'm smiling, Patson, but it doesn't seem to be helping," Grace whispered, gripping my hand tightly.

In the face of his blank, hooded eyes, I tried to make my voice as strong as possible. "My name is Patson Moyo. We need to go to Marange."

The man considered me silently, his bloodshot eyes never leaving my own. Both of his cheeks carried scars, ridged and glossy, like two frozen tear lines. I had heard of the initiation rites where the cheeks of fourteen-year-old boys were branded with a heated needle after they'd proven themselves as warriors. He dismissed me and shifted his gaze to Grace.

"Please could you show us the way?" Her voice trembled.

My father joined us; the Wife followed, still swearing loudly.

"Why you want to visit the eye?" the man asked my father, in a deep, foreign-sounding voice, looking down at us as if we were prey not worth eating.

"I'm Joseph Moyo." My father offered his hand. "My family needs to get to Marange before dark."

The man spat another stream of red saliva at my father's feet and ignored his outstretched hand. "I can't help you. If you love your family, Joseph Moyo, follow that track to the highway and go back to where you came from. The eye is not for you. Once you go in, you will never come out," he said, and walked away.

My father did nothing to stop him. I knew that if this man left us, we would be alone in the bush and would have to walk back to the main road. I had noticed that he had glanced curiously at Grace, and I was sure I had seen a spark of compassion.

"James Banda will pay you lots of money if you take us to him," I said.

The man stopped at my words. He turned around and his black eyes bored through me. "James Banda? You know Banda?"

"James Banda is my brother," said the Wife, producing her most luscious smile. "The boy is right, my brother will pay you."

He glanced at the Wife, at our pile of luggage, and then back at Grace and me. I could see his brain ticking over, weighing up his options. If he left us and we managed to get to Marange and told James Banda that he had abandoned us in the bush, it could be very bad for him.

"Take only what you can carry," he said finally, clearly irritated with the decision he had made. "Hurry. You have a long walk ahead of you."

The Wife protested immediately, but for once in his life my father spoke firmly to her. "We have no choice, Sylvia. Do as he says."

Quickly we sorted through our luggage, repacking it into the smaller bags. The Wife fussed about what shoes she should take, while my father sorted through his books and teaching materials. Grace selected one of her soft toys and packed the others away. "I will come pick you up soon," I overheard her whispering to those she was leaving behind.

I surveyed all that I owned dispassionately. Spread out on the ground against the vastness of the bush, my belongings seemed insignificant: jeans, T-shirts, a couple of underpants, and socks. The first things that went into my backpack were my pens, my phone, my diary, and my best pair of running shoes.

Finally, we were ready. The Wife and my father had stopped their arguing. He would carry one of her suitcases. The other three, mostly packed with her clothes, were tossed into a hollow space inside the baobab tree.

"Tomorrow, when you have a car, well, I cannot say, but they might still be there," said the man, shrugging, and speaking in a lyrical way, which I ultimately recognized as a French accent. "Now we start to walk."

"What is your name?" asked Grace.

"Boubacar," he answered.

"And how far is it to Marange?" asked the Wife.

"There's no need to worry about that," said Boubacar. "If we are caught, they will shoot us and bury us until the wild animals carry our bones elsewhere. If you want to worry, worry about getting to Marange alive."

3

We walked through the forest for what seemed the longest hour of my life. At every rustle in the grass we fell to the ground, waiting until Boubacar gave us the all clear. The bags I carried grew heavier and heavier and blisters bubbled up on my palms. My feet ached but I walked on, never losing sight of Boubacar's broad back. All around us the bush noisily prepared for night: The barking and scuffling of a troop of baboons heading for high ground, the mournful caw of the night crows nesting in the trees, and the scratching and burrowing of smaller animals reminded us that we were not alone. The sun had disappeared behind the hills; baobab trees towered over the forest like giant watchmen. Night was only moments away.

Before each clearing, Boubacar stopped until he was sure there was no danger and then signaled us forward. His cautious progress from one clearing to the next and his watchful silence had infected us all. Darkness spread over us from the horizon, all shadows faded away, and above us stars began to pinprick their way into a dusky, ink-smudged sky. I was surprised to see the Wife struggling with her luggage without complaining. My father quietly urged Grace on with promises of chocolate and rest, and although he smiled at me, I saw the worry in his eyes. Elephant Skull was no nearer. The driver had lied to us. It seemed a lifetime ago that I had wanted more than anything to get out of the car to stretch my legs, but now I longed for its safety and comfort. Once again Boubacar raised his hand and we dropped to the ground, crouching next to our luggage.

"What are you watching for?" I asked, crawling up as close to him as I dared. "If you tell me, I can help you."

"Policemen. Soldiers. *Mailashas*," he whispered, scanning the clearing for any movement. "They will call the syndicate guards and you will stand no chance. Now stop talking and tell your mother—"

"She's not my mother."

"Tell her she must leave those bags behind," he continued. "She is slowing us down. We still have a long way to go."

"When will we get there?"

"Five, maybe six hours' time."

I glanced back at my family. My father was pulling Grace to her feet. He had tied her bag to his own and was dragging them along the ground behind him. The Wife rose slowly, sweat trickling down her face.

"They can't walk for another six hours," I whispered.

"You would rather sleep out here in the wild?"

There was no further discussion and we trudged on. I glanced up at the sky: The Milky Way arched across a canopy of millions of glittering stars, brighter than anything I had ever seen in the city. As beautiful as it was, the night must have been full of terrors for Grace. I offered to give her a ride, and slung my backpack around to rest on my chest.

"I'm fine, Patson," she said, but I knew she was only trying to be brave.

"But I'm not. I need you to hug me tight," I answered, insisting she climb up onto my back. Grace was the one person with whom I could truly be myself. I never had to worry what she thought about me; I never had to explain myself to her. I was her Big Brother with capital letters and that was all that mattered to her. I didn't tell her everything, not anymore, but I told her a lot of stuff that I wouldn't tell my father or even some of my friends at school. I liked the way she listened to me, with seriousness and complete attention, as if for that moment, I was the only person in the world talking to her. It was a habit she had inherited from my mother, and I loved her for it.

Grace clambered onto my back and wrapped her arms tightly around my neck. "I'm scared of the bats, Patson," she whispered into my ear. "One almost flew into my face. And Boubacar scares me too."

"How old are you, Gracie?"

"You know how old I am."

"I forgot. You're seven or eight years old, right?"

"No, I'm not! I'm ten."

"Ten?"

"Well, almost ten."

"Then you must know that bats are the butterflies of the night. They sleep during the day and can't wait to stretch their wings at nighttime. Imagine sleeping through the whole day and only waking up when the sun goes down. You'd be hungry and stiff when you woke up. That's why they zip through the air once the sun sets, eating mosquitoes and playing with one another. They can't do anything to you. And as for Boubacar, he just looks scary."

"He speaks funny."

"That's because he speaks French. He'll look after us. He knows where he is going."

In the distance the violent crack of a rifle shot frightened a flock of herons from a nearby tree. They launched themselves from their sleeping perches, exploding in a shower of white feathers.

We fell to the ground.

"We must move," urged Boubacar. "Come on. Get up."

The terrain was uneven and difficult to negotiate in the dark. I stumbled forward with Grace on my back. Another round of gunfire crackled through the night. Grace's grip tightened around my neck but I ran on. Glancing over my shoulder, I saw lights from a vehicle, scudding through the bushes, closing in on us. Loud voices headed in our direction. Then someone broke cover from my right and ran across my path, followed by two more people, their frightened faces lit by the headlights.

"We must run now. Leave your bags. Leave everything," ordered Boubacar as he swept Grace off my back and started running with her in his arms. My father clung to his briefcase and, grabbing the Wife's hand, pulled her along behind him. But she would not leave her suitcase, so he gathered it up, and pushed her forward in front of him. I dropped the suitcase I was carrying, swung my backpack higher onto my shoulders, and followed Boubacar. My stomach knotted in fear of what might happen to us, and somehow a new power surged in my legs.

Gunshots boomed across the bush as the lights from the vehicle grew brighter.

The wail of a baby hurriedly silenced; a scream of a woman in pain.

All around us people were running, darting from tree to tree. For hours we hadn't seen anyone. Now, suddenly, flushed out by guns and beams of light, people were running with us. Where had they come from? Boubacar must have known that there were others heading for Marange. He must have seen them, yet made sure we avoided them. Our cautious progress had become a noisy, full-on flight with vehicles pounding through the bush behind us.

Keeping up with Boubacar was hard but I had to stay close to my sister. I would not lose her to this chaos of the night. With no warning, Boubacar herded me into an outcrop of rocks, and my sister scrambled out of his arms and into mine.

Tears streamed from her eyes and I held her hard against me, trying to still her trembling. "It will be okay. Shhh, don't cry."

More gunshots, more frightened voices.

"Over here!" Boubacar beckoned to my father and the Wife, sprinting toward us. My father's face was gleaming with sweat. I had never heard him breathing so hard, yet he clung to his briefcase, then dropped it to sweep Grace into his arms and lay with her flat on the ground.

"Under the rocks. Keep your heads down," ordered Boubacar as we scrambled into the shelter of the rocks as best as we could.

Boubacar quickly disappeared among the rocks above us. My father squeezed Grace into an even smaller space hidden by grass and wedged his briefcase in front of her as if it were a magical protective barrier. The Wife whimpered as male voices barked orders and came closer. Two vehicles converged near our hiding place and a second pair of lights swept past us. Without warning, three soldiers ambled from the cover of the bush, their automatic rifles held loosely in front of them. A black-booted, gun-metal presence filled the clearing not more than ten meters away. One of the soldiers held a red-tipped cigarette, pulsing in the darkness. They seemed unhurried and talked in low murmurs. Then the trees across from our hiding place blazed in the harsh onslaught of headlights, and I realized if the soldiers were to look in our direction they would be blinded by those headlamps. Boubacar had chosen our hiding place well. My father firmly squeezed my wrist. I didn't need his words to understand this was the moment of our greatest danger yet. Grace was safe behind us, and the Wife's trembling hand was clasped over her mouth. I was grateful to her for that.

Four young men and a woman stumbled into the glare of the jeep's headlights, clutching bags to their chests. Three soldiers, rifles pointed at them, were close behind. A second jeep stopped abruptly, its driver descending on the group trapped in the light.

"Lie down!" the driver screamed, and a young man fell to the ground, covering his head with his hands. "Now stay down because you do not think when your head is upright." With the sole of his boot, he ground the man's face into the dirt, while the soldiers ripped into the bags of the others. The men were ordered to take off their shirts and trousers, and a soldier, with his rifle now slung over his back, carefully searched their clothes.

"What are you doing here?" the driver asked the man trapped under his foot as if he were talking to a child. "Where are you going?"

A jumble of terrified gibberish came from the ground, and the driver smashed the butt of his rifle onto the man's legs. The crack of wood against bone, the cry of agony, as he jerked into a tight ball. The driver sauntered over to the other three men and the woman.

His rifle burst into life, spitting flames as bullets bit into the dirt. The deafening noise echoed off the rocks. But it wasn't dead bodies or silence that followed. Instead the night filled with very-much-alive screams of terror as the men and the woman clung to one another.

"Yes, you are alive. Now go and never return, or you will be dead," said the driver, prodding the men with the tip of his weapon. "Not you," he said to the woman and nodded to one of the soldiers. Without further words, she was thrown into the back of one of the jeeps, while the terrified men lifted their wounded companion and dragged him away. Out of the jeep's lights, the night swallowed them whole.

"You find anything?" the driver asked his comrade, rifling through the clothes and bags.

"Nothing. Perhaps she can tell us," he said, pointing to the woman in the jeep.

"Perhaps not, but it will be fun to find out," said the driver as the others chuckled knowingly. They clambered into the jeep beside her and drove away. The second jeep followed, and soon the throbbing of their engines faded; the beams of their bobbing headlights grew smaller.

We did not move. My father's grip softened on my wrist and he wiped the sweat from his face. I scanned the darkness for any movement.

"I think they've gone," I whispered.

My father did not answer. He inched forward on his stomach.

"Patson?" Grace's small voice came from behind the briefcase.

"Have they gone?" asked the Wife.

"Stay where you are." What if Boubacar had fled? I shuffled forward to peer at the rocks above us. "Boubacar?"

At the sound of my voice, my father raised his hands to silence me. I pointed upward, and he cautiously rose to his feet, keeping an eye on the clearing.

"Boubacar!" he called.

No one answered.

4

I scrambled out of our hiding place and stared into the darkness. My father called out Boubacar's name again, panic in his voice. Out here his book knowledge could do nothing to help his family survive. He clambered up the rocks, calling Boubacar's name louder and louder. Grace slipped out from behind the briefcase and stood up.

"I don't like it here, Patson. I want to go home," she said, a sob catching in the back of her throat.

"We can't go home," said the Wife, looking wildly about her. "We have to get to my brother. James will help us. There is no other way. We have to find James."

As much as I hated to admit it, I agreed with the Wife. The option of going home had long passed. We had no choice but to find Marange and then James Banda, the man responsible for us running through the bush away from soldiers, hiding under rocks, terrified for our lives. Diamonds for everyone, he had said to the Wife. He hadn't told her about the roadblocks or about the soldiers attacking people in the night. He had forgotten that part.

And then my father appeared, grinning, with Boubacar by his side. Grace ran to him and threw her arms around one of his legs. "Thank you, thank you for coming back for us."

Boubacar rested his hand on her head and bent down to look into her eyes.

"I didn't leave you, Mademoiselle. I had to see if the soldiers were gone."

"Who were those poor people?" I asked.

"Those boys wanted to be men. It is the way here. When you have worked the mines, you are no longer a boy. If you make it into the eye, you are seen as a man."

"And they did not make it?" my father asked.

"No, their luck ran out. They were found camping in the valley near the diamond fields, waiting for a chance to fill their sacks with soil. It was as close as they could get to the fields."

"What did those soldiers want from them?" I asked.

"Diamonds. The police usually patrol this area, but I have never seen soldiers before. This is something new. I don't know why the army is here."

"And the woman with them?" asked the Wife, but he offered her no answer.

"Do we still have far to go? I'm tired," said Grace.

Boubacar crouched and laid his hands gently on her

shoulders. "I need you to be brave, Mademoiselle Gracie, and when you are tired, I will carry you. You do not need to be afraid," he added. "While I am here, you can wear my magic tie. Whoever wears it cannot be harmed. Would you like that?"

Grace nodded and Boubacar solemnly took off his tie and placed it around her neck.

We gathered what was left of our luggage and again walked out into the night, knowing better than to ask how much longer it would be to Marange.

A full moon rose above Elephant Skull and bathed us in a silvery glow. I had lost all sense of time and space, the shimmering sky too bright to find those stars that might have marked our progress. We had walked for three, maybe four, maybe five hours, I could not say. I remember stopping briefly and drinking foul, dark water from a muddy pool. I remember the Wife weeping on the ground and my father putting his arms around her, before dragging her to her feet. I remember tripping over tangled roots in the dark, falling over and rolling down an embankment and Boubacar lifting me off the ground, dusting me off, and pushing me forward.

Uncle James was responsible for all of this. Uncle James Banda. Diamonds for everyone, he had said. I concentrated on putting one foot in front of the other and staying awake. The heaviness of sleep deadened my arms and legs. My neck seemed incapable of holding my head erect and it dropped of its own accord onto my chest until I jerked it upright. This must be sleepwalking, I thought. I stubbed my toe, grazed my arm against a thorn bush, and awakened only long enough to again walk, walk forward into the dark night. I dreamed of cool fridge water and clean, soft sheets and Sheena.

Although the forest around us was eerily quiet, I had an unnerving sensation that we were being watched. Every flickering shadow threatened. The moonlight illuminated shapes that seemed to move but then when I looked again they went still. It was difficult to make out what was solid and what was not. All animal noises had been silenced and we walked on, on through a sleeping forest.

And then I glimpsed a shadow in human form staring at me. The ash-gray figure was no taller than me and stood at the foot of a hulking mimosa tree, leaning on a pair of crutches. I could not tell if it was a girl or a boy, alive or dead, or whether I was dreaming or awake. But it stared at me with eyes that were real enough. The figure lifted its dust-gray arm and pointed back to where we had come from, its lips moving with words I could not hear. Moonlight spilled through the branches, forming a halo of silver around its head.

I was so tired, I was not afraid. I moved toward it just as the figure turned away and disappeared into the low-hanging branches of the mimosa tree. The forest was as silent as an empty church. Boubacar's pace had never slowed. Grace's arms were flung limply around his neck. She slept like a rag doll on his shoulder. My father dragged the Wife behind him, still clinging to the last of the four suitcases she could not live without. I trudged on, barely able to keep my eyes open.

I was too exhausted to think about what I had seen or what it had meant. That would come later, but now all I could think of was sleeping. Boubacar suddenly stopped and raised his hand. Once again we fell wearily to the ground, no longer concerned with the noise we made. He whistled—three short notes—like the call of a nightjar. Grace did not stir. I wished he would carry me. My eyelids drooped shut.

Behind me, the Wife's whispered urgency roused me. "Look, Joseph, look!"

A single flame rose from beneath the ground and floated in the air only ten paces ahead of us.

I rubbed my eyes as, one by one, small flames rose out of the earth and hovered in the air. In their flickering light, figures emerged from the ground. Their faces were stained with gray dust and sand, their bloodshot eyes illuminated by the light from wax candles they held in front of them. Some carried long iron rods; others bore pickaxes upon their shoulders.

My skin prickled the rest of me awake.

Wordlessly they stared at us through the darkness, their gray faces all holding blank, incurious expressions. I had heard of zombies roaming the earth after midnight but had never believed those stories until this moment. Their silent presence was unworldly. If Grace had been awake, she would have screamed. Could I still be asleep and dreaming of the undead rising from the earth? Was the figure I had seen standing under the mimosa tree one of these creatures? Boubacar had not moved since the figures emerged from the ground. He whistled the same three short notes again, and from the darkness a voice responded in a language I had never heard before.

"Wait here," whispered Boubacar, crouching down beside me and laying Grace gently on the ground without waking her. "If anything happens to me, you take your sister and run for your life. You do not look back. You do not wait for your father or his wife. You run. You understand, Patson? You run faster than you ever have before."

There was no doubting the warning or the large knife in the palm of his right hand. He quickly pulled a short iron bar from his bag and rose to his feet, walking slowly toward the waiting figures. He concealed the blade behind his back but carried the iron bar in full view. I glanced at Grace, still protected from these zombies by her armor of sleep. More glimmers of candlelight emerged from the earth and moved gradually toward us, until we were surrounded. The murmuring of a strange language covered us, huddled as we were on the ground. I strained to hear a familiar word or make sense of imminent danger in the tone of the speaker. Fully awake now, my body hummed with tension, fear, and wonder. At the first indication of danger from Boubacar I would sweep up Grace, and run directly toward the flames. I would scatter these zombies with a scream of the living and bring my sister to safety before she woke up. They would not devour her, or drag her into their shallow graves.

"Shhh, Patson," whispered my father. "Easy, son. It's all right."

My father's words jolted me out of my fear. "What are they, Baba?"

"They are diamond miners working at night, Patson. We must have entered the diamond fields of Marange. Look, hundreds of them digging through the earth."

More figures emerged from a different hole only a few meters away. They were oblivious to our presence, intent only on their work. In the dull yellow light of lanterns and candles, they lifted large, heavy sacks onto their heads and slowly disappeared into the forest that fringed the field.

"But why at night?"

"I don't know, son," he admitted, squeezing my arm.

"They'll take me to my brother," declared the Wife. "We'll be all right once we get to James. James will look after us." She made to stand up, but my father held her in place.

The foreign voice barked an instruction and one by one the flames disappeared back into their holes beneath the ground. A blanket of darkness descended once again over the field. Boubacar returned. He no longer carried his knife.

"The Mazezuru syndicate has an understanding with Banda. They have allowed us to cross their section of the field and go on to Banda's camp." Turning to a thin man standing silently by his side, Boubacar said, "This man will escort us."

Leaning on a long iron rod, his bony frame didn't seem capable of holding the heavy sack on his back. He looked as exhausted as I was.

"Thank you," said my father. "Thank you very much."

The man did not respond; instead he turned away and, in a maneuver that suggested he had done this a hundred times before, adjusted the weighty sack on his back. He stabbed his iron rod into the ground for support, and made his way through the field, skirting its shallow craters. Boubacar picked up his bag, packed away his own iron bar, and carefully lifted Grace into his arms to follow closely behind our new guide. I allowed my father and the Wife to go ahead of me and took up the rear.

Another man clambered out of a hole, blew out his candle, and, after a brief exchange with our new guide, joined us. He, too, carried a sack on his back, and used an iron rod for support. A short distance away, I turned to look back at the diamond field that now seemed dark and empty and a bit less frightening.

"They mine at night to avoid sharing their ore with the police," explained Boubacar. "Some do work during the day— the Live Show, they call it—but then they are watched by the police, who breathe down their necks looking for *ngodas*."

"*Ngodas?*"

"Raw diamonds."

"And the iron rods?" my father asked.

"They are sharpened to chip away the rocks and break the earth. Then they load the ore by hand into those sacks," said Boubacar.

"Basic artisan mining techniques," mused my father. "The diamonds here are low-quality industrial diamonds often found in shallow alluvial deposits. They are accessible to anyone with a sharp tool, plenty of muscle, and an abundance of optimism."

"Shut up, Joseph," snapped the Wife. "You're showing off."

5

The Wife got a second wind, now that we were closer to her brother's camp. She left my father and walked next to Boubacar, who ignored her endless chatter. I dared to hope that our journey was coming to an end. Climbing into the car early yesterday morning was now wrapped up with the faraway past of leaving Bulawayo. With each step through the darkness toward the Banda camp, I was moving farther away from the life I had had in the city. How could I ever tell Sheena anything of what had happened to us since then? She would be waking up soon, having breakfast, putting on her school uniform, and walking the familiar road to Milton High School, refreshed and ready for just another ordinary day, whereas I had no idea what was waiting for me in Marange.

The guide stopped, cocked his head as if listening for an

imagined sound. He whispered hurriedly to the man behind him and pointed at figures running toward us. A loud police whistle blasted the night air and was followed by angry voices. The men dropped their ore sacks and metal rods and sprinted away, leaving us standing out in the open. If this was the end of our journey, caught by the police and driven away in the back of a van, then so be it. I had had enough of this long night.

Boubacar passed the sleeping bundle of Grace to my father and instructed the Wife to stand behind him. He swung his backpack to the ground and lightly twirled his iron bar in his left hand. The knife was again in his right hand as he stood tall, waiting for the police, treading heavily toward us.

But they were not police. Instead, four men wearing balaclavas and armed with knives and rods, and one with the handle of a pickax casually slung over his shoulder, approached us.

"*Magombiro*," said Boubacar, raising his knife before him. "Miners who failed as diggers and who steal from others. The worst kind of Marange parasite. We'll see if they have the stomach for a fight."

The four men stopped. They spread out to surround us. My father pulled me close to him, while the Wife clung to his arm. Boubacar merely stood his ground as the beam of the flashlight lit up a look of scorn on his face.

"What do we have here?" said the one who appeared to be the leader, a police baton twirling from his wrist. "Trespassers? Stealing what doesn't belong to them?"

Boubacar, his gaze firmly fixed on the masked man in front of him, did not reply.

"You know what we want, big guy. You can't be as stupid as you look. We can take it with blood or without. The choice is yours."

Boubacar's size, stance, and silence unsettled the leader enough that he had stopped a healthy distance away. The other three men moved cautiously to the side of their leader. Boubacar's resolute stand was not the response they expected.

"You step aside," the leader demanded. "Do you hear me? I mean what I say."

"Does your father know what you are doing, boy?" Boubacar finally replied.

The man's head jerked as if Boubacar had slapped him.

"Does he know you prowl the night like the coward hyena? What would he do to you if he found out that you prey on those who cannot defend themselves, stealing their day's honest work?" Boubacar's tone left little doubt as to what he thought of these *magombiro*.

"And do you give your father anything of what you steal?" Boubacar lifted his knife and pointed it slowly at each of them in turn. "Or do you and your friends hide it from the Banda syndicate?"

Unsettled by Boubacar's questions, the men glanced nervously at one another.

"And what would your father do to your friends if he found out you're running your own little business on the side?"

Boubacar goaded the leader. "Have any of you clowns ever thought about that?"

The leader adjusted his balaclava to get a closer look at Boubacar.

"Boubacar?" he exclaimed, pulling off his mask and gesturing to his companions to step back.

He laughed, a tight, high-pitched snuffle that seemed even scarier than his anger. He quickly stuffed his balaclava into his back pocket, while the police baton swung loosely from his wrist. Boubacar, however, did not lower his knife as he approached.

"Musi?" The Wife broke away from behind my father. "Musi Banda, is that you?"

The man froze at the mention of his name.

"It's me. Auntie Sylvia. You remember me? Sylvia from Bulawayo," she said, with a girlish laugh. "We should have arrived yesterday but that driver deserted us after the first checkpoint. We had to walk. It's been a terrible journey."

Confusion, laughter, embarrassed embraces, and hurried introductions came rapidly. Musi had transformed himself from a dangerous thug into his family's welcoming representative. With all the noise, Grace woke up and looked around in a daze. Boubacar stood to one side, letting Musi take charge, sending one of his friends ahead to wake his father. But before we were swept along, two of the men quietly hid their sacks behind a clump of rocks and covered them with a bush. Then Musi ordered them to carry our luggage. He talked loudly, laughing at the misunderstanding, shaking my father's hand more vigorously than was necessary and embracing the Wife as if it were he who had rescued her.

"My father will be so pleased I found you, Auntie. I come here only to watch for strangers in our fields. Everyone steals from everyone else. I thought you were *magombiro*. You'll tell him that, won't you?"

"Of course, Musi, of course," said the Wife, leaning on his arm. "We'll tell him exactly that."

"And your face, little cousin," he said to me, cuffing me painfully on the shoulder. "You looked like you had seen the devil himself!"

Boubacar, forgotten in the excitement, put away his weapons and stood apart, observing our strange family reunion. He motioned for me to follow my family, but before I did, I slipped off his tie from Grace's neck and looked up into his scarred, ugly face, which was no longer the least bit scary.

"Thank you, Boubacar." I handed him his tie.

"We would never have made it without your magic tie," said Grace.

He fixed her with his sternest gaze but a flicker of a smile played on his lips. "I hope you will like your new family," he said, glancing at Musi, who was now leading the way. "You will have a new life, Patson, one that will require all the courage you have inside you."

"I will never forget what you did for us," I promised.

"You can have my necktie, Mademoiselle Gracie. It will keep

you safe." Boubacar slipped the tie back around her neck and turned to leave.

"Boubacar, where do you come from?" asked Grace.

"The Congo," he replied. "Go now. Tomorrow is here already and your uncle will be pleased to have another pair of hands working in his syndicate."

6

When I finally woke up nine hours later, my cousin Jamu was sitting at the foot of my bed. The first thing I noticed was his smirk. I'd seen expressions like his before on other boys, sometimes mean, sometimes superior, but always hiding some insecurity. His face was round, with thick lips and a stubby, flat nose that looked like he'd come up short in a long fistfight. His chubby legs were covered with gray dust and his shins and bare feet were coated with mud. Then I saw the reason for his smirk: He had been reading my diary.

"My father says you're lucky to be alive."

The contents of my backpack were strewn about the floor and he was flicking through the pages of my diary like it was a magazine.

"Give me that. You have no right—" I lunged at him.

"You write lots of stuff," he said, waving the notebook, then tossing it onto the pile of my clothes.

"It's mine. And it's private."

"You didn't bring much, but your phone is cool," he said, pulling my phone from his pocket. "Who is this Sheena chick?"

I sprang out of bed and grabbed my phone. Jamu fell backward, slamming his head on the corner of a cupboard. When he took his hand away it was sticky with blood. Like a baby he wailed in pain and ran out of the room calling for his mother. Serves him right, I thought, and angrily stuffed all my things into my backpack.

My father entered the room. "Patson? What's going on?"

"He was reading my diary and he took my phone."

"Remember we are guests here, son."

"But that doesn't mean he can—"

"Patson, I know you to be better than this. I want you to apologize to Jamu."

I hurriedly dressed, smarting at my father's rebuke and the unfairness of it all. I followed him down a corridor and into a lounge that looked more like a toolshed. It was filled with pickaxes, iron rods, sieve trays, and ore sacks. Musi and one of the men from last night lounged on an old leather couch drinking beers. The large flat-screen television mounted on the wall was on mute, showing the strutting moves of a rock star with bling flashing from his wrists and ears. From the backyard came the *thump-thump* of a huffing generator. Grace was working in the kitchen and ran to me, but the Wife pulled her back to the sink, scolding her to finish her work. Another woman was standing at a stove cooking. Jamu was being attended to by an older woman who scowled at me as we walked into the room.

"Jamu," said my father, "Patson has something to say to you. I trust it's not a deep cut, Prisca?"

"Deep enough," the older woman replied. "It's still bleeding." Her hair was cut short like a boy's and she wore a loose T-shirt and red boxer shorts that didn't quite cover her bloated belly. Her legs were coated with the same dust that marked every member of the Banda family. This was not the normal dress of Shona women; but this was no normal family.

The younger woman left her cooking to peer under the cotton wool pressed to Jamu's head. "You'll be all right," she said brightly.

"I suppose so, Amai," he mumbled.

"It's nothing to worry about, Joseph. I'm sure it was an accident," she said.

"Thank you, Kuda," said the Wife. "But Patson must apologize. He is your guest, after all."

"Yes. Guests. Mmm," said Prisca, not taking her eyes off me.

"Joseph?" demanded the Wife.

My father gently pushed me forward and I stood before Jamu, who glared at me. I mumbled my apologies.

"I can't hear him, Amai," complained Jamu.

"I said I was sorry you hurt your head." My father squeezed my shoulder painfully. "And that I pushed you."

"He's not really sorry, Amai. Make him say it again. Properly," Jamu protested, grinning at me the way a cat plays with a bird.

48

"Jamu, did you take something that was not yours?"

Every head in the room turned toward James Banda, sitting at the head of a table and bent over a small pile of stones spread on a black velvet cloth. A cylindrical magnifying glass seemed stuck in his right eye, and made his whole face look like a dried-up prune. With a pair of tweezers, he plucked a dark green pebble from the pile and studied it intently. He was a large man, with a thick, flabby neck and broad shoulders. His shaved head glistened with oil.

The Wife had often told us that her brother had once been the heavyweight champion of the Mutare region with sixteen knockouts to his credit. Although he had long since lost the muscles of a prizefighter, there was no doubting he could still knock out a man with a single blow. Yet his thick, gnarled boxer's hands handled the tweezers and small stones as delicately as a surgeon's.

"Come here and bring your cousin," he said, not looking up from the table.

His words had an immediate effect on Jamu. The smirk slid from his face and he scrambled off the chair, pushed away the fussing hands of his mother, and dragged me toward his father. Uncle James continued sorting the pebbles, examining each briefly, then placing them, one by one, in smaller piles on the table.

Jamu and I stood before him, and Musi swiveled on the couch to get a better view. Then he pointed two fingers at me and cocked his thumb like the hammer of a gun. I wanted to wipe the stupid grin from his face with a shovel.

"Now, Jamu, you must answer me truthfully. I will ask you again. Did you take something that did not belong to you?" Banda spoke softly, like he might be asking about nothing more important than the weather.

Jamu was clearly terrified. Suddenly I felt sorry for him, being so afraid of his father.

"I was only looking at his phone," mumbled Jamu.

"So you didn't take his phone?" Uncle James lifted another stone toward the light.

Jamu hesitated.

"Jamu?"

"I took his phone."

"Good, Jamu, you have spoken the truth. Now I will show you what happens when you take something that does not belong to you."

"It was my fault, Uncle James," I blurted out. "I left the phone lying around and I knocked him off the bed."

Uncle James popped the magnifying glass out of his eye.

"So, the son of the schoolteacher defends the weak," he said, looking at me for the first time. "Your name is Patson?"

I nodded.

"I hear a young lion in your voice, little prince. I shall remember that." He pointed the tweezers at me. "Musi, come here. Bring Xaba. I want to show you something."

The two young men ambled over to the table.

Uncle James indicated the pile of pebbles on the velvet cloth. "I'm disappointed with yesterday's work. Mostly *ngodas*. One or two that might be low-grade *girazi* but it was a day of poor-quality ore. What do you think?" he asked, inviting them to inspect the stones.

The two of them leaned over the pile. Musi's eyes gleamed and the tip of Xaba's tongue flicked over his lips.

"Look closer but no touching," said Uncle James, lifting his hands away from the table.

As Musi and Xaba bent lower, Uncle James clamped his hands onto their necks and smashed their foreheads into the table. With the crack of bone on wood, the pebbles leapt from their piles. Musi cried out in pain and reeled away holding his forehead, while Xaba struggled under Uncle James's iron grip.

In the next moment, Xaba's whimpering grew louder. Uncle James had inserted the tweezers into his nostril and was gripping the corner of his nose. He slowly turned the tweezers, twisting the fleshy part of his nose, forcing the man to his knees. A dark pearl of Xaba's blood fell onto the table.

"So, Jamu, what have you learned?" asked Uncle James.

"You shouldn't...I mean...Never take what doesn't belong to you," stammered Jamu.

"Good. And, more importantly, never take what belongs to *me*. If you do, I will hurt you badly," he said, yanking out the tweezers and releasing Xaba.

"Come here, Musi," he demanded as he carefully wiped the tweezers on the edge of the velvet cloth. "I won't hurt you again, but next time you think about playing *magombiro*, I will. Now you two will return the sacks you stole last night and apologize to Alfred Mazezuru. Then you and your friends will spend the rest of today and tomorrow working for the Mazezuru syndicate. I will be proud to hear that you have sieved sixteen sacks each." As the young men turned to leave, Uncle James added, "And, Xaba, instead of listening to the boss's son, use the brains God gave you and make your own decisions. Now, get out of here, both of you."

Halfway out the door, Musi shot me a glance as if I'd been the one who caused him this humiliation. Before I could even think to object, Uncle James had turned his attention back to me.

"Patson, come here."

I took only a small step toward him, eyeing those tweezers warily.

"No, no, you don't need to be afraid," he said, and chuckled. "You've done nothing wrong. I want to show you my diamonds." Uncle James lifted a few stones and dropped them into my hand. They looked like coarse chips of broken beer bottles: dark brown, black, and a strange shade of darkish green.

"You are holding over three thousand Usahs in your hands, Patson. Yes, that's right. Three thousand American dollars," he said, explaining the word *Usahs* to me. "Your son has never seen such wealth, hey, Mr. Schoolteacher?" He glanced at my father, standing at the other end of the table. "With those ugly *ngodas* you can have anything you want. Look closely at them, Patson, beyond their colors, feel their knobbly, smooth shapes. These are the stones of *midzimu*, the land spirits of Marange. If you are good to your ancestors, they will guide you to *ngodas*. Once your *shavi* allows it, finding such stones as these is easy. But first, you have to be pure in your heart, Patson, or your *shavi* will hide from you. Are you pure of heart, Patson?"

I studied the tiny stones. It was hard to believe that I was holding three thousand American dollars in the palm of my hand. It was a fortune beyond imagining. These stones could be mine. I could own all that money.

Uncle James gripped my wrist and turned my palm firmly, until the rough, uncut diamonds fell back onto the table. I stared at the stones, no longer in my grasp. A fortune had slipped through my fingers. Uncle James studied me for a moment and then removed a small leather pouch hanging from around his neck. A single glassy stone, the size of my thumbnail, fell onto the velvet cloth.

"Come closer, Patson," he said. "You want to see my most precious of all stones? This is the greatest of gifts from the *midzimu*. A *girazi*. This little beauty was one of the first diamonds found here. Cut and polished, it's a gem of tremendous quality. At least eight or nine carats, worth over fifty thousand Usahs. Think what a stone like this could mean to your family, Patson?"

I didn't understand why he was asking me that question. He seemed to be testing me but all I could see was the sparkling white light of the stone, which he twirled lovingly between his thumb and index finger.

"This stone you cannot hold. You have to find your own, Patson, and it will define your future."

I was vaguely aware of my father clearing his throat. He called my name, softly, as if he was reminding me of something. I ignored him, even though I knew it was wrong to do so. Had

I been an obedient son, I would have listened to him. I should have stepped back from the table, away from that *girazi* glittering between Uncle James's fingers. Instead, all I seemed able to do was imagine what a gift like that from the land spirits could do if it belonged to me. Fifty thousand American dollars. The sum of money seemed unimaginable. The things I could do with fifty thousand American dollars, the things that money could bring to my family. It would change all our lives forever. We could eat meat every night. We could buy a house. My father could have a car. I could go to university and my sister could go to a private school. An endless list of possibilities raced through my head.

"You do want to be a man, Patson?" Uncle James lifted the *girazi* to the light again.

I nodded, mesmerized by the diamond.

Then it vanished into the leather pouch around his neck. "Your initiation into manhood begins on the diamond fields. There you will learn what it is to become a man."

"Patson," said my father. "Come here, son. My boy will be going to school, James. The mines are not for him."

I could be a miner. I could find my own stones. I didn't need to go to school.

"Just a moment, Baba," I said as Uncle James folded the corners of his velvet cloth over and around my future.

7

The Banda family lived on Kondozi Farm, thirty kilometers away from the town of Mutare. The farm had once
belonged to a prosperous white farmer, the largest tobacco and
wheat producer in the district. Then the war veterans came
and invaded the property, ran off the family without letting
them pack up their belongings, and claimed the land for themselves. The rambling thatch-roofed farmhouse bore traces of
that family: A glass-framed collection of faded photos still hung
behind the toilet door; two smiling blond-haired boys with farm
workers beside them; a boy sitting on a tractor in the lap of a
tanned, burly man in a bush hat. In another photograph these
same white people sat around a table laden with food, wearing paper Christmas hats and smiling at the camera. Mounted
on the living room wall were the heads of a bush buck and a

kudu, with glassy eyes that stared serenely over what used to be. I wondered where this family had gone and what they would think of Kondozi Farm's new occupants and all the dirty tools in their lounge.

Later, I found out that after the war veterans had moved on, the farm had been inhabited by local people who did a poor job of farming, and then diamonds were discovered nearby. Uncle James offered everyone living on the derelict land the chance to join his mining syndicate as long as he took over the farmhouse. With Kondozi Farm as his headquarters, Uncle James doubled the size of his syndicate workforce, and soon became one of the richest men in Marange.

But it was the food the Banda family ate that made the biggest impression on me. All morning I had been distracted by the delicious smells coming from the kitchen, and when we finally sat down for our first meal in Marange I decided that I, too, wanted to be as rich as Uncle James. Kuda darted in and out of the kitchen, with large bowls of stewed meat, cornmeal, and mounds of *sadza*. Uncle James was served first, then Prisca, then Musi, Jamu, and finally the Moyo family. I had never seen such a feast, and I struggled to keep my hands under the table, as my mother had taught me.

Grace poked me in the ribs. "You're drooling, Patson."

While we ate, Uncle James kept looking from my father to his sister and made disapproving clicking noises in the back of his throat. It seemed as if he couldn't believe how his pretty sister could have married my dour father. To my eye, the Wife seemed overdressed for lunch. She wore a low-cut yellow summer dress and her face shone with freshly applied makeup. She entertained everyone with her version of our journey, how she berated the driver for abandoning us, how she was the one who found Boubacar and ordered him to show us the way. Her story went on and on, how she hid her luggage in the hollow baobab tree and how she had made all the decisions when her husband was too terrified to do anything at all. Uncle James kept on shaking his head and laughing.

"I know that place," he said. "I will send someone to collect your things from Father Baobab."

"Oh, James," said Kuda. "Can Sylvia and I go into Mutare to get her some new clothes? I'm sure the luggage has been stolen by now."

I remembered overhearing the Wife tell my father that Uncle James had two wives. Prisca must be the senior wife, mother of Musi, and Kuda—the junior wife—was Jamu's mother. Only a very wealthy man could have two wives. My father listened passively as the Wife continued to embroider her role as protector, but interrupted her when she suggested that Boubacar had abandoned us.

"I believe he was close by at all times, Sylvia."

"Well, it certainly felt like he ran off when the soldiers started beating up those people," she replied, squinting at my father.

"I know this Boubacar. He is a bodyguard for Farouk Abdullah, one of the richest diamond dealers in Mutare. He is an out-of-work mercenary from the Congo who fought on the side of the rebels in DRC. There was a strange story about him recruiting child soldiers. I'm not sure of the details, but he can't be trusted," said Uncle James, drinking from the beer bottle Kuda handed him.

"Oh, but he can, Uncle James," insisted Grace. "He carried me on his back all the way and let me wear his magic tie."

"Hush, Grace, it's not polite to interrupt." My father laid his hand on her arm.

"But, Baba, Boubacar helped us. Without him we would never—"

"That man was nothing but rude to me," interjected the Wife.

"Him and Abdullah wanted to pay me peanuts for my diamonds," said Uncle James, waving his knife at my father. "Boubacar is not welcome on Banda Hill. You can't trust the Congolese."

"I agree, brother. Joseph wouldn't listen when I said the very same thing," chirped the Wife.

Throughout the lunch, Prisca eyed the Wife, while Kuda fussed over her as if she were a film star. Kuda was not quite as beautiful as the Wife, but they were roughly the same age. She seemed to have a kind word for everyone and never stopped smiling. Prisca, on the other hand, was older and, despite the softness of her large stomach, she had a hard, thin mouth and a face like a squeezed orange. I couldn't help wondering if she wasn't jealous of Uncle James's prettier, more pleasant second wife. But there was no mistaking which one of them was the mistress of the house. While Kuda talked about shopping and dresses with the Wife, Prisca was all business, interrogating my father with short, sharp questions.

"If the work was so bad in Bulawayo, why did you not go back to your village?" she demanded. "Sylvia says you have land there."

My father paused in his meal and looked at the Wife for an explanation.

"No, no, Prisca, we wanted to come here," interrupted the Wife quickly. "To Marange. The stories were all over Bulawayo about how good things are here. Besides, I haven't seen my dear brother in ages."

Prisca would not be distracted. "When do you start at the government school?"

"Mr. Ngoko said I should come as soon as I arrive."

"The headmaster of Junction Gate High School? He left," Prisca said, glancing at her husband, who was dishing up a large second portion of food.

"Junction Gate High School?" said Jamu, his mouth full. "That's funny."

"And where will you stay?" probed Prisca, ladling still more delicious-smelling stew into my bowl. I planned to make up for all the meat we hadn't eaten in months.

My father frowned. "I believe government housing was mentioned."

Uncle James slapped the table with the flat of his hand and laughed loudly. "Government housing. That's a joke. The school's broke, shut down. Not working. No pupils. You're better off working the fields. Patson looks strong. I could use him on the mines."

I glanced up at the mention of my name.

"My son will be going to school, James—"

"But I could work on the mines after school, Baba," I interrupted, ignoring my father's frown. "Just think of all the money—"

"That's enough, Patson."

"My boys haven't gone to school for six months. Not worth it," said Uncle James. "They learn more on the fields. Isn't that true, Jamu?"

Jamu nodded eagerly at his father, and I was able to sneak a glance at him to see if he was still angry at me. He was piling more stew into his bowl, the wound on his head long forgotten.

"My father says that going to school is the most important thing in life," Grace declared, wiping her bowl with a piece of bread. "You don't just learn stuff in books; you learn how to understand the world."

"I would like Jamu to go to school," began Kuda, but when Uncle James raised his hand she stopped talking, and the smile slipped from her face.

"Is that so, Grace? And that's why your father brought you all the way to Marange?" Uncle James raised his eyebrows at my father. "To understand the world better?"

"I've tried to talk sense to him, brother, but he doesn't listen. What's wrong with having a nice house, or a brand-new car,

Joseph?" needled the Wife. "My husband has something against being successful. Look how well James has done. You wouldn't say no to having a motorbike one day, Patson, would you?"

I didn't respond to the Wife because if I answered truthfully it would seem like a betrayal of my father. I couldn't understand why he was so reluctant to become a miner. He had seen all the diamonds that Uncle James owned. Here was proof enough that there were diamonds for everyone.

"We will visit Mr. Ngoko this afternoon," said my father, ignoring the Wife's huff-puffing and eye-rolling.

"You go and then, when you come back, we can talk," said Uncle James.

"Bring more meat, Kuda," ordered Prisca. "Our guests are still hungry."

Junction Gate High School was only a short distance from Kondozi Farm, but Prisca offered us all a lift in the back of her pickup truck. Despite my father's excitement about his new school, I couldn't help feeling uneasy about the visit. Prisca dropped us off at a path that led to a series of green thatch-roofed rondawels behind a fence. Jamu, who had taken the seat in the cab, watched us in the mirror as we climbed down from the open back of the truck. We still hadn't spoken to each other since that morning, but I did catch him glancing in my direction after lunch. I was hoping that meant there might still be the possibility of a truce.

"Your school's over there," Prisca said, dismissing us with a wave.

"Thank you for the lift," replied my father, adjusting his old university tie and dusting off the only black jacket he still had.

Prisca clicked her tongue and shook her head, laughing. "Listen to my husband and you can look after your family. Properly. Like a man should," she said, turning the steering wheel in the direction of the farm.

"I'm sure Mr. Ngoko will be pleased to see me," he called out after her.

Watching her speed off, I wished I were the one sitting in the cab of the truck, leaving my father and Grace in the dust. I hated myself for the thought but I knew how pathetic the three of us must have looked to Jamu. My father picked up his leather brief-case, took Grace's hand, and together we walked up the path toward the school.

I checked reception on my phone. Three bars and two messages from Sheena.

> R u there yet? What's up? I got into X-country
> team.

And:

> u still there !?

My thumbs danced across the keypad:

> School ama-Zing! Gr8 new home. ☺ Gr8 job for
> my dad! ☺

Prisca was wrong. The school was not deserted. A woman was washing clothes in a tub in the playground. Dripping laundry hung on a washing line strung between the empty flagpole and a wobbling netball post. She looked up as we approached.

"Not open now. Come back tonight," she shouted, beating the washing against a board.

"Excuse me. I'm looking for the reception. For Mr. Ngoko," my father said.

The woman glanced over her shoulder and clicked her tongue. "Ngoko. Who's he?"

Another woman stood in the doorway wearing only a purple bra and shorts. I couldn't help staring at her breasts and her oiled thighs. She eyed us through a haze of cigarette smoke.

"What do you want, mister?" she asked.

"The headmaster of the school. Mr. Ngoko," said my father primly.

The women glanced at each other. The one doing the laundry shrugged and shook her head. The purple-bra woman blew a thin wisp of smoke into the air. "There's no school here. I've never heard of this Ngoko chap."

"Is this Junction Gate High School?"

"It used to be a school. Not anymore," she said. "What are you looking for?"

"I am Mr. . . . I mean," my father stammered as the woman pushed away from the doorway and approached him. Inside the classroom I saw another woman asleep on a mattress, her arm thrown over her face, her dress pulled up past her thighs.

"Come on, Patson," called my father over his shoulder as

he turned around, gripped Grace's hand, and walked quickly toward another, bigger building.

"We have school for adults later on tonight, Mr. Teacher. Why don't you come for a private lesson?" shouted the purple-bra woman.

"You can always learn something new at our school," added the washing-woman, laughing and flapping a wet dress behind us.

We stopped at the dilapidated office and peered through the broken windows. More mattresses. Sheets separating the room into sleeping quarters. The smell of grease and fried chicken feet.

"What you want here?" barked an old woman sitting on a can in what was once the office foyer. She was chopping up a large piece of liver on a block of wood.

"I am looking for Mr. Ngoko. The headmaster of Junction Gate High. I've come to teach at this school."

"Here, there's no other work than cooking. You know the belly of people? They eat when they are hungry. That's all. We sow corn. We sow pumpkins in our fields. Mmm. But nothing comes but stones. Truly, we are suffering. You look for corn. You look for pumpkins. But there is nothing. When the rain didn't fall, heh! We didn't find those things," said the woman, slicing cleanly through the purple liver, peeling off the thin membrane and dropping it piece by piece into an oil pot bubbling on a gas burner.

My father looked wildly around him. He walked down the corridor, opening doors, calling for Mr. Ngoko. Grace and I stood fascinated by the woman's wrinkles, her small hands, and her knife blade flashing through the meat.

"I sit. I cry. I finish. I look for firewood. I go home. I cook. Yah. I cook for the boy who must eat or he dies. This soul, it wasn't happy. Hoh. That fella. He left two weeks ago. No children, so no school. I needed a room. Photocopying, they say. Okay, I say. That will do for medicine."

"Baba," I called after my father. "The *gogo* knows something."

I was beginning to feel uneasy at how she jabbed her knife in my father's direction, and the cooking smells of fried liver turned my stomach.

"You know something about Mr. Ngoko?"

"I saw you talking to those low-down women. They're no good. We don't want them here. They bring trouble. There's trouble enough. Mmm," she said, now waving her knife in my father's face. "They've come from Harare. They all want money. Hoh-hoh. They wait for the men who work the pits of fury. Mmm. Those that drink the breasts of Banda. Eeee, I say to myself. Not going to happen. Not today. Not tomorrow. No way."

"About Mr. Ngoko?" my father reminded her.

"Ask him. He knows," she said, pointing to me.

"She said he left two weeks ago. There were no students."

"No children, so no school. That's right. We needed the rooms," confirmed the old woman, plopping the last piece of liver into the pot and stirring the broth with a stick.

My father dropped his briefcase and slowly slid to the floor like a tall building collapsing in slow motion. He closed his eyes, lifted his knees, and his head fell into his hands. He drummed his fingers against his skull and mumbled something I couldn't understand. He seemed to have trouble breathing, until I realized he was taking in great deep sobs of air.

"Baba?" Grace ran to him, gathering him in her small arms.

"Let's go, Baba," I said. "Come on. Let's go." I shook his shoulder gently, aware that for the very first time I was touching my father in a different way. I wanted him to stand up, to reassure me that everything would be all right. I wanted him to straighten his tie, jab his glasses up his nose, and smile at me over the rim, in the way he always did when faced with a problem.

Instead, he gave way to his despair.

I couldn't bear seeing this man, my father, sitting on the ground in his black jacket and university tie so close to the old crone stirring her pot of foul-smelling liver stew.

"Baba, Baba, get up, please," Grace pleaded, shaking his arm. "Please, Baba. I want to go home."

Slowly he lifted his head. He stared through us, with a black hollowness in his eyes. Then he pulled Grace into his arms and hugged her fiercely. "It's okay, Gracie. I'm fine. This is just temporary, just a temporary setback."

"That's all you have in the end," said the old woman, sipping the smelly broth from her pot. "Your children. Mmm. You're a lucky man. All I got is a boy who's dead already. Dying every day. The sickness. Mmm. But I've got food for him tonight. That's good. You want a taste?"

I lifted my father up off the floor, picked up his briefcase, and together we left the foyer, stepping into fresh air and blazing sunshine.

"Who were those women, Baba?" asked Grace.

"Washerwomen, Grace, washerwomen," replied my father, loosening his tie and slipping off his jacket.

"You forgot this," I said, raising his briefcase, wanting to hand him back his dignity.

"Yes, thank you. You are a good son," he said. "I won't need that anymore."

My world tilted. It was unimaginable that my father would give up his briefcase.

"Baba?" prompted Grace, but our father was somewhere beyond hearing.

We walked on in silence, Grace holding his hand, and me his briefcase. I didn't want to ask the obvious question, but it tumbled out after the silence became unbearable.

"What are we going to do now, Baba?"

I dreaded he might say we would return to Bulawayo or that he would search for another job as a teacher. But my father's answer, which came quietly, and in his characteristically calm manner, was completely unexpected. "We're going to become diamond miners, son. That's what you want, isn't it? That's what Sylvia and Uncle James want. Diamonds for everyone and when we have enough money, we'll go to Harare. I'll find a teaching job there. You can finish school, go to university. We'll get us a nice house and all will be fine again. Yes, it will. All will be fine."

He gripped my hand far more tightly than I imagined he could. "This is only a temporary setback. We mustn't be downhearted. No, not at all. There is opportunity here, for us all."

They might have been the words I wanted to hear, but somehow they sounded all wrong coming from my father.

It cost my father a great deal of pride to ask Uncle James if he and his family could join the Banda syndicate. He must have known that in Uncle James's eyes he was now no better than those who begged for work. Asking to join the syndicate was an admission that he had failed to provide for his family, a thing every Shona man saw as his duty as head of the household. I think my father must have felt that for a man who had been to university, worked in a professional occupation, digging in the dirt was a humiliating end to his career.

When we returned to Kondozi Farm, my father sat on the edge of the couch, his back book-straight, his hands covering both his knees, while Uncle James drank beer and watched the television. He took a deep breath before he raised the issue, and true to character, used far too many words.

"I was wondering, James, whether you might consider me useful in your mining operation. I don't want to be an imposition, but if there was a role that I might be able to play, it would be greatly appreciated." He should have stopped there, but instead he felt it necessary to display his book knowledge, which I knew counted for nothing in this family. "I have been reading extensively on the extraction methods of alluvial mining, which I would be happy to share with you and implement in the field. Or perhaps as a bookkeeper. I'm quite competent with figures."

I was embarrassed for him, ashamed too. Why couldn't he ask straight-out what he wanted? He spoke so earnestly, like a schoolboy asking permission to leave the classroom. Kuda and Prisca exchanged knowing glances and I squirmed at how silent the room became as all eyes turned to Uncle James to see how he would respond.

"You'd like to work for me?" Uncle James considered him blankly, giving nothing away.

My father swallowed. "Yes. If you think there might be a place for me."

The Wife's response was typical. "What took you so long to see what everyone else could, Joseph?" She raised her eyebrows and then added, with a glint of triumph in her eyes, "That's what I always said you should do."

"That is the best decision you have ever made. You won't be sorry, Mr. Teacher, and you can start demonstrating your extraction methods tomorrow," Uncle James said, mocking my father's words. "Now, Jamu and Patson, come here." He gripped our forearms and pushed us together until our shoulders touched. "Do you want to become a miner, Patson?"

I could see the stones back in my hand again but this time they were sparkling, bright with promise. Without thinking, I nodded. "Yes, Uncle James. I want to be a miner."

"Patson," my father interrupted, and when I turned to him I saw his face was stricken, his brow furrowed.

"And you will teach me in the evenings, Baba. I promise you I will not abandon my schoolwork."

"It's a man's work," said Uncle James, ignoring my father's interruption and gripping my arm.

"I'm not afraid to be a man."

"We shall see, boy, we shall see. Jamu, I want you to show this prince-cousin of yours around the mines and teach him everything I taught you," he commanded. "And, Patson, I'm expecting great things from you. I think you've got the eye. You will be proud of your son, Joseph, wait and see. Now you two will be friends. Yes?"

Jamu smiled lamely at me as I offered him my hand. We shook solemnly. This was the way things worked in the Banda family. No one disobeyed James Banda.

◆ ◆ ◆

Marange

Kondozi Farm

20 February

I'm in bed writing by the light of my phone.
Jamu's snoring. The farmhouse is quiet;
outside crickets chirp. I don't know if my
father is disappointed or pleased with me.
All day he listened to the Banda family,
but didn't say much. He seemed a hundred
miles away, and then, after everyone had
gone to bed, I heard the Wife telling him
that he should be more grateful to Uncle
James. She's never satisfied.

Today I held three thousand US dollars in
my hand! I don't understand why my father
doesn't want me to become a miner. If we
had three thousand US dollars he could do
whatever he liked. He wouldn't have to sit
in front of Uncle James like a schoolboy.
If he had money he wouldn't have his wife

on his back the whole time. What is wrong with having plenty of money? Money makes things happen; money makes you feel good about yourself. It can buy you knowledge and respect; it can inspire you to do good things for others. When I leave the mines, I'm going to be rich and I will show my father that I can be a man.

Tomorrow—the mines of Marange.

♦♦♦

MINING

8

My introduction to the diamond fields began the very next morning. Jamu took his responsibility seriously, and I didn't mind playing Wide-Eyed-Dumb-Pupil to his Mister Know-It-All Teacher. If I wanted to find diamonds, I would need to know everything I could about mining and I didn't care who I learned it from.

"There are three main mining areas in Marange—PaMbada, Mafukose Munda, and Banda Hill," Jamu said as we struck out, running through the empty furrows of a long-forgotten tobacco field. "Let's start at PaMbada. Yah, I know you don't know what that means. But if you're going to fit in here, Patson, you're going to have to learn a bit of miners' slang. We use a whole new language on the mines. The quicker you learn it, the sooner you'll fit in. *PaMbada* means 'where the leopard hunts' and it was where the first *girazi* was found."

Ten minutes later we had scrambled up a small rise and looked down at another hill carved into chaos by a thousand pairs of hands.

"PaMbada is run by the Mazezuru syndicate," explained Jamu, clambering up a pile of gravel to get a better view. "The Banda and Mazezuru syndicates are the two biggest ones in Marange."

"How does a syndicate work?"

"People who trust each other work together. They protect one another and they all share the profits."

It wasn't long before I saw a pattern emerging at the foot of the hill occupied by an army of ant-people: Pickaxes, shovels, and iron rods dug into the hill; sacks of ore went to small pools of water; sieves washed the ore and the waste was discarded on mounds.

"You see that man down there?" Jamu pointed toward a stool with a red umbrella. "That is Alfred Mazezuru. The man next to him is a policeman. All the sacks of ore are sieved in front of them. Any *ngodas* they find are supposed to be shared with everyone working in the syndicate. If you find a *girazi*, you get a larger share than anyone else."

"Nobody steals them?"

"Some people try but if they get caught they get beaten up."

"And the policeman?"

"He gets his share. When the police started guarding the diamond fields they could easily be bribed with a pack of cigarettes or a can of beer, but now they want more. Mazezuru is lucky. His policeman is a family member. If he weren't there, they would all be working at night."

"I thought the police were here to stop illegal diamond mining?"

"Huh! That's a joke. They're making thousands of US dollars out of our work. My father says they're supposed to guard the mines, but there are too many miners and too few of them. Remember, you can never trust a policeman; he will cut you open for a diamond. Where there's a policeman's boot, there's always money," he said, pursing his lips and sounding exactly like his father; then he lifted his hand against the glare to scan the hillside. There must have been more than two hundred miners—men, women, and children—working the side of the hill, yet Jamu spotted exactly the one he was looking for. "There's Musi," he said, pointing to a group of men violently pounding their iron bars into the side of the hill. "You'd better watch out for him. He's got a mean temper. He said you ratted on him. Did you?"

I studied the group of men working in rhythm, the chime of metal against rock echoing across the valley. I couldn't pick out Musi. "No. I didn't, but your brother did try to rob us."

Jamu's face hardened. "I think he must have shat in his pants when he realized it was Boubacar with you. Nobody messes with him."

I wasn't exactly sure if Jamu was talking about Boubacar or Musi, but it was clear that Jamu feared Musi as much as his father. Where Musi was tall and muscular, Jamu was short and plump. As the son of the junior wife, life must have been hard for him. His strategy for survival seemed to be to please everybody and most particularly anyone who could do him harm.

"Come on, I want to take you to the Live Show," he said as we skidded down the gravel heap.

"What's that?"

"People who are brave enough to work the mines during the day. They don't have enough money to bribe the police, so they have to take their chances. Come on, you'll see."

"Are you really a prince?" Jamu asked as we walked through the blazing heat, trampling the tall grass on our way up another hill. Below us a brown river snaked around the bend, disappearing into the forest.

"What are you talking about?"

"Auntie Sylvia says you're a prince. She said she married into a royal family."

I had to laugh at the Wife's ability to polish a half-truth into a gleaming lie. I climbed up the rock and sat down beside him. In the distance the valley was green and lush, but below us brown patches of barren, dry land marked the miners' territory.

"Well, I guess I'm sort of a prince but it doesn't mean anything to anybody," I said, wondering how to explain my complicated family.

"She made it sound as if one day your father would inherit a kingdom," he said, flinging a stone into the air.

I watched it tumbling, bouncing, and skipping down the hillside. "That's sort of true, but not really. My father is from the

Lozi tribe. His father was a chief and had only one son. They were wealthy farmers, lots of cattle, with lots of land," I explained. "If my father returned to his village, he would have to sit on the king's council and be responsible for overseeing the traditional lands. But when he married my mother there was a problem. His family didn't want him to move to the city to become a teacher and, more than that, I think, they didn't want him to marry my mother."

I still wasn't comfortable enough with Jamu to tell him about the trouble my mother's totem had caused. When my mother was still alive, and I would ask my father why we never visited his family, he would only sigh, slide his glasses onto his head, and run his hand over his face. It was as if he were wiping away a bad memory.

"You explain it to him this time," my mother had said. "He wants to hear it from you, Joseph."

"Patson, come here," said my father. "Now, what have you learned about how people came to this earth?"

Like every other eight-year-old Shona boy, I knew the answer to that question. "All life came from the Great Pool," I said, sitting on his lap. "And the Shona people divided themselves into clans, which are represented by totems. Some totems are animals and other totems are parts of the human body," I recited.

"Yes, that's right. And what is the Moyo totem?"

"The heart."

"Good. *Moyo* means emotion, soul, or spirit and—"

"I know, Baba, you don't need to tell me," I had said, eager to impress him. "*Moyo* is also the title for kings or queens. A ruler."

"Literarily speaking, the Moyo is the soul and spirit of the palace, Patson. But you are correct and you get full marks. Now, who can a Moyo not marry?"

"Those people belonging to the lion totem—the Shumba. That's you, Amai. Right?"

And my mother smiled at this conversation she had heard a hundred times and, reaching for me from my father's lap, she folded me into her arms. "That's right, my little lion. You are a half-and-half. And that's a good thing," she added cheerfully, kissing my father.

"The best thing that ever happened to us," said my father, stroking her cheek.

I remember seeing them together, the two most important adults in my life, and feeling strangely excluded. It was as if I lacked the essential password to understand the secret smile that passed between them. I suppose like all children, I was having a hard time imagining them as independent people and not parents serving the needs of my universe.

"Then I am a lion-heart," I announced with pride, wriggling between them, jealous of their affection for each other. I remember so clearly how I'd made my father laugh and how he'd encircled us both with his long, strong arms.

The memory hurt.

It was sometime later I learned the other reason my father's family disapproved of his marriage. My mother's family was poor. How could a Moyo, a university graduate, a future chief, marry into a family that lived on the outskirts of a poor village?

When my mother died, I stopped asking my father these questions, and he stopped talking about how much they had loved each other. There didn't seem to be any point to it, especially when, just two years after my mother was laid in the ground, he married the Wife.

I picked up a stone and stood to hurl it into the sky. I watched its trajectory as it looped downward and bounced off the rocks below, splintering into a hundred pieces.

"How did your mother die?" asked Jamu.

"In a road accident."

A head-on collision with a bus on a dark country road; a phone call that broke my father.

"How old were you?"

"Ten."

"So it wasn't long ago?"

I didn't want to talk about my mother. Not here. Not now. And not to someone whom I had only known for a day or so.

"Yah, I think I get it," said Jamu after a moment.

How could you? I thought. You've got two mothers. How could you possibly understand?

"I didn't know what to expect, from a prince. Auntie Sylvia said—"

"She makes things up to impress people. Like how we got here. None of that stuff was true. Boubacar did it all. We would have been lost without him. She was peeing in her pants the whole way."

He looked sideways at me and I thought I had gone too far.

The Wife, after all, was his aunt, but then he laughed. "Yah, she tells a good story, that one. I can imagine she must have smelled pretty awful when you got here," he said, grinning.

So the Wife hadn't fooled Jamu, I thought, as we continued to climb to the summit.

Jamu pointed at a large, barren stretch of land dotted with people working in the dirt. "That's Mafukose Munda. *Munda* means a crop field, but down there, harvesting diamonds is the only crop they know. They say this place is as big as the township outside of Harare. Welcome to the field of dreams."

9

Mafukose Munda was crawling with people. Everywhere you looked, miners were sifting through sand, walking with sacks of ore on their shoulders, stepping out of craters and pits, or tunneling shallow trenches into the ground. The sun pounded down on a land stripped of all trees and bushes, and the heat was like being licked by the hot tongue of a fire. Every miner wore either a cap, head cloth, or floppy hat, and all were powdered in a fine gray dust. They looked like pilgrims of some religious sect searching for the stone that would change their lives forever.

We walked freely through the open Mafukose mine and I stared at mothers cradling their nursing babies with one arm and sifting sand with their free hand, at small children crouched over baskets, raking their little fingers through stones, and at an old man scratching through a pile of gravel shaded by his sieving basket. The deep pits were all carved by these men and women, the ridges flattened and shaped by their feet, and the large mounds had grown from thousands of baskets of soil they had carried on their shoulders. For in every hole they dug, every pile of gravel they searched or sack they carried, was the promise of a very different future.

I remembered those ghostly columns of miners rising out of the ground on the night we arrived in the fields: the zombielike creatures sifting through sand by candlelight. And to think I'd been so afraid of them that night, but now, in the harsh light of the day, they were nothing more than poor, desperate people.

"Yafa Mari! Yafa Mari!" shouted one of the miners.

"What is he saying?"

"We, who have nothing, have uncovered a diamond, now money will surely follow," answered Jamu. "It is the call every miner loves to make but hates to hear."

A few people huddled around the miner as word of his discovery spread. Everyone else within earshot looked enviously in his direction, and then, one by one, returned to their sifting, sifting, sifting.

"Is it really as easy as that?"

"No, it's not. Your *shavi* must be happy with you and it's very hard work. You have to be lucky and you can never stop looking," said Jamu.

"Have you ever found one?"

"One day I will," he said. "One day."

"How long have you been looking?"

"Six months," he said, and then as if reading my mind, he

continued. "Yah, I know you're thinking that's a long time to not find anything. But once you start you can't stop searching, because if you do, someone else might find what was meant for you. I'm still looking for that pile of mud that will make my father happy."

"I know this place. This is exactly where we were when we first met Musi," I said, recognizing the shape of a large crater. "How did it get so deep?"

"That's the eye of the mine. When the diggers come to a rock too big to break, they light fires on it to crack it open and the eye grows bigger. Come on, Patson, follow me."

We scampered down the side of the crater and gravel fell onto the men working below. They cursed and shouted at us but Jamu ignored them. Crouching on his heels, he slid down to the men digging at the center of the eye. I followed cautiously, trying not to dislodge any more loose gravel. At the bottom of the pit, five men with iron rods gouged at the earth. Women scooped up the soil and packed it into baskets that were passed, hand to hand, along a long line, until they were dumped into heaps at the surface. Then an endless stream of empty baskets made their way in reverse back into the pit.

The women sang as they worked:

> Mother and father, do not cry that I am gone,
> I chose to come to these fields,
> And with your spirit watching over me
> I'll find the girazi that shines,
> that brings food to our table.

"Who are all these people and where do they come from?" I asked as I scanned their faces.

"Nurses, bus drivers, farmworkers, goat herders, and teachers with big dreams. They come from everywhere."

"But where do they live? Where do they sleep?"

"In the hills, in the bush, or in camps hidden in the forest. Anywhere close to water." He paused and clicked his tongue. "It's becoming a problem. My father says there must be ten thousand people working these mines, and that many people attracts attention. Sooner or later, the wrong kind of attention," he added.

"You sound a lot like your father, Jamu."

"Well, it's true, isn't it? Look at them. Ten thousand people looking for diamonds. It can't go on forever."

What chance would I have to find any diamonds with all these people working the mines? It would take a special sort of luck, magic even, for me to find a diamond. I didn't have the strength to do this donkey work, or the patience to sift through piles of gravel. I would have to think of another way—a smarter way—to find my *girazi*.

"Come on, Prince Sort-Of," Jamu said. "This place is for losers. I've saved the best place for last. Tomorrow we'll go to Banda Hill."

By the time we got back to Kondozi Farm, the Moyo family had been moved out of the house into empty tobacco-drying sheds at the back of the farm. The house wasn't big enough for all of us, Prisca had explained, and once we became part of the Banda syndicate, we were no longer honored guests. She said the matter had been discussed and everyone had agreed. I found it hard to believe that we had spent only one full night with our new family before they evicted us, but this was decided while I was learning about the mines from Jamu.

"Jamu, take Patson to the sheds," Prisca ordered, and a little dazed, I went to Jamu's room to collect my bag only to find the Wife busily placing her clothes into the cupboard.

"Did Uncle James tell you of the new sleeping arrangements, Patson?"

"No, Auntie Prisca did."

The Wife had taken over Jamu's room and had packed all of his stuff into an old cardboard box. The desk was now cluttered with her pots of creams, makeup, hair extensions, brushes, and a large mirror. The suitcases abandoned in the baobab tree were on the bed, next to a heap of shopping bags. Once again the Wife had gotten exactly what she wanted.

"Jamu, dear, your clothes are in your mother's room. Here you go, Patson, I think this is yours," she said, handing me my backpack.

I refused to give her the satisfaction of saying thank you or asking where my father would sleep. I simply stared at her with all the loathing and scorn I could manage.

"You don't expect me to live in a tobacco shed, do you?" she asked in mock horror. "My brother's looking after me now. Once your father has found us better accommodation, well, who knows? But for now this just makes so much more sense."

"And Jamu? Where will he sleep?"

"With his mother, of course. She's so sweet. I think Prisca gives her a hard time, doesn't she, Jamu?" She lowered her voice and slipped her arm around Jamu's shoulders. "But we know who the favorite wife is. Right?" She hugged him in a way that made Jamu squirm out of her embrace before he picked up his box.

"I'll see you outside," he said to me, and hurriedly left the room.

"I'm sure you'll be comfortable," I said to the Wife as dryly as I could manage.

"Oh, I'm very comfortable, thank you, Patson," she replied. "Now run along, I'm a little busy. I don't know how I'm going to fit these new clothes into this tiny cupboard."

As I left the house, I passed Prisca and Kuda working in the kitchen.

"Good-bye," I said.

"Good-bye, Patson," answered Kuda, frying a delicious meal of onions and meat that I assumed I would not be eating tonight. Prisca was kneading dough and ignored me as I left the farmhouse.

I checked my phone.

> Found any ♦♦♦ yet? X-country team misses u.
> We lost today ☹ against Sec High. And hours of
> homework. ☹ When u rich, don't forget me!! ☺

How could I forget Sheena? Her hands on her hips, grinning

at me as she challenged me to run ahead of her up Uggy's Hill. We always ran together, the length of our steps perfectly matched. She was a good running partner; she never spoke when we ran. All I heard was her steady breathing at my elbow, and our feet tapping in rhythm with each other. I missed her and the comfortable sameness of our ordinary days at Milton High.

> I will never forget u >!< Working the mines.
> ♦♦♦ for everyone! It's ama-Zing here. ☺ Found
> lots of small ♦♦♦! Easy. ☺ Life is good. ☺

How could I tell the truth about this strange world? I didn't know what else to say. And if she wanted to forget what happened in her bedroom, then there was nothing I could do about that either. We were alone in her house, the afternoon was hot, and I was leaving in two days. It happened so fast: One moment we were only looking at each other and the next we were pressed together and kissing as if we would never see each other again. But the next day at school we both pretended that nothing had happened. I was fine with that but it was all very confusing.

> Missing u. U ok? I'll never forget that last
> afternoon…

I read the text. My thumb hovered over the Send button but then I deleted it. If she wasn't going to bring it up, then neither would I.

Outside, Jamu was waiting by the gate. He didn't look very upset at losing his room, but somehow I still felt responsible for the Wife's behavior. "I'm sorry, Jamu, if it wasn't for us you would still—"

"It's not your fault," he cut me off. "Anyway, my mother doesn't sleep in her room much. So it will still be like having my own room."

We walked on in silence while I pondered the sleeping arrangements of the Banda adults. "Does Prisca have her own room?"

"Oh yes. My father doesn't sleep with her anymore. He hasn't done so in a long time. Would you want to sleep with Auntie Prisca?"

"No." I laughed. "I'd rather sleep with a buffalo."

"I'd rather sleep with a warthog."

Our laughter took the edge off my anger and we walked the rest of the way, listing animals that were preferable in shape and size to Auntie Prisca. But at the rusty gate with an old KONDOZI TOBACCO sign hanging off it, Jamu stopped.

"The sheds are over there." He pointed to four squat cinder-block sheds standing next to one another in the tall grass. "Some of the other miners live there, too."

"See you tomorrow, then," I said.

"Yes, Banda Hill. The best for last."

I watched him run back the way we came, half hoping he'd stop and invite me to share his room with him. But he ran on without looking back and I clamped down my disappointment. He's a strange one, I thought.

Children were playing in a clearing and looked up as I approached. I heard a yell of delight as Grace recognized me.

"Patson!" she called, running to greet me. She was trailed by four children. "Look at all my new friends. This is Lovely and Maka and No Matter and Sidi," she said, lightly touching each of the children's heads. "We are playing scouts and Girl Guides. And look what our scoutmaster gave me!" She pointed at a green scarf around her neck.

The children grinned shyly as Grace took my hand in hers and explained that I was her big brother, and how happy she was to be out of "that old stinky farmhouse with the dead animals on the walls," and that this was a much better place, and that Baba was happy, and that moving to Marange was the best thing in her life. Her enthusiasm was infectious and I could only laugh as she rattled on as we walked up to our new home.

The four cinder-block buildings shared a flat corrugated roof and each shed had a pair of large metal doors, which opened onto a long, narrow, dark interior. We walked past the entrance of the first block, numbered one and two, where a woman was chopping up tomatoes on a table. Next to her an old man was sitting on a stool watching a small black-and-white television. I greeted them but they ignored me. In the next block a woman was plaiting another's hair and next to her a man was sleeping on a mattress near the entrance of the shed. We passed a woman carrying a table loaded with pots and plates. She glared at me as I greeted her and mumbled something about strangers taking what does not belong to them.

"That lady doesn't like us," whispered Grace. "Uncle James's men told her that she had to make way for the Moyo family. She was not happy even when Baba offered to help her move. All she said was, 'Go back to Bulawayo.'"

At the entrance of the last shed my father was energetically washing himself over a basin of water.

"Baba, Patson is here," called Grace, pulling me forward. "We are in number six shed." The children hung back.

"Hello, son. I'll be with you in a moment," he said, squinting at me through the soap suds still on his face.

I walked past him and stepped into a shed that was no more than two meters wide and ten meters long. Metal crossbars, once used to hang drying tobacco leaves, laced through the hot air rising to the ceiling. There were no windows, no source of any ventilation, and the stale smell of tobacco leaves made me cough. Three thin mattresses were laid out head to toe down the length of the shed, and Grace's collection of soft toys hung from hooks on the wall, like Disney characters in an abattoir. Boubacar's tie hung over one of the mattresses, presumably the one Grace had chosen. Laid out on the ground near the entrance were three plates, mugs, and spoons, a large container of water, potatoes, onions, and a box with cornmeal. Water was bubbling in a pot on a small gas stove.

Uncle James had moved us to a foul-smelling tobacco-drying shed. No wonder Jamu acted so strangely. He must have known. So much for my new family, I thought bitterly. Well, we were not going to be staying here for long. I would find diamonds and get my family out of here as quickly as I could.

My father dried his face and grinned at me as I stepped back out into the fresh air. "It's temporary, Patson, don't look so sad. This is all temporary. We have to work hard and soon we'll move somewhere else."

"How could you let them do this to us? And your wife has left you too." I couldn't hide the resentment in my voice.

"No, no," he said, laughing. "Sylvia can't live here. It makes sense that she stays in the big house. Once we have a proper place, we'll all be together again. There's no room for all of us in the farmhouse, Patson, and we can't expect Uncle James to feed four extra mouths."

"You said they would look after us, Baba. You said we would have a schoolteacher's house. We can't live here. Look at this place."

"Don't talk to me like that, son. You know better." He turned away from me, and put on his shirt. "Sometimes you have to make sacrifices that are painful but necessary."

Grace scattered the children and took my hand, pulling me toward my father. I wanted to jerk away, but she held on to my hand tightly.

"Auntie Kuda gave us a stove and all these things. She was very kind, Patson. I saw her slip some chocolate in the box. She told me what I should do about making food. We've got potatoes, onions, and goat's meat. Are you hungry, Baba?"

She took my father's hand and he turned around to face us both: the circle of my family, Grace connecting us.

"Like a lion," he said.

"And you, Patson?"

Grace squeezed my hand and I couldn't stay cross in the face of her enthusiasm. "I could eat a horse," I replied.

"Good." She laughed. "I will make a feast for all of us." She dropped our hands now that peace had been restored and left the two of us together. My father studied me silently and then took out a package from his briefcase.

"I bought you something. I expect your old one's nearly full," he said, giving me the package and leaving the shed.

I unfolded the wrapping paper, which revealed a leather-bound diary. I flicked through the blank pages and came across the inscription written in my father's neat handwriting:

For my son
Write your way into another life.
Your father

He must have carried this in his briefcase all the way from Bulawayo. It was a typical gift from my father. Always, as a young boy, I was initially disappointed with his presents and only after all the other toys broke or had lost their appeal would I appreciate the value of his gifts, the ones I had slighted. Last year he gave me a black moleskin book for my fourteenth birthday and taught me how to write a diary. "Writing in your diary is a way of interpreting the things that happen to you, more than just a record of your day," he had told me. "You could write *and then I went to school and then I came home and then I had porridge*, but it's much more interesting to write *how* you felt about school, what it *meant* to go to school, and *why* the porridge tasted good." For the first six months I didn't know what to do with all the empty pages, but soon I learned to write a paragraph, then a page, and before long I had finished the book and wanted another one.

I got my old diary from my backpack and went outside to sit down next to my father. Without saying a word I flipped through the pages until I found the section I was looking for and then started reading aloud:

"Today Baba made a decision that will change all our lives. We are to go to Marange to stay with the Banda family. I think this is a good idea, because we need to change our situation. I am excited and scared at the same time. Excited to go to a new place. Scared because I don't know what it will be like. But I trust my father. He knows what is good for us."

I closed my diary. "Thank you for my new diary, Baba, and I'm sorry. I was wrong to blame you. It's not your fault that we landed up here."

My father put his arm around my shoulders and hugged me. "I am excited and scared, too, Patson," he said. "Excited because I think being here can change our lives, and scared because it might not. I don't want to be a miner, son, but if it's going to help our family, well, I will do it gladly."

"I can help, too, Baba."

"I know, Patson, and I will allow you to be a miner during the day, but during the night you are to be a scholar. Can we agree on that?"

"Yes, Baba, and we can start with the lessons tonight, right after supper."

He laughed. "That's good to hear. It will be a pleasure to have you and Grace as my pupils."

Sitting next to my father, at the end of the day, the Wife gone, Grace preparing the food, I realized how little time I actually spent alone with him. Here in Marange, learning had no value; his profession was scoffed at. The Banda family did not understand him. It must have been hard for him to realize that all the values of his Shona tradition were ignored in a place where all that mattered was the discovery of diamonds. Perhaps living away from the Banda family would be a good thing after all, but not in these smelly tobacco sheds. I was going to become a diamond miner and get us out of here as soon as possible. The Moyo family will not live in a shed forever.

"And I have a feeling we won't fail as miners, Baba," I said. "The Moyo *shavi* will look after us. I know the ancestors are happy with you."

"I haven't thought of my ancestors for a long time," he said. "I suppose now would be a good time to address them."

"They'll help us find the stones. I know they will."

"And then we'll go back to my university town and I will get work there, in Harare. We should work the fields for only one term. If we are lucky we should have enough money by then to start over. You and Grace are both good students. You'll easily make up the lost time in school," he said.

I told him about everything Jamu had shown me that day and he told me about how the first diamonds were discovered here. There was a man who had been fired from the De Beers Diamond Trading Company along the Skeleton Coast in Namibia. It was a massive alluvial diamond field that runs two hundred miles along the Atlantic coast. He was visiting his father in Marange when he saw something shining on the ground. He recognized it as a diamond and immediately started looking for more.

"Nobody believed him at first, but after six months West Africans, Lebanese, and Israelis came to buy the stones he'd collected. And that's how the diamond rush to Marange started."

"Where is he now?"

"He's dead. He got drunk in a bar and crashed his BMW into a tree."

"That's a terrible end to the story, Baba. I thought you were going to say he has a beautiful mansion and lived happily ever after," and I laughed at the deadpan expression set on my father's face.

Then he smiled too. "That only happens in storybooks, son. Real life is a bit different."

"The food is ready," called Grace.

My little sister served up a meal of goat's stew and potatoes and proudly beamed when we asked for second helpings.

"You see, Patson. It won't be so bad," she said. "This is almost as good as the food at the Banda house, don't you think?"

"Much better," I said, licking up the last bit of gravy off my plate and feeling strangely happy to be alone with my real family.

While we were sitting at the entrance of our shed finishing our meal, a young man walked up and greeted us. Around his neck was a green scarf similar to Grace's. He had a broad smile and twinkling eyes. He shook hands with all of us and handed a plastic bag filled with avocados and litchis to my father.

"My name is Determine Ludozwa. I live in shed number one," he said. "We want to welcome you."

"Hello, Scoutmaster," Grace called, and then turned to us. "This is the man I was telling you about. He was teaching us how to march. I'm going to be a Girl Guide, Patson."

"Thank you, Determine. I am Joseph Moyo and this is my son, Patson. It is good to meet you. Are you working the mines?"

"No, that's not for me. It's too dangerous. I'm studying accountancy at Mutare Polytechnic. When I finish, I plan to go to South Africa. I have an aunt in Cape Town."

"You can't go, Determine. We just got here," protested Grace.

My father looked at the young man with interest. "I'm glad to hear someone in Marange believes in studying. What year are you in?"

"Well, I've completed my first year, but for lack of funds I couldn't go into my second. I'm always looking out for ways of making money and next year I hope to continue," he said, smiling. "In the meantime, I'm working on the fruit farm," he added, pointing vaguely in the direction of Mutare.

Their conversation faded and I, for the first time, thought to check if my mobile reception was any better here. But the battery was flat and how was that possible?

"Grace," I called, following her back into our shed. "Did you play games on my phone?"

"I was bored, Patson. It was only a couple of minutes."

"And now the battery's flat," I said, irritated, tossing it onto the mattress. "You must ask me before you use my phone."

"If I had my own phone, I wouldn't have to ask you," was her pert reply. "But don't worry, the old man in the first shed has a television set. I can ask him to charge it. I know how," she said, darting out the door.

"There's no connection up here," said Determine, watching Grace leave with my phone. "You'll have to go down to the road."

A thought struck me as I watched Grace talking to the old man, three doorways down. "What do we do about Grace when we are working, Baba?" I remembered those children working in the dust at Mafukose Munda. I didn't want Grace sifting dirt in the diamond fields.

"She must go down to the farmhouse with Kuda," suggested my father. "Or she can stay here. There are children here she can play with."

"We have scouting in the afternoons," Determine said. "I don't mind looking after her." And with a great, warm smile, he added, "She is welcome to join us."

10

The next morning Jamu was waiting for me on the steps of the old farmhouse. I had risen early after an uncomfortable night on the thin mattress to discover that my father had already left the sheds and that Grace was on her way to the big house.

"Auntie Kuda told me you can eat breakfast with us," she said as we walked down the path toward the farmhouse. "Come on, Patson, I know you're hungry."

"Nah, I'm okay, Grace. Maybe tomorrow. You go ahead. I'll see you later."

Jamu didn't ask about my first night in the tobacco shed, how I had slept or how I felt about us being dumped there. Instead he adopted his schoolteacher voice and continued my education about the mines. As we ran down the path toward Banda Hill, he explained how erosion had washed the diamonds from their underground pipes—"They're called kimberlitic pipes"—and scattered them much closer to the earth's surface. He gave me a regular geology lesson but I was only half listening as we walked up to the gates of the diamond mine.

Banda Hill wasn't really a hill but rather a series of mounds in a warren of paths that led down to a muddy brown tongue of water snaking through the open mine field. Around its edges piles of sand had been flattened by men patrolling along the fence that marked the mine's perimeter. A few men were busy repairing a section of barbed wire under the watchful eyes of two policemen.

"Welcome to the richest mine in Marange," said Jamu proudly as we approached the main gate. "That's why we need a fence and a security team. Everyone wants to work on my father's mine."

I followed him as we strolled up to the security guards, who nodded at Jamu, but then eyed me suspiciously.

"He's with me," said Jamu to one of the guards. "He's my cousin."

The guard stepped aside and we walked into the mine.

"They're all ex-policemen who were tired of getting paid with suitcases full of worthless money," said Jamu, referring back to the guards. "We've also got the police working for us. My father pays them to leave us alone."

Banda Hill had fewer miners than PaMbada and Mafukose and although the process of mining looked the same—the pits, the baskets, iron rods, and sieves—here it somehow seemed more organized, more urgent.

"We have our own source of water. The Odzi River washes the silt down those water channels, and higher up we have the purest ore, better even than PaMbada." Jamu talked on and on but all I could do was stare in wonder at the bustling activity of the mine. Everywhere I looked people were digging, sifting, shoveling, sorting, raking, burrowing, tunneling, and turning the earth with their bare hands: all determined to harvest a precious stone.

I spotted James Banda sitting under a large red and yellow beach umbrella close to the eye of the mine. He wore sunglasses, a white panama hat, and a brightly colored open-necked shirt and had his phone pressed to his ear. At his feet, two men were crouched over a pile of washed stones, studying each one with the same kind of magnifying glass Uncle James used. Although he was still talking on his phone he beckoned us closer with his free hand.

"Whatever you do, don't put your hands in your pockets," whispered Jamu. "When you're on the mines, he has to see your hands at all times."

While we waited for Uncle James I stared at the heap of stones and wondered if I could spot a diamond before the men could. My fingers itched to rake through this pile of promising pebbles.

"Morning, boys," greeted Uncle James, slipping his phone in his pocket. "Jamu, you showed Patson the mines?"

"Yes, Father."

"Is he clean yet?"

"No, we came straight here."

Uncle James frowned.

"I know. We'll do it today," Jamu promised quickly.

Then Uncle James's phone jangled in his pocket and he waved us away.

"You can't touch anything," Jamu warned. "It will bring you bad luck. You must first be cleansed."

"I washed this morning, Jamu," I protested.

"That's not what I'm talking about. Prophet Ubert will get you right," he said, climbing up one of the embankments to the middle of the mine. As we ran past a line of men handing baskets of mud to one another that had been excavated from the center of the eye, one of them called out my name. I looked more carefully into their muddy faces.

"Patson! Over here!"

I recognized my father's voice instantly. He was standing halfway up the slope, looking just like everyone else, covered from head to toe in brown mud. His feet were bare and he wore an old, dirty T-shirt and short pants. Uncle James had started him in the assembly line; the most menial of all the miners' tasks. I'd seldom seen him in anything other than a crisply ironed white shirt, thin black tie, suit coat, and trousers. But most surprising of all, his ever-present black-rimmed glasses were missing. How could he possibly think he would find a diamond without his glasses? He struggled with a heavy basket of mud while on either side of him the other miners cursed loudly. He seemed out of place; the weak link in a chain of strong and able men.

"Baba?"

"Don't look so shocked," he said. "You'll look like this soon enough."

"Have you found anything yet?"

"No. But I will. You'll see," he said, with his eyes glinting and a white smile flashing from his mud-splattered mouth. "I still have to work out a more productive method of gathering ore, but I'll find a way. See you later, son. Don't worry about me. I'm fine."

My father returned to the work he clearly wasn't very good at, and I followed Jamu, aware that in this mine, the miners' energy was quite unlike the others. Here, the men worked hard, silently, and with keen purpose. I would have to do better than my father.

"Hey, Fatso, you planning on working today, or you too busy playing tour guide?" one of the miners shouted at Jamu.

"Get lost, Chipo," Jamu shouted back and then pointed to me. "My dad's given me an important job to do."

"Oh, crap, not another hard-luck story!"

"I knew it wouldn't be long before you spotted us," Jamu relented. "Chipo, meet Patson."

I nodded at the miner and looked closer. Inside the too-large cap, the dirty shorts, and muddy T-shirt, Chipo was a girl. She was slightly taller than me, but I guessed, like me, she must be about fifteen years old.

"Hey, Arves!" she called, eyeing me suspiciously. "Arves! Kamba! Come over here. Fatso's picked up a stray."

Two young miners walked over, one thin and small boned with wiry arms and the other stockier, with one slow-moving eye and a jaw the size of a peanut butter jar. They both looked me up and down as if I'd fallen from outer space.

"What do you think, Arves?" she said, hands on her hips.

"Definitely too clean," the thin one answered.

"He'll be vulture meat in a week," said Jar-Jaw.

The boys circled me, while Chipo shook her head. "A week? No way, Kamba, he won't last two days."

"Patson is family," announced Jamu. "He's my cousin."

"Oh, so this is the prince we heard so much about," Chipo jeered.

"Doesn't look like much of a prince to me," scoffed Kamba. "What do you think, Arves? Royal blood or grape juice?"

"Looks more like a teacher's pet," observed Arves. "That new guy dropping baskets in the line, is he your father?"

We all turned to look back along the ridge of the eye. There was my father, on his knees, carefully lifting handfuls of mud into a basket while men in the line passed more baskets over his head.

"He won't last long in Banda's syndicate," predicted Chipo.

"Yah, he carries on like that and he'll be scratching dust on Mafukose Munda," agreed Arves.

"Banda hates slackers," Kamba chipped in.

To them my father and I were just four more hands looking for the same thing they were. Obviously we were not going to be welcomed with open arms. Not in this place where every stranger that walked onto the mine could be the lucky one who left a millionaire. I glanced back at my father, who had been passed over and now sat to one side, his head in his hands. I saw myself as different from him, though I didn't quite know how, just yet. But if I was going to be different, I would have to be that way right from the start. This interrogation and standoff with the *gwejana* of Banda Hill had lasted long enough.

"We are here to stay," I announced. "So, you guys better get used to us Moyos being around. Yah, and one other thing. Jamu's right. We are family. I'm part of the Banda family and James Banda is my uncle. I'm sure all of you have enough brains between you to understand what that means."

They stared at me. Even Jamu's mouth hung open. Then Chipo laughed.

"Well, that shut us up. I like your style, Prince," she said and, turning to Jamu, added, "I think your cousin is going to fit in at Banda Hill just fine."

"Come on, Jamu," I ordered. "I want to get this cleansing thing over with. It's time I got dirty."

Prophet Ubert Angel strode up and down a long yellow cloth, swatting invisible flies. He wore a purple velvet jacket with large pockets over a white smock that hung to his feet. His face shone with exultation as he talked to his god and received His Direct Message. Women wearing white headscarves and robes knelt in rows four deep on one side of the cloth, and men in long white tunics, holding long shepherds' staffs shaped like question marks, sat in rows on the other. The service was held outdoors, and a red cloth trimmed in white with a large cross at its center, stretched taut and held aloft by two acolytes, provided the temporary walls of the church.

"I am with the spirit. I am in the vision. We are traveling. By the power of the spiritual navigator you must be cleansed of your disbelief," the prophet shouted to the blue sky, his fingers moving dials on his imaginary switchboard to heaven.

Jamu sat next to me, transfixed. His eyes never left the prophet. All around us this strange congregation shouted out their "hallelujahs," the women bowing forward and back, and the men pounding their sticks in complete agreement.

"If you are poor, it is because of evil spirits," said the prophet. "But my god is a rich god, a generous god. Why should his children be poor?"

A rumbling of "hallelujahs" and "amens" rose from the assembly. A woman lifted a Bible in the air and it was quickly snatched away by the prophet.

"The hand of the angel of God is on this book," he said, smacking its cover. "He says raise your money in the air and he will double and triple what you offer him. Everything you have will be double-double, money double-double, cars double-double. Woh-woh—raise your money, people. Let God see what you give, so that it can be doubled."

Jamu handed me two American dollars. "Wave it above your head," he said. "It's from my father. You can pay him back later. Do it! Now."

All around me people were waving notes above their heads as the prophet walked through the crowd, gathering the money, which disappeared into his purple pockets. He laid his hand on people's heads, fanned them with the floppy sleeves of his smock, and gave one man a quick rap on the forehead. The prophet was like some microwave exorcist: Everyone he touched turned hot and shouted, "Hallelujah."

"You have been blessed, brother. Go to your *girazi*. It waits for you."

He zapped a man, who fell to the ground.

"Thank you, brother. You are cleansed."

And another, who flung his arms in the air.

"Mine is a rich god," he chanted, taking people's money with one hand and knocking them to the ground with the other.

"Why should his people be poor? Thank you, sister. You are cleansed. God is your *girazi*. Find him in the fields."

"Wave your money," said Jamu. "Otherwise he will pass by you."

I waved the two dollars above my head and in the next moment Prophet Ubert Angel lifted me to my feet, rested the sweaty palm of his hand on my forehead, and pushed.

"Your *girazi* is there, child. God wants you to find its blessings. Hallelujah!"

As I fell to the ground, the prophet moved on to the next miner, and Jamu shouted, "Hallelujah."

The two dollars were gone. The women across the yellow cloth were on their feet, singing, dancing, swaying from side to side. The men were chanting, pounding the ground with their sticks. The prophet withdrew behind the red cloth canopy, and the ceremony was over.

"And now I'm cleansed?" I asked as we headed back to Kondozi Farm. "That was it?"

"You don't need to believe, Patson, but remember, finding a diamond is more than a matter of luck. The cleansing works. Why do you suppose some people are luckier than others?"

I didn't have an answer to that. But if Jamu was cleansed in this same way, why hadn't he found anything? Could it be simply because of who he was, or was it really nothing more than bad luck?

"The miners also use spirit mediums," he said. "There is a powerful one from Mozambique who lives at Junction Gate who can speak to your ancestors. She gives me the creeps, but a lot of people go to her. You've got to have something extra, Patson, otherwise you'll work for months and all you'll find is rock and sand."

"But I didn't give the prophet my money," I said. "It was your father's money."

"You could have kept the dollars, but you didn't. You surrendered them to God. Now you can start working the Banda Hill mine," he said. "You'll see, Patson, it will work. Prophet Ubert Angel is connected; he knows what he is doing."

"You make him sound like he's got his own cell phone to God."

"Sometimes I think he has," said Jamu seriously.

I didn't know what to think. I didn't want to be skeptical in case my doubts somehow canceled out the prophet's blessing. All I knew for certain after seeing those purple pockets fill with other people's money was that Prophet Ubert Angel had come to Marange and found his own version of a *girazi*.

11

I soon had four friends in Marange. It took some time before they trusted me enough to let me join their syndicate, but after a month of working shoulder to shoulder with them in the mud, as hard as any of the adult diggers, I became part of the *gwejana*, a secret syndicate within the Banda syndicate. Every day the five of us met at Banda Hill, picked up our tools, staked out our working area, and turned the soil, searching for the elusive *girazi*. We shared information with one another, debated mining techniques, whispered gossip, and developed our own secret language and means of protection. One day Kamba and Jamu would dig, Chipo would carry, Arves and I would sift and sort. The next day we would change the rotation and so our days took on a familiar pattern we believed superior to the methods used by the adults. We focused on areas that they ignored, and we sifted in pairs, our fingers nimble and quick over the stones. We kept to ourselves and when the call of *Yafa Mari!* filled the air, we didn't waste time in admiring the find, but redoubled our efforts. At the end of each day, before I went back to the shed for my night lessons with my father, we would meet at Gwejana Rock, our camp up on the hills overlooking the mine, to share our stories, relax, and plan the following day's dig. It felt like we were playing the treasure-hunt game that I had so enjoyed as a child. But working here in Banda Hill, there was the real possibility that lying under the surface, waiting for each of us, was a *girazi* worth a fortune.

Although it was never said, it was understood that even though Jamu was family and Kamba was reliable and Chipo was a girl, Arves was my best and closest friend. He was a skinny stick of a boy who talked so rapidly he would break into a coughing fit because he forgot to breathe between sentences. His eyes always twinkled with some nonsense or crazy idea, and I have never known anyone who was able to grab life by the collar and shake it up and down so vigorously.

Arves had been born HIV-positive and lived with the sickness like it was nothing more than a pesky mosquito hovering over him. His real name was Tendekai Makupe, but everyone called him Arves because every day he had to take his ARVs— the antiretroviral drugs that kept him alive. Both his parents had died from AIDS and he was orphaned, until his uncle moved to the diamond fields, where they lived with his grandmother in one of the rooms at Junction Gate High School. Arves was one of the first miners to find a true *girazi* in the early months of the diamond rush. When James Banda heard about the discovery, he met with Arves's uncle to make him an offer in exchange for the stone. The deal was simple: Arves and his uncle could join the Banda syndicate and in exchange for the stone they received a six months' supply of food.

"Of course, Banda was smart. He knew that someone taking antiretroviral meds needed to eat regularly. Otherwise, the treatment doesn't work. I was as dumb as a donkey's arse in those days," Arves explained to me as we washed and sieved stones together in the muddy water. "I didn't know then that the *girazi* I handed over could buy a four-by-four, the latest Nokia, a business-class trip to anywhere in the world, a Harare whore for my uncle for life, and enough change for fried chicken and chips on the side. And neither did my uncle.

"He's not the brightest bulb in the socket. He was only too pleased to join the Banda syndicate for a while, and so we handed over my *girazi* as happily as a monkey picking nuts in a cashew tree. We had no idea of its true value. So what if all I got was a bowl of *sadza* and meat every day? I'm alive, right? And that's a good thing, I suppose. I eat regularly and the antiretroviral drugs are keeping my T-cell count stable, but where's the fun in that?"

"And what happened to your uncle?" I asked, pouring wet pebbles into a sorting tray.

"He left to join the gold mines in South Africa. I told you he wasn't very bright."

"And the *girazi* you found? How big was it?"

He lifted his hand out of the water and showed me his blackened thumbnail. "That big. The purest, brightest, loveliest thing you've ever seen."

"I've seen your *girazi*, Arves," I whispered. "Only now it's cut and polished. Banda keeps it in a leather pouch around his neck."

He stopped working, his eyes glazing over at the memory of his precious stone. "Yah, if only I'd known what I was giving away. If only I had more brains than a rabbit, I wouldn't still be here. But, hey, there's plenty more where that came from, and if I could find one, then I can find another."

Arves angrily piled another handful of ore into his basket and dunked it in the water. He sieved with such force, as if he believed he would find another *girazi* in the very next basket he held in his hands.

"Patson, listen to me." He dropped the empty basket in the water and gripped my hand. "If you find a *girazi*, you don't give it away to anyone. You hear me?"

I glanced around to see if anyone else was listening. "Arves, are you crazy? This is the Banda syndicate, remember? Nobody dares steal from James Banda. And what about sharing what we find with Chipo, Jamu, and Kamba? It would be stealing from the *gwejana* syndicate too."

He shook his head. "Yah-yah, we all share our *ngodas* for the good of both syndicates, but a *girazi* is different. The *girazi* finds you, because you have done something good in your life. You deserve the *girazi* that comes to you. It's like winning the lottery. You've got one chance and everybody here knows that. Look, Patson, a mine is just a hole in the ground with a fool at the bottom and a liar at the top," he said. "You're not a fool, Patson, you're clever. You've got more than monkey nuts for brains. I've seen you checking out the security, eyeballing the way the stones are collected. You're watching with one eye, and planning with the other. You can't fool me."

He was right. Throughout my first month on the mine I had watched the men on Banda Hill who were not mining. All day they walked up and down the high ground, peering down on us, always watching, searching for any suspicious behavior. Banda had at least twenty pairs of eyes ensuring that no one slipped a diamond into his pocket. I realized I'd have to be even more careful. If Arves could spot me scheming, why couldn't any one of the eagle-eyed guards see it as well?

It took a whole month of shoveling and sieving alongside my new friends before I learned exactly how the *gwejana* kept some of the *ngodas* they found for themselves. It was the end of another long day on the mine and we made our usual trek up to Gwejana Rock, as we did at the end of most days, to discuss the day's events before we all went our separate ways home. Arves and Jamu took up their usual positions on the flat rock overlooking the mine, while Kamba filled a bowl with water and began washing the mud off his arms and hands. Down below, the miners were packing up and leaving Banda Hill for their own camps.

"All those stones down there were left to us by our ancestors," proclaimed Chipo, from her usual perch at Gwejana Rock.

Chipo Nyati was born in the town of Mutare and she felt that everyone who came to Marange looking for diamonds was an invader. Her mother had a market stall in town, selling tomatoes and vegetables but never making enough to pay rent or feed Chipo and the other three children. Chipo moonlighted as a diamond miner, and even though her mother hated the thought of her oldest daughter working the fields, she couldn't argue with the money Chipo brought home. Chipo liked to brag that with no fathers, brothers, or uncles around, she was the man of the household. Nobody disagreed with her except when she started lecturing us on how the diamonds only belonged to the people who had always lived here.

"The land spirits of Marange are our ancestors," continued Chipo, throwing stones down the hill in disgust. "The people in this area have been suffering too long, and now these foreigners are taking what belongs to us."

"I come from the Bvumba Mountains, Chipo," said Kamba, scrubbing his arms. "You can't call me a foreigner."

"But you don't come from *here*," she insisted. "And what's here belongs to us."

"My father comes from Chiadzwa," said Jamu. "If you tell him he's a foreigner, he'll cut off your balls. Oh, sorry. I forgot. You don't have any, Chipo."

"Oh, yes, she does," chipped in Arves. "She just hasn't found them yet."

We all cracked up, except for Chipo, who squinted at us and then coolly strode over to Arves and slapped him across his head.

"How many sacks did you get through today, Arves? You going to be able to eat tonight? Don't come crawling to me for food when you have to take your pills," she said. "And you, fat boy? What's your father going to say when you show him the worthless pebbles you found today?"

Jamu squirmed. We all knew James Banda expected Jamu to work the hardest of all the miners. Then she turned her gaze toward Kamba and me.

"I didn't say anything, Chipo," I said, lifting my hands in defeat.

"Me, too, Chipo, not a word," added Kamba.

"But you two laughed like a hyena whose arse was being tickled by a feather," she said, dropping a stone into the bowl and splashing Kamba.

"I was laughing at the idea. Not at you," I defended.

"Yah-yah," she said, scuffing dirt in my direction. "And one day your brains are going to get you into a lot of trouble, Patson."

"But seriously, Chipo," said Arves. "Your people were loading *girazi* in catapults and shooting birds down from the trees, before someone from someplace else told you they were diamonds. It's a bit late now to claim something someone else discovered."

"Oh, I feel a delivery coming," said Kamba, suddenly getting up off the rock and wiping his hands dry on his T-shirt.

"Another one?" asked Chipo.

"Yah, early this morning, and now it's making its move," he

said, jumping on one leg. He picked up his sieve and a bottle of water and disappeared behind some nearby rocks.

"Can't you do that a little farther away?" called Chipo.

"Okay, stop complaining," he shouted back.

"What's Kamba's problem?" I asked.

Chipo and Arves glanced at each other and I caught the slightest nod from Arves. Jamu, meanwhile, picked up a stone and tossed it up and down in his hand nervously. Then he stood up, checking the hill behind us and scouring the path leading up to our camp.

"Relax, Jamu. There's no one watching us up here. We're cool," said Arves.

"Hey, guys, what's going on?" I asked, feeling uneasy at how tense everyone had become.

Kamba groaned behind the rocks.

"We've been watching you this last month, Patson, and we think you're ready," said Chipo. "Well, Jamu thinks you're ready and he's the one who counts. Like you said, you're a part of his family, so if he trusts you, so do we."

They watched me closely. "What?" I said, uncomfortable under their gazes.

"Go get them, Arves," ordered Jamu.

Arves cleared the bushes away from where they had hidden the camp's supplies. He unpacked the bottles of fresh water, a Nokia cell phone, a box with bandages, acetaminophen, a bottle of Dettol disinfectant, a bag of raisins and nuts, a couple of old blankets, and their very own loupe. He took a hand shovel and dug into the earth. After a moment he returned with a small tin box, which he, almost ceremoniously, placed on the rock before me.

Kamba returned, grinning. "It's a beauty," he said, holding a dark green pebble between his fingers.

"You swallowed that!" I gasped at the raw industrial diamond he held in his hand.

"We all do," said Arves, opening the tin box. "You have to be careful it's not too big, otherwise it gets stuck. Ask Kamba about the time he had to drink two cups of salt water to get one out."

"Un-com-fort-aaaa-ble," he said with a look on his face that said it all.

Inside the box were at least twenty tiny *ngodas*. They looked exactly like the stones Uncle James had shown me on the black velvet cloth, only a little bit smaller.

"Still warm, but clean," Kamba said, handing the stone to Arves.

"Time for the Nokia test," he said, holding the stone between his fingers and taking a photograph. The phone flashed, the stone sparkled.

"You photograph all your diamonds?" I asked.

"Nah." Chipo laughed. "This boy is so green it hurts."

"Only Nokia phones work," said Kamba.

"It's the flashbulb they use. It gives a blue light, which shows whether a stone is a real gem or a fool's diamond. And this beauty is definitely a gem. Well done, Kamba," Arves said, dropping the stone with a *clink* into the tin.

"You want me to swallow stones?" I asked, looking from face to face.

"Yah, you get used to it after a while," said Arves. "But don't ever put your hand near your mouth while you're working. That's what Banda's security is watching for. In Mazezuru's syndicate they caught a man swallowing a *girazi*. They got him later that night, cut him open and squeezed the diamond from his intestines."

"So how do you do it?" I said, trying not to imagine the agony of that mutilated miner.

"Chewing gum," said Chipo. "Lots of it. Once you've chewed it soft, you stick it in your clothes. When you find a small enough *ngoda* you cover it with the gum and hide it behind your ear, in your hair, wherever you're most covered in dust. Kids like us are allowed to chew gum, but obviously you've got to be casual about it. Make sure they know it's only gum."

"So how much is all this worth?" I asked, running my fingers over the *ngodas*.

"Maybe three thousand Usahs," said Chipo.

"Nah, I would say maybe two," said Arves. "If you get a dealer you can trust."

"That's a fortune," I said.

Chipo laughed again, shaking her head. "This boy's got no idea, has he? I thought you said he was bright, Arves? Patson, this is nothing. People are making millions of US dollars on these mines. Soon the army will get here, then the politicians, and then the corporations will squeeze all of us out. Our president has built an airfield only twenty clicks from here. Every night planes are landing and loading up our diamonds. Don't you read the newspapers? Everyone around the whole world now knows about the diamonds of Marange."

"Surely you've heard the planes?" Kamba asked, then turned to the others. "Let's go tonight. We haven't been in a long time. We've got to show Patson the planes."

Kamba's name meant "water tortoise" and it aptly suited him. He viewed the world cautiously, sticking his neck out only when it was safe to do so. He had lived in one of the small villages high up in the Bvumba Mountains with his older brother, Hondo. The brothers had looked after goats on the slopes of the mountain, living a slow village life until Hondo had heard about the diamond fields. When they arrived at Banda Hill, Kamba was unused to the crowds of people and the noise and pace of diamond mining, and stayed close to his older brother. They worked together until Hondo heard about an airstrip, torn out of the forest and flattened by bulldozers, not far from the mine fields. He became fascinated with the planes that dropped out of the sky at night, clattering down the runway to a corrugated warehouse, guarded by policemen.

From the safety of the forest, Hondo and Kamba watched the small, faraway lights in the sky grow into the gray steel-winged Dakotas that swooped down onto the dusty airstrip with a clattering roar of their engines that turned into a drowning idle. They saw the tail ends of the Dakotas lift up as large crates of what must have been ammunition and weapons were off-loaded, in exchange for much smaller crates of diamonds. And they watched as papers were signed and passed between Chinese men in uniforms.

"Hondo wanted to know everything about these planes," Kamba said, when I asked him why he wanted to go back to the airfield. "And then, one day, he ran across the strip while the soldiers weren't looking, sneaked inside the plane, and hid among the crates. I was too scared to move. The doors closed, the plane turned around, and, with Hondo on board, took off down the runway and disappeared into the night sky."

"Where did it go to?" I asked, amazed at the courage of Hondo.

"China, I guess," Kamba said sadly. "I think Hondo's gone to China."

That night Kamba lost his protective shell and became a member of the *gwejana* syndicate.

"Kamba, stop telling the story. You know how upset it makes you. We'll go to the airfield another time. Just not tonight," said Chipo, and Kamba's face fell.

"Someday he'll come back," Kamba said to no one in particular, pouring out the bowl of dirty water.

In the distance the sun sank slowly over the faraway hills as the day drew to an end. It was cool and quiet up at Gwejana Rock, a good place to unwind after a day of digging and sieving. No one talked for a while as we watched the line of people being searched one by one before they left the mine. James Banda did not allow anyone, including us kids, to leave his mine without a full-body search. I had learned so much about mining in the last month but still hadn't found any diamonds, not even a tiny *ngoda*. I wanted to add my own *ngodas* to the tin box and prove to the *gwejana* that I was as good a miner as any of them.

"Jamu, what if your father finds out about the *gwejana* syndicate and how many *ngodas* we have?" I asked, watching the men being searched below and remembering James Banda's tweezers, and the sound of bone being slammed against wood.

"He's never going to know," said Jamu, his face set tightly in a hard, grim mask. "We hand over all the larger *ngodas*. He doesn't need these small stones. Like Chipo says, there's enough for everyone. Those *ngodas* in the tin box are ours."

12

The first *girazi* came to me because of anger. It was two months after the Moyo family had come to Marange, and Uncle James was acting as if he had swallowed a snake. He was obviously troubled but no one knew why. He strode up and down the paths of Banda Hill, talking angrily on his phone. Some said a local chief had complained that the graves in the diamond fields were being destroyed. Every Shona knew the importance of the revered ancestors they worshipped, and if a grave had been disturbed it was serious business. Others said it was Banda's razor wire that he had set up around the mine that had offended the *midzimu*. No one had the right to fence off land, and everyone knew if the land spirits were angry, there would be no more diamonds. A few of the bolder adults whispered that Banda had become too greedy.

Uncle James shouted into his cell phone and then abruptly the conversation ended. He picked up a shovel and smashed it on the ground. Miners scattered as he moved through the pit, swinging his shovel like a punch-drunk boxer.

"Faster! Work faster," he shouted at a man working next to me who had left three sacks of untouched ore lying beside him. "What are you doing on my mine? You're wasting time!" Uncle James gripped the man by the arm and struck him across the face with the handle of the shovel and then kicked one of the sacks. "Get this man off my mine," he called to Musi. "Patson, take his place!"

I ran over and tried to lift the unconscious man out of the water. Musi walked up and pushed me aside. "Get out of the way, boy," he ordered as others from the security team ran down and hauled the man through the mine.

"Get back to work," screamed Uncle James at the diggers gawking at him. "What are you looking at?"

We all quickly returned to our work. I scooped up the ore from the sack Banda had kicked, dumped it into my sieve, dipped it under the water, shook the basket, and lifted it onto the bank. I had done this too many times to count but this time a *girazi* was sitting on top of the wet gravel, the size of my big toe.

The trouble was controlling my breathing; a surge of excitement exploded in my chest. I tamped it down, aware that the slightest sign of exhilaration would draw unwanted attention. I had to keep working in a slow, steady rhythm; I had to remain calm.

I dipped the basket back into the swirling, caramel-colored water, glancing up to see if anyone was looking in my direction. All eyes were on Musi and the guards carrying the unconscious man out of Banda Hill. It was then that I noticed his shoes lying on the bank, and offered up thanks to my *shavi* for bringing me both the *girazi* and a way of getting it off the mine. Without considering the danger, I placed the sieving basket next to the shoes, palmed the *girazi*, picked up the shoes, and followed the guards carrying the man.

I figured it would take me about three minutes to walk to the entrance. There, I knew I would be searched. I had to work quickly, but at the same time everything had to be done without anyone noticing anything unusual. I paused to drink at the water station, buying myself more time. The guards had dumped the unconscious man a short distance away, just outside the mine entrance. Musi was having a heated discussion with his father. None of the miners dared to look up from their work. As the guards started walking back into Banda Hill, I ran toward the entrance, now guarded by only one man.

"I got his shoes," I said, waving them in the air.

The guard who had been watching them drag the man across the field turned to search me. I lifted my arms up in the air, spread my legs, and opened my mouth.

"Boss man is crazy today," he said, warily looking over my shoulder at Banda, who was shouting at Musi.

"If he's got problems, we've all got problems," I said as the man ran his hands over my body, checked under my tongue, glanced at the ragged shoes I held in front of him, and then nodded for me to pass.

I ran up to the man lying on the ground, praying that he would still be unconscious. As I approached, he stirred, flinging his arm to one side in an effort to stand. At any moment he might open his eyes and see what I was doing. I slipped my hand into the shoe where I had stuck the *girazi* with chewing gum and pried it loose with my left hand. The man groaned and opened his eyes and I knelt down beside him.

"You were unlucky today," I said, handing him his shoes. "Pray to your ancestors that you will find what you want at Mafukose Munda." We both knew he would not be returning to Banda Hill.

The man blinked at me, took his shoes, and staggered away.

Walking back to the mine, I pretended I needed to have a pee. I turned around and trotted to the nearest set of boulders. With my back to anyone who might be watching, I carefully checked the size and shape of the nearest thorn tree, the relationship between the rock I was peeing against and where the sun set. I dropped the *girazi* and surreptitiously scuffed as much sand as I dared over it. And then just to be absolutely sure I would find it later, I made as if I was wiping my hand on my T-shirt but instead I tore off a scrap and dropped it into a nearby bush.

When I returned to my station, Arves, Kamba, Jamu, and Chipo all looked up, like a family of meerkats, and watched me pick up the sieving basket and start working again.

"You good?" asked Chipo, walking over.

"Just fine," I replied.

"You took the guy his shoes?" asked Jamu.

"Uh-huh."

"Why did you do that?"

"'Cause maybe he felt sorry for him, Jamu," chipped in Arves.

"Was he hurt badly?" Kamba didn't really sound concerned.

"He's okay. Sore head, that's all." I hauled the sack Banda had kicked and poured more ore into my sieve.

"You took him his shoes. 'Cause you felt sorry for him?" Jamu again.

"Nah, not really. I just took him his shoes." I didn't look at Jamu but felt his eyes on my back.

"Hey, Jamu, why's your father so pissed?" asked Arves. "He's making everyone jumpy."

"Yah, what's going on?" Chipo joined in.

Jamu glanced around to see who was within earshot.

"He was shouting at Musi," said Kamba. "I thought he was going to hit him with his shovel."

We all looked at Jamu, waiting for an answer. Finally I felt I could look up from my work without giving away the elation that was flowing through every muscle and nerve in my body. In the last month I had found my fair share of *ngodas* and made my contribution to the *gwejana* by adding several stones to the tin box, but finding a *girazi* was different. This diamond was mine and mine alone. I wasn't sharing it with anyone. I was going to be rich. And now that I had found one, I knew I would find another and another.

"The army's coming," Jamu finally said. "The soldiers could be here by the end of the week."

At the end of the day we all headed up to Gwejana Rock in a somber mood. Jamu's news about the possibility of the army coming to Marange made us realize how precarious the situation was at Banda Hill. I hated the fact that the Moyo family was still living in the sheds and that when I got home tonight, I would have to fetch water for a bath, lie down on a hard mattress, and breathe in the stale smell of old tobacco. But now with the *girazi* I found we wouldn't have to stay there much longer. All afternoon I had been daydreaming about the new Moyo house we would live in—it would be bigger than Kondozi Farm, with a swimming pool and two garages.

"I've been thinking," said Kamba as we jumped from rock to rock on our way up to our camp. "If the army comes here, how are we going to cash in our stones?"

Kamba articulated what I had been worried about: turning my anger-stone into cash. If the army came, it might make that a lot more difficult.

"That's going to be one big problem," said Arves. "The army is far worse than the police and everyone knows we all work for Banda. If any of us are caught selling stones to any of the dealers around here, Banda will find out. You can never trust a dealer. They're like hungry hyenas and Mutare is full of them."

"We could sell them at night along the highway that passes

Marange," Chipo suggested. "I heard there were a lot of foreigners on the road coming to Mutare and they won't know or care who Banda is."

"Yah, I suppose we could try that," said Arves.

"No! You don't want to go to the highway. It's too dangerous. There are soldiers in the bush. I've seen what they did to people who were trying to come to Marange," I said, and then the idea popped into my head. "If you're looking for a diamond dealer, I might know someone who can take us to one."

Everyone stopped climbing and stared at me. "You know someone who could help us sell our stones?" Kamba asked.

"He's a French guy from the Congo. His name is Boubacar. He brought us through the forest to Marange and he works for a diamond dealer. A Farouk somebody."

"Abdullah. His name is Farouk Abdullah. Everyone around here calls him the Baron," said Jamu. "And Boubacar is his bodyguard. It's not a bad idea, Patson. My father hates the Baron and won't do any business with him, so if you're careful, he'll never find out. But you had better know how to haggle. My father says the Baron doesn't negotiate."

"Hoh-hoh, Patson, you are full of surprises." Arves grinned at me as we made it to the top and he handed me a bottle of water from our supplies. "Didn't I tell you this guy was going to be great for the *gwejana*?"

"But how are we going to find him?" asked Kamba, pulling out a packet of dried nuts and fruit, which he handed around.

"Oh, that's easy enough," said Arves. "Everyone knows about

the dealers that hang out at the Dairy Den in Mutare. And they will all know where to find the Baron."

"So how much are we going to ask him for our *ngodas*?" said Jamu, placing our tin of small industrial diamonds on a rock before us. "I can't go. I might be recognized."

We sat around the tin box, lifting up the individual stones, counting them, discussing how many carats each stone had and their different colorations. Everyone had his own opinion as to how much our stash might be worth, but it was Kamba who surprised us all with his simple logic.

"Come on, guys, of course we think they are worth thousands of Usahs, but look at us. We're just kids," he said, raising his voice. "Most of the dealers will simply take our stones and walk away. And what could we do about that? Go to the police? I don't think so. Patson should find this Boubacar guy and maybe together they could speak to the Baron, and we'll just have to be happy with however much money he brings back."

No one could say anything after that. Kamba's words made me realize that finding a *girazi* was one thing but getting someone to give you money for it, without stealing it from you, was another thing altogether. My *girazi* was still just a stone as long as I was unable to find someone to pay me money for it. Finding a diamond was hard enough, but selling it was harder, and more dangerous too.

"And if the soldiers come to Marange, who knows what will happen. You're going to have to get to the Baron as soon as possible," Chipo said as she wrapped up the tin in an old newspaper, stuffed it into a carrier bag filled with nuts and fruits, and handed it to me. "If we're going to have any chance of cashing in our *ngodas*, you should go to Mutare tomorrow, Patson."

"And 'cause I know Mutare like I know every trench and hole in Banda Hill, I'll go with him," offered Arves. "You can't trust those Dairy Den diamond dealers; they'll eat this chicken alive if I'm not there to protect him."

13

The town of Mutare lay at the foot of the Bvumba Mountains, some two hours west from Marange. Arves and I had to hitch three lifts to get there; first a maintenance truck that dropped us off at a rock called the Stone for Girls, where six girls had been killed by lightning; then a white guy Arves knew from his Family AIDS clinic who dropped us at a taxi depot. And, finally, a taxi driver who agreed to take us the rest of the way free of charge after Arves slipped him a small brown paper packet.

We drove past Sakubva township, past a roadside market of mounds of exhaust pipes and secondhand clothes, along the ilala palm–lined Herbert Chitepo Avenue, and were dropped off opposite Meikles Department Store at midday. Naked white mannequins stood behind the glass windows, frozen in a different age. I peered into the shop at the rows of empty shelves.

Election posters for the opposition party, the MDC—Movement for Democratic Change—were stuck in the corner of the window. The people of Mutare did not vote for President Mugabe, which was probably why this shop was empty.

"Come on," said Arves, dragging me away from the window. "It's time for me to eat." We ran across the busy street, dodging cars, until Arves spotted a woman selling roasted corn on the cob.

Munching the corn, we headed down one of the alleys off the main road and passed shops with makeshift signs announcing BABYLON INVESTMENTS, LUCKYFIELDS ENTERPRISES, and GIRAZI GIANTS. "No, not here," Arves said as I tugged at his shirt. "Banda sells his stones to all of these guys. The dealers at Dairy Den will know where to find Boubacar and the Baron."

"Hey, Arves, stop holding on to the bag like that," I warned, throwing my cob into the gutter. "People will know you have something worth stealing."

"I'm still hungry," he complained, tossing the bag more casually over his shoulder, and heading for another street vendor. "*Sadza* and relish?"

Sitting on the pavement with a pile of hot, clean-white *sadza* with spicy atchar between us, Arves and I ate handful after handful, washing it all down with a can of Fanta grape. It was one of the best meals I'd ever had. I pulled my phone from my pocket. Four messages from Sheena.

> School's out. Don't want to talk about school. U there?

And:

> Going crazzzy thinking about u. Hmmm, any
> friends? Girlfriend?

And then the text that took my breath away:

> Do I mean anything to u?

And then the last one:

> Ignore that. Nvm.

I thought for a minute, put down my can, and texted back. Arves watched me carefully, wiping up the last of the gravy with a handful of *sadza*.

> School is great. Lots of homework. Got no time
> for running. Yah, good friends. No girlfriend.
> Yes, u mean a lot to me. Xxx

"Girlfriend problems," stated Arves.

"Nah, just an old friend from Bulawayo."

He shook his head and looked at me with pity. "When you come to the fields, Patson, better you forget your old life. Nobody really understands what happens to you when you get here." He pointed a sticky finger at me. "It's like we're living two lives—the one on the fields, which is all about hard work, and the one in our imagination, which is all about the good life we think we're going to have. When you come to the fields, you enter the *girazi* zone and become a zombie digger under the spell of *girazi*."

"Arves."

"Uh-huh?" He wiped his mouth with the back of his hand and looked up at me.

"Stop talking crap."

"Okay. But you know I'm right." He chuckled. "You said this Boubacar guy came from the Congo. Jamu said that he was a mercenary. You're sure we can trust him?"

"Sometimes you got to trust somebody," I said, putting my phone away, pleased with the text I had sent to Sheena, and slipping Grace's tie from my pocket to my neck.

"What's with the tie?" asked Arves, licking up the last of the atchar and *sadza* with his tongue.

"Lucky charm."

"Let's go." He jumped up, full of energy, and headed off down the pavement. "Come on, Patson, hurry up. We don't want to get back to Marange in the dark."

I hoped that Boubacar would remember me. It was unlikely that Uncle James would have paid him anything for bringing us to the fields. He might not even want to see me, but I had kept these doubts to myself and then, seeing his tie hanging above Grace's mattress, I brought it along, sure that Boubacar would remember "Mademoiselle Gracie."

"The diamond dealers of Dairy Den," announced Arves as we turned a corner and stared at the shiny Mercedes-Benzes, Hyundais, and BMWs that stood gleaming in the ice-cream parlor parking lot. The men, dressed in the latest gangster style— gold chains, baseball caps, wifebeater vests—leaned against their cars talking into cell phones, with their beefy arms draped over the thin shoulders of long-legged women wearing bling from head to toe. Waitresses from Dairy Den bustled to and fro serving ice-cream sundaes to the women, and burgers and beers to the men; street kids washed cars that blared hip-hop music; a crowd stood around a man holding an open black briefcase chanting auction-speak. Across the road, a police van idled in the shade of a government building, its blue light whirling its silent warning.

"Watch and learn," said Arves, handing me the precious bag. "When I find out where Boubacar is, we'll find Baron Farouk Abdullah. I want you to follow me at a distance. If anything happens to me, you run and I'll meet you at the naked mannequins. I know how to deal with these goat herders turned millionaires."

"But, Arves," I protested. "What if—"

"It's going to be cool. I'm sure they'll know where the Baron hangs out."

"Arves, I want to come with you."

"Relax. Who's going to hurt a skinny kid with HIV? I get a lot of pity and sometimes sympathy can be useful. I'll give you the thumbs-up when it's safe but it will be better if you keep your distance."

Arves sprinted across the road, heading for the group of street kids washing a midnight-blue Isuzu Trooper. After a brief exchange with the washer-boys, he approached a man talking on two cell phones simultaneously.

The radio chatter coming from the nearby police van made me nervous, and I realized how tightly I was holding the bag. Before we left the mine, the others had warned me about the dreaded plainclothes officers of the Central Intelligence

Organisation who roamed Mutare searching for dealers. Diamond dealing was illegal. You had to have a permit but nobody knew how to get one. If you were caught with stones, you were arrested and thrown into the back of a police van and never seen again. Remembering this and my own advice to Arves, I slung the bag more casually over my shoulder. I tried to ignore the parked police van but its slow-moving, silent blue light made my skin prickle and then I noticed the reflection in the shop window.

A scruffy boy with legs and arms brushed with light-gray powder stared silently back at me. The boy reminded me of those other boys standing on the side of a highway who had lifted their hands to form the shape of a diamond. Now I had become a *mailasha*—a smuggler of diamonds—just like the boys I had seen in the long grass trying to sell me their *ngodas*. The words of the driver returned: *signing their death warrants by sticking their necks out like that. They'll be dead in a week.*

I shivered and scanned the street for Arves.

He had moved to a woman lounging across the hood of a car. He offered her something that she looked at with interest, before slipping it into her brassiere and handing him her ice-cream cone. Then she pointed to a man with a nest of fat dreadlocks, lounging on a sofa in the back of a brand-new Nissan pickup. Arves walked up to this open-air office and hiked himself up onto the open tailgate, swinging his legs and licking his ice cream as if he were on holiday. They talked for a while and then Arves got up, tossed the man another small brown packet, and wandered away. He didn't look back at me but I noticed him scratching his head with his thumb.

That was our signal.

I started moving but then I noticed that Dreads had called one of his men, a man with baggy basketball shorts and dark glasses, and pointed at Arves strolling up the street. Dark Glasses nodded and headed off behind Arves.

Why had Dreads sent a man to follow Arves? I crossed the road, keeping both Dark Glasses and Arves in my sight. Arves turned a corner; Dark Glasses followed. I crossed the road and saw that Arves had stopped before a shop's entrance. He looked up at the building, glanced in my direction, scratched his head with his thumb, and then took off running through the traffic and disappeared down an alley, leaving his ice cream melting in the doorway. Dark Glasses ran across the road and narrowly missed being run over by a speeding taxi. By the time he got across the street, it was too late. Arves had disappeared. Taking off his glasses, the man looked up and down the street and then, after a while, shrugged and strolled back toward the Dairy Den.

I waited until he disappeared around the corner, scanned the street for any sign of Arves or shiny shoes and large watches. Did Arves want me to go into the shop alone? Suddenly, I felt that everyone looking at me knew I was carrying diamonds. I had to keep moving, so I crossed the road and paused at the puddle of melting ice cream.

Above the door was a sign: FAROUK SPECTACLES.

Arves had found the Baron.

14

A bell jangled as I opened the door and greeted a woman who sat behind a glass counter reading a newspaper. She looked up, pinning me with a glare.

"No hawkers," she said. "And no car wash."

"I've come to see Boubacar," I answered.

"And you are?"

"Patson Moyo. He helped my family get to Marange. He knows me. This is his tie."

She looked more closely at me, and then picked up the phone, indicating that I should wait in the corner. I sat on the edge of the chair and looked out the window. There was no sign of Arves. My hands started to sweat. The woman dropped the phone back in its cradle and returned to her newspaper. For a spectacle shop, there were very few on display.

The silence was hot. Sweat trickled down my back, and my leg was twitching up and down. I leaned hard on my knee and at that moment Boubacar stepped through a beaded curtain. He stared at me with a bemused expression.

"Patson?"

I'd forgotten how ugly he was but I had never been happier to see those scars and his broken nose.

"Can we talk?" In the background a police van hurtled down the road, its siren blaring.

"Come." Boubacar parted the beaded curtain and led me up a flight of stairs. We stopped on a small, dimly lit landing outside a heavy door. Our precious tin of *ngodas* wrapped in newspaper and stuffed among nuts and fruit seemed to be burning a hole in my bag.

"Grace wanted to come with me," I said. "She says hello."

He nodded. "But that's not why you came to see me."

"No."

This was the moment I had to take the plunge. After all we went through to get to Marange I felt I could trust Boubacar. "I found some diamonds," I blurted. "I need your help to sell them."

Boubacar's black hooded eyes bored into my own. "On Banda Hill?"

I nodded.

"And your uncle knows that you are here?"

I shook my head, suddenly embarrassed, as if I had been caught out in a lie.

"Does your father know?"

Again, I shook my head, unable to answer or even look at Boubacar.

"Patson, what you are doing is a very dangerous thing. Diamond dealing is not for children. Do you think that if you are caught the police will treat you any differently from an adult? No, they will not. Now, before I can help you, you had better tell me everything. Okay? And no lies."

I could not refuse Boubacar nor could I lie to him and so I told him how we lived in the tobacco sheds behind Kondozi Farm, how my father did not get the teaching job, and how he now worked on the mine for Uncle James. I told him how the Wife had left my father. I told him about the *gwejana* syndicate, how we operated secretly within the Banda syndicate, how we swallowed the stones, and how we all needed money to help our families.

"We live in a tobacco shed, Boubacar. I've got to do something to help my father. Once we have enough money we will leave this place. But I don't know who to sell our *ngodas* to and so I thought of you. Please, can you help me?"

"Let me see your stones."

I hauled out the tin box and handed it over. This was the moment Kamba had spoken about. What would I do if Boubacar pocketed the tin box, picked me up, and threw me down the stairs and out onto the street?

He opened the tin and studied the small stones.

"You *gwejanas* have a big appetite," he said, with a flicker of a smile. "I will help you on one condition: that you behave like a man in there and speak the truth. Yes?"

142

I nodded.

"Then we go to meet the Baron." He rapped twice on the door behind him before we stepped into a carpeted room with shelves of books on every wall. Sitting at a desk in one corner in a haze of smoke, a gray-bearded man, a pair of glasses on his head atop his small white cap, was studying a pile of stones, the now-familiar loupe stuck into his right eye. A cigarette burning in an ashtray curled a tail of smoke through the eerie light of a green lamp.

"Mr. Abdullah, we have a visitor." Boubacar walked over to the desk and placed the open tin on the table. "This is Monsieur Patson Moyo. He would like to do some business with you."

"You know I don't do business with children, Boubacar." The old man popped the loupe from his eye and lowered his glasses to study me.

"I know this young man," said Boubacar, moving to stand slightly behind Farouk Abdullah. "You can trust him."

"Hmm, so you say."

Farouk Abdullah picked up a pair of tweezers to move the tin box closer. Then he plugged the loupe back into his right eye and deftly picked up stone after stone with the tweezers, studying them briefly and dropping them with a *clink* back into the box. "A neat little collection of low-grade industrial diamonds, cloudy and flawed. Insignificant weight, with poor light. No, I would say not worth more than a hundred US dollars." He sniffed, closed the lid, and pushed the box toward me.

Only one hundred dollars. My heart sank. I glanced at Boubacar but his ugly face gave away nothing.

"I might have a hundred here, somewhere," Abdullah said, patting his pocket and producing a crisp Ben Franklin, which he laid next to the tin.

I was about to take the money, but then I remembered the advice my father gave me when I was tormented by a bully at school. "In circumstances where you find yourself powerless, words are always your best weapon, Patson," he had said, gently applying a dishcloth packed with ice to my blackened eye. "You can always argue your way out of a tight corner by using the bright light of logic to defeat dull, dim thinking. If you get them listening to you, it is the first step to victory. Words are powerful, Patson. Put in the right order, they can move mountains."

I didn't want to move a mountain; I only wanted the Baron to change his mind.

"I heard a rumor that the army is coming into town," I began cautiously. "James Banda says they could be here by the end of the week. When the soldiers come, smuggling diamonds out of the fields will be a lot more difficult, a lot more dangerous too." I paused to allow this information to settle in the room. My leg wouldn't stop trembling and I hoped that the Baron did not notice. I glanced up at Boubacar to gauge his reaction. His face remained impassive, but I detected a glimmer of encouragement in his eyes.

"I was right beside Mr. Boubacar when we saw what the soldiers do to men with illegal diamonds," I continued. "They stripped them, beat them, and made them wish they'd never left home. Boubacar knows, and he can surely tell you worse things than I can."

The Baron raised his cigarette to his mouth, inhaled, and slowly blew out a trail of smoke, which curled above his head. He sat very still, listening to me. Then he shot a glance at Boubacar, who nodded.

I picked up the tin box, opened the lid, and took a deep breath before speaking again. "Perhaps there will be a day when such a box of little diamonds will be worth more than a hundred dollars. I will have to wait for that day or perhaps find someone at Dairy Den who knows what James Banda is saying is true and has no problem doing business with children...while they still can." Then I stood taller as if I had made a decision and said, "Thank you, Mr. Abdullah," and snapped the box shut. "I am very sorry to have wasted your time."

"Wait a moment," said the Baron, raising his hand. "I don't know why young people are in such a hurry all the time." He sighed, sliding his pile of stones into his desk drawer. "Boubacar, tell your friend to sit down," he ordered, offering me the stool beside his table. "And make us some tea. I will take some Darjeeling and make the same for young Patson. Perhaps he might like a biscuit too. I see we have a real businessman here who understands that with every transaction there is a process of negotiation. And that process works better when both sides take a little refreshment and the time to understand the needs of the other. Come, sit, and show me those stones again. Perhaps I was too hasty."

I sat at the table while the Baron looked again at each of the stones and provided a more detailed running commentary on their individual size, clarity, and value. Boubacar, meanwhile, brought a tray with two delicate porcelain cups, a matching container filled with small white sugar cubes, and a teapot painted with small pink flowers. He placed the tray at the center of the table and swirled the teapot gently. Was this the same Boubacar I knew? The one who carried a large knife? Yet he seemed perfectly at ease pouring tea into dainty cups. When he passed a cup to me, I noticed a slight twinkle in his dark eyes, though his face remained as impassive as ever.

"Now, I'm sure you have a figure in mind for these hard-earned stones," said the Baron, placing three lumps of sugar into his cup and stirring it slowly with what looked like a baby spoon. "What would that figure be?"

"Three thousand," I said.

The Baron sipped his tea. "Overestimating the worth of stones is a common occurrence in Marange. Those Dairy Den boys will laugh at your price, take your stones," he said with a thin smile, "and then slit your throat. But here at Farouk's Spectacles, I offer you tea and biscuits. As you can see, I am a reasonable and cultured man."

I placed two cubes of sugar into my cup, stirred it slowly, and sipped the still-bitter tea. "And your reasonable offer is?"

"One thousand five hundred."

My stomach flipped. That was a fortune. I took another sip, trying to keep my hand from trembling. I glanced at Boubacar, who stood directly behind the Baron. I thought I saw his eyebrows rise.

"Two thousand five hundred," I countered.

"Oh no, my boy, that is still too much for these stones. But I will concede that they are worth something. Perhaps this first transaction could lead us to a more permanent arrangement in the future?" His eyes never left my face. He replaced his cup on the tray, Boubacar refilled it from the rosebud-painted pot, and no one spoke until three more sugar cubes melted beneath his spoon. Only then did his eyelids blink when he said, "I think you need someone you can trust. Am I right?"

"Go on," I said, sipping more of the tea, now enjoying its delicate sweet-and-sour taste.

"I know Mugabe's army will be here soon and I have heard of their brutal ways of doing business. If you take all the stones you find to Boubacar, you will not need to run on the streets selling them to strangers or deal with those thugs at Dairy Den. There is no love lost between James Banda and me," he said dismissively. "I give you my word that our business arrangement will remain a secret."

What do you look for in a face when you need to trust someone? The spark of sincerity in the eyes? The honest shape of a mouth? Or do you listen to the tone of voice and the impact the words have on your heart? All I knew about this gray-bearded man was that Uncle James Banda didn't like him and Boubacar worked for him. He served the Baron tea as if it was the most natural thing in the world. I trusted Boubacar with my life; it made sense, then, that if this man was his boss, I should trust him too. What the Baron had suggested was the perfect solution to our problem. There wasn't much more to think about but, just to be sure, I glanced up at Boubacar and caught another of his almost imperceptible nods.

"Let's agree on two thousand two hundred," I said, placing my cup back on the tray.

"Two thousand US dollars is what I am willing to pay for these stones," said Farouk Abdullah firmly. "And this represents a down payment on our partnership. Do we have an agreement?"

Before I had a chance to answer, the phone on the table rang, followed by a commotion from the shop below. A woman screamed and there was the sound of someone running up the flight of stairs. Boubacar moved quickly to the door, his knife appearing in his hand. He swung the door open.

15

Arves burst into the room, looking wildly around him.

"Patson! I've been looking everywhere for you. Your father's on his way and Uncle James is right behind him. And the police are coming right behind them, and then the CIO, so you guys had better not touch my friend," he shouted.

Boubacar grabbed him by the back of his shirt, and lifted him off the floor. Arves swung at fresh air, his feet scrambling to make contact with the floor.

"He's a friend of mine," I shouted. "I know him."

Boubacar lowered Arves but still held him tightly by the scruff of his neck. The woman from downstairs appeared in the doorway.

"I'm sorry, Mr. Abdullah, he slipped past me—"

"You were taking too long, Patson," said Arves. "I didn't

know what was going on up here. I was going crazy walking up and down the street. The CIO goons are everywhere and the police have raided Dairy Den, the dealers are heading for the hills, so I thought I would hurry things up a bit. We've got to get out of town, it's not safe here. Mr. Baron, can you please get your gorilla goon to let go of my neck or I'm going to have to take a great big bite out of his arm and he'll die a horrible HIV death?"

"This is Tendekai Makupe," I interrupted.

"This is why I do not deal with children, Boubacar," said the Baron, with a sigh. "No manners and far too loud." He dismissed the woman and indicated that Boubacar should let go of Arves.

"Your father? James Banda?" said Boubacar.

"Arves, it's okay. Tell us the truth. Are they really outside?"

He shook his head and grinned. "It was the only thing I could think of. I didn't know what happened to Patson. Sorry, Mr. Abdullah."

"Patson, do we have an agreement?" asked the Baron.

"What agreement? What's the deal?" asked Arves.

"Shut up, Arves," I hissed, gripping his arm tightly with one hand and offering my other to Mr. Abdullah. "Yes, we have a deal."

The Baron shook my hand with a grip that reinforced our arrangement. Then he opened the desk drawer and our hard-won *ngodas* disappeared inside. He counted out the dollars underneath his desk, folding them tightly to fit inside our tin box.

"That concludes our business for today, Patson," he said. "Boubacar, please show the young men the back way out."

"One more thing," I said. "If we should find a *girazi*, will the same deal apply?" I tried to phrase the question as casually as I could, knowing that these men, with all their experience and stealth, could easily sense when someone was hiding something.

The Baron stopped; Boubacar stared at me as if he could see right through me.

"A *girazi* is another matter entirely, Patson," said the Baron quietly. "You have found one?"

"No, no." I raised my hands defensively. "I just wanted to know if we could come to you in the same way."

"Oh yes, but with extreme caution," replied the Baron. "One *girazi* is worth a fortune and many men would go to extraordinary lengths to get one. There are many hungry eyes on the diamond fields and selling a *girazi* requires a completely different set of arrangements."

He nodded at Boubacar, who opened the door and led the way down the stairs, only to stop when Arves popped his head through the beaded curtain.

"Next time we come back, we'll buy some Ray-Bans," Arves said to the woman behind the counter.

I dragged him back to the staircase and we joined Boubacar outside in a dusty back alley. Arves couldn't stop talking about the CIO raid on Dairy Den, the police vans converging from three sides, the dealers scattering throughout the town.

"It was chaos out there, Patson. Dealers running down the

street chased by police, sirens blaring! Something's happening in Mutare. This is not normal. Something's going on."

"You helped me in there," I said to Boubacar, fumbling blindly through the notes in the tin box deep inside my bag. I got hold of one, and passed it to him inside a grateful but casual handshake. "Thank you."

He looked at the money without comment, but I could see he was pleased.

"How will we contact each other?" I asked him.

"Give me both your numbers."

Arves and I recited our numbers to him while he typed them into his phone.

"Text me on this number and I will come to Marange. Traveling to Mutare is too dangerous," he said, handing me a slip of paper. "How will you boys get back? You are carrying a lot of money."

"Rent a helicopter," joked Arves.

"Taxi ride or hitchhike," I answered.

Boubacar frowned. "This is not a good idea," he said. "If anyone saw you coming into this shop, they will know you have money. I will take you to Marange. We meet here in five minutes."

Boubacar went back inside, while Arves and I waited in the alley.

"Patson, how much did you get for us?" Arves could hardly contain his excitement.

I told him.

"Two thousand Usahs? Do you know how much money that is in Zim dollars?" His voice rose an octave.

"Keep your voice down," I urged. "You want the whole of Mutare to know how much money we have?"

"I can't believe it!" he mock whispered. "And it's just the beginning, Patson. Through Boubacar you have a direct line to the Baron. Everything else we find now turns into instant Usahs. Two thousand Usahs! I feel like singing. Like dancing. Like tearing open the sky and flying to the moon. We did it, Patson. You did it! Come on, get excited."

He shook my arm and we both started laughing until I had to wipe tears away. Arves laughed like a hyena with a bone stuck in his throat, which made me laugh even more. He was right. We had pulled off the impossible. If the Baron gave us two thousands Usahs for those little stones, how much would I get for my *girazi*? This was our start back to normality. The Moyo family was going to move out of the tobacco sheds. We were going to live in a decent house; my father would buy his car. It felt so good that I gave myself over to an uncontrollable, air-gulping, stomach-aching fit of laughter.

"And did you see how easy we got rid of that goat herder who was trying to follow us?" said Arves as he recapped the events before he burst into the room.

"What was in the little brown packets you were giving to everyone?"

"*Ganja*. The magic herb that makes pain disappear."

"You smoke marijuana?"

"Yah, smoke it or chew it, same difference. When the sickness gets me down, it's good to have a bit of *ganja*-happiness handy. It's also a great way of getting people to tell you stuff you want to know," he said, and then he held out his hand. "I want to look at the cash."

I opened the tin and we stared at the pile of American dollars. We counted out the money and divided it up into five equal parts. Arves slipped an elastic band around each healthy roll of cash and I took my share, placing it back into the tin. The *gwejana* syndicate had made its first real money. The others would be pleased.

"You've found one, haven't you?" said Arves, suddenly serious.

"What?"

"A *girazi*. You've found one. I know you have."

I didn't know what to answer. A part of me wanted to tell Arves about my anger-stone but I hesitated, and in that moment, as he looked deeply into my eyes and saw what I was not saying, Boubacar returned. I had hesitated and Arves's question remained unanswered. I hated seeing the disappointment in his eyes. He was my best friend after all, yet I still didn't want to share my *girazi* with anyone. It was mine. For my family. My *shavi* had sent it and it belonged only to me.

"Let's go," ordered Boubacar. "I want to get to Marange and back to town before it's dark."

I stuffed the tin back into the bag and we squeezed into the front seat of the pickup truck. As we pulled into Herbert

Chitepo Avenue, two police vans roared past us, sirens blaring, blue lights whirling. People were still running in the streets and two blocks past Dairy Den there were several police vans setting up a roadblock. Boubacar swung a hard right and drove down a side alley.

"Mr. Boubacar," said Arves, in the most charming voice he could manage and with his winning smile broadly in place. "Before we go back to Marange, there's something Patson and I have got to do."

"It will have to be quick. There is a lot of police action in Mutare."

"We'll be superquick, but it's very important," said Arves.

"What's so important?"

"Shopping!"

Boubacar pulled up before the old TOBACCO FARM sign and let the engine idle. We had dropped Arves off at Junction Gate High School after Boubacar promised us we would see him soon. Arves had solemnly offered him his last brown packet but Boubacar refused, saying he didn't smoke roasted cow dung.

It was late afternoon and the sun had dipped over the hills. Tiny motes of dust glowed in the fading light and the smell of cooking drifted down from the sheds. I was weary and hungry and elated all at the same time.

"Grace and my father would be pleased to see you," I said, in the ear-humming rumble of the truck's interior.

Boubacar hesitated, checked his watch, and then switched off the motor and opened his door. Together we walked up the path to the sheds. When Grace saw us, she ran and flung herself into his arms, almost knocking him over. For the first time that day I saw a smile on his face.

"I only gave Patson my tie because he told me he was visiting you," she said, slipping her hand into his. "Baba! Baba, look who's here!"

My father stepped out of the gloom of the tobacco shed. The exhaustion that lined his face disappeared the moment he saw who stood at the entrance.

"My word, it's Boubacar. How good it is to see you again," he said, shaking his hand and pulling out the only chair we had.

Boubacar sat down but seemed uncomfortable with all the attention. A few of the other shed dwellers looked in our direction, but after the excitement of the unexpected guest had passed, they returned to their preparations for the evening. I handed Grace two carrier bags filled with groceries, including vegetables and meat for our evening meal.

"Next time you have to take me with you, Patson," Grace insisted. "I don't like being stuck at the sheds the whole day." Peering into the bag, she gasped. "Real bread."

"And your favorite cool-drink, Grace," I said as she pulled out two tins of red Sparletta.

"Son?" my father asked.

I handed another small package to my sister. "Now you can run your own battery flat."

Grace took out the pay-as-you-go cell phone as if it were

treasure, looked up in amazement, and then hugged me hard. "Thank you, Patson. You're the best big brother in the world!"

"Now remember, you can't make any phone calls, but I downloaded Mxit and as long as you have ten cents on the phone you can send as many messages as you like. And I got this for you, Baba." I handed my father a copy of Credo Mutwa's *Indaba, My Children*. I had found it in a book shop in Mutare, knowing how much it would mean to him. He held the book in his hands, turning the pages slowly.

"Son, how did you manage this?"

"I found some stones, Baba," I said quietly, knowing Boubacar would not mention the *gwejana* syndicate. "Boubacar helped me sell them. It's good news." I took out the tin box and showed him the money.

"You gave him this money, Boubacar?" asked my father.

"No, my boss did. The Baron—Mr. Abdullah. He was impressed with your boy," he replied. "He will give him more money, if he finds more *ngodas*."

"Does the Baron live in a castle?" Grace asked, without looking up from her phone.

"No, he owns a spectacle shop without many spectacles in it." I laughed. "This is for you, Baba," I said, handing him the tidy pile of cash.

Silently my father took the money, looked searchingly at it and at me, and then slipped it into his book. "That my own son should give his father so much money." His voice caught on the final word. "My ancestors remain unhappy with me. All I find is mud and rocks. But your *shavi* is strong, son. He shows you what I am unable to find."

I hated to hear my father sound so sad. Ever since that day at Junction Gate High School, when he sat sobbing beside the old woman, he had developed the habit of frowning and staring into the middle distance.

Grace eased herself under the wing of his arm and took his hands into her own. "Tomorrow will be a good day, Baba. You will find your diamond. I know you will." She turned to Boubacar. "You must stay for supper. My brother has brought enough for us all and tonight is a special night."

He hesitated, made to get up and leave, but Grace persisted and he sat back down again. Boubacar's unease vanished when Grace served him tea and biscuits and we sat together enjoying the cool of the evening.

"Joseph, your children are a credit to you," he said to my father. "They are a finer treasure than any stone you will find in the diamond field."

"You're right, Boubacar. That's a good thing to remember."

At that moment I wanted to tell my father everything, about the *gwejana* and the *ngodas*, even about my *girazi*. But looking at him as he stared at his hands, shaking his head, I didn't have the heart. I had hoped that my success with the *gwejana* would cheer him up, but all I saw was despair in his eyes. It was enough that we now had food for the month and that I had brought them gifts.

As the sun set and the lights in the sheds went on, and while Grace cooked a meal in our midst, I took my first giant step away from childhood. My father had silently pulled up a seat for me and indicated that I should join him and Boubacar. He directed questions to me, listened to my answers, and, in so doing, something shifted between us. He had invited me to take my place in the company of men. We spoke as equals about all of the things that happened on the mines: extraction methods, the Banda Hill syndicate, the problem of the fence that Banda had erected, the police raids in Mutare and what that might mean for the fields.

"And what if the army comes to Marange, Boubacar?"

"The army is here already, Patson. I have reports of the Fifth Brigade camping only a few miles from here. Those soldiers we saw on the night we came here, they are from the Number One Commando Regiment. They are also heading in this direction."

"But why are they coming to Marange?"

"The government has run out of money and can't pay the army. Our president may be old but he's not stupid. He knows the fields are making money, money he can pay his army with."

"That is not good news," said my father. "Our president will not look kindly on ordinary people and foreigners stealing Zimbabwe's mineral wealth."

"Soldiers are not miners," countered Boubacar. "They will need people to find the diamonds."

"Enough of soldiers and mining," announced Grace. "Let's eat."

How I wished I could capture moments of life, wrap them up and keep them safe to relive at a later time; the soft clink of spoons against empty tin plates, the smells of a delicious meal; the twinkle in Grace's eyes as she teased my father about his mining mishaps, the signs of affection; the deep tones of Boubacar's rumbling laughter, the sound of friendship; my father gently tapping the book with US dollars hidden between its pages, his recognition of my success.

If I had known how special that evening was, I would have paid more attention to my father, and written all he had said in my diary and how it felt to be acknowledged in this new way. But I was too full of pride about the money I had earned for my family. All through the meal I schemed about how I would get more money for my *girazi*.

My *girazi*; our family's fortune.

Later, after Grace had gone to bed, as we strolled back from saying good-bye to Boubacar, I told my father about my *girazi* and how I had hidden it. Once again, he responded in a way I least expected.

"Patson, you must be very careful," he said quietly. "Sell it and then we can leave this terrible place."

"No, Baba," I said, emboldened by his acceptance of my new manhood. "This is exactly why we cannot leave. I will find another one. I know I will. I have been cleansed by Prophet Ubert Angel and I am one of the lucky ones. As you said to me, my *shavi* is happy and helping me."

"Who have you told about your *girazi*, Patson?"

"No one," I said. "Only you, Baba."

He frowned. "Remember, Patson, telling a secret to an unworthy person..."

"Is like carrying grain in a bag with a hole," I said, finishing the Shona proverb.

"If anyone finds out you have a *girazi*—"

"They won't. I will give it to Boubacar. Mr. Abdullah will buy it from me. He has the money."

"People will kill for a *girazi*. I've heard terrible stories about what men will do to own a *girazi*. We must get away from here before—"

"I am staying, Baba. I know I will find more stones. This is the chance we have to change our lives," I said, surprised at how strongly I felt about this. "We can't leave now. We will be rich. You will have all the good things you want for our family."

I had never challenged my father so directly. He studied me silently and then laid his hand on my shoulder. "You remember what happened to the man who found the first diamonds in Marange?"

"Yes, he drove into a tree and killed himself."

"He lost control of his life, Patson."

"But that's not going to happen to me," I insisted.

"I hope not, son, I hope not."

And that was the end of the conversation. I had thought my discovery would have pleased my father. However, he seemed unaffected by my news, which left me feeling deflated. I had wanted to hear his praises, not his anxiety. I wanted him to be excited, but instead, we arrived at the door of our shed in silence, my father deep in thought.

As we approached, Determine stepped out of shed six and looked up at us in surprise.

"Mr. Moyo," he said, shifting awkwardly. "I wanted to speak to Grace. She's sleeping now."

"It's late, Determine," said my father. "What do you want?"

"Nothing important. Just tell Grace that we will meet at the usual time tomorrow afternoon. Sorry for the trouble, Mr. Moyo," he said, embarrassed for no reason I could see. "G'night, Patson," he mumbled, walking quickly back toward shed number one.

My father watched him leave, and then entered the shed briefly. "That's strange," he said, standing in the doorway. "Why would Determine be inside our shed?"

I was too lost in my own thoughts to question him. Instead I walked past without a word, stripped off my clothes, and lay down on the mattress.

"Are you ready for your lesson, son?" He lit the paraffin lamp and took out the books from his briefcase.

"I'm tired, Baba. It's been a long day." I rolled over, turning my back on my father, waiting for his inevitable response.

But he said nothing. Instead, I heard him packing away the books, taking up the water basin, and leaving the shed.

I listened to the steady breathing of my sister and the sounds of my father washing outside. I don't think either of them had yet realized how grateful they should be to me. Our lives would be different now all because of my hard work. I had found the stone that would change our lives. I would find more diamonds. This was just the beginning. I was the one who had found our way out of this place. I stared up at the iron rafters disappearing into the gloom of the shed, restless and not yet ready for sleep. This wasn't the way I wanted to end a perfect evening; my father's fretting had spoiled everything. I heard him throw out the water, enter the shed, and close the metal door behind him.

"Patson?"

I pretended to be asleep. He blew out the lamp and I heard him lying down on the mattress.

"Never let the stones become more than you, Patson," he said into the darkness.

I did not answer him.

"Good night, son. I'm proud of you."

Once I heard him sleeping, I picked up my running shoes, and by the beam from my cell phone, found Grace's small vegetable knife among the dishes. I slipped outside and sat down under the sallow light above the shed door.

The night was still; I was alone.

I inspected the soles of my running shoes and carefully cut out a hole the size of my thumb from the inside of the right shoe. The rubber proved too tough to cut cleanly, so I returned to the shed and found the gas stove. I heated the knife until the tip was red-hot. Now the blade cut cleanly through the rubber and I gently prised a plug from the sole and made a hole deep and long enough for the length of my entire thumb. Once I was satisfied, I shortened the plug, replaced it over the secret cavity, and laced on my running shoes.

I knew exactly how long it would take me to get to the bush tagged with a scrap from my T-shirt.

Finally, I was going for a run.

◆◆◆

Marange Diamond Fields

Gwejana Rock

A Day in March

I thought today about the old life I left
on a shelf back in Bulawayo. Every day
putting on my school uniform, and walking
up the tree-lined entrance to Milton High
School. Sitting on the steps with Paul,
Max, and Thaka before the school bell
rang, watching the Grade 9 girls walk past,
loaded down with their school bags.

How normal to listen to a teacher standing
in front of the class; how ordinary to take
out my trigonometry book and turn to a
new page. The quiet concentration of thirty
students bent over a mathematical problem
with sunshine streaming into the room. And
the pleasure I got from working out the
sine—the opposite side over the hypotenuse—
of a right-angle triangle. (I remember the

formula still.) And the funny, lyrical way we greeted Mr. Sampson in unison—"Good-after-noon-Mis-ter-Samp-son"—at the end of the period before heading out to the playground to play soccer and kick the ball to each other until the bell rang. And then, lining up to drink water from the water fountain, and straightening my tie as I saw Sheena heading for the library. How I would pass a note to her in a book about the Romantic poets and she would write back with a note hidden in The Mating Habits of the Animal Kingdom.

The idea of putting on a school uniform, listening to a teacher, working out the sine, playing soccer at break time, and study period in a library all seem so strange now. The habits of my old life were all so important. But now they are as insignificant as the discarded pebbles that pile up next to the trenches on Banda Hill. That life in Bulawayo is over. I am no longer a schoolboy but a diamond miner.

◆◆◆

SOLDIERS

16

They came without warning. Four helicopters appeared above the hills like huge metal locusts. The gray gunships swooped down upon the diamond fields, rotors whipping up dust storms, guns firing upon the miners. Arves and I were working together in one of the pits, and at the sound of the machine guns we dropped our tools and scrambled to the top of a mound, only to see one of the helicopters peeling away from Mafukose Munda and heading directly toward us.

"Run! They're coming this way!" shouted Arves as we bounded down the mound.

The helicopter bore down on Banda Hill, preceded by two lines of gunfire tearing up the earth. The noise was terrifying; the chaos immediate.

A man who had been digging next to me tried to collect his bag of ore and a bullet went right through his head. Miners scattered before the oncoming helicopter, clambering out of their holes, scrambling over the fence, yelling, running in all directions. The helicopter hovered over Banda Hill, filling our eyes and ears with the dust storm from its rotors and the blasts from its machine guns. It rotated slowly, its guns blazing. In a blind panic I staggered forward, falling over bodies of miners, and rolling down the side of a mound.

Arves grabbed my hand and pulled me to my feet. The whites of his eyes were showing and his mouth was moving. Our screams went unheard, even to ourselves. In the roaring tempest of the assault we were trampled by fleeing miners as they dashed toward the main gate, desperate to escape.

Kamba and Chipo were huddled by the fence.

"Come on," I shouted, dragging Arves back to his feet, dodging people running toward the gate. "Chipo! Kamba!"

Kamba was trying to pull a corner of the fence up from the ground, his face straining with fear and effort. Chipo was on her belly, working her way under the wire. Arves and I grabbed the fence, and together we were able to lift it just enough for Chipo to crawl through.

"Go! Go!" I shouted as Kamba wriggled to the other side, then stopped long enough to hold the fence up for us. Chipo was ahead of us, running across the plain toward Gwejana Rock. In the distance, two helicopters hovered over PaMbada, their tracer bullets slamming into the hillside and ricocheting off the rocks.

"Look," shouted Kamba.

Across the plain, soldiers on horseback herded a group of miners before them, firing their rifles over their heads. Dogs ran alongside the horses, snapping and barking at the heels of those trying to escape. We sprinted toward our hill. At Gwejana Rock we would be safe. But the soldiers were everywhere. All around us, ear-crushing gunfire, barking dogs, whirling rotors, and screaming people. Two jeeps came barreling down the banks of the Odzi River, heading straight for us. A man stood at the back of one jeep, firing at miners in the water.

"We're almost there," cried Kamba.

Another round of machine gun fire, closer now, crackled through the air.

Up ahead, soldiers appeared at the top of our hill, holding their rifles in front of them. They had spread out ten paces apart and were marching steadily toward the mine. Behind us the hovering helicopter spun slowly above Banda Hill.

We were trapped.

"What do we do?" Chipo cried.

"Split up," shouted Arves. "They can't catch all of us."

"No," I cried, my heart pounding. "Stand still. It's too late."

A miner heading up the hillside saw the soldiers and tried to hide between the rocks. Not far from him, a soldier casually raised his rifle and fired. The man's body jerked, spun around, and fell to the ground.

"Don't move," I said. "Don't do anything."

Fear is not one thing alone. It was the hardness of the ground we sat on; the pain in our arms that came from hours of holding our hands on our heads; it was the trembling of Kamba's shoulders and the smell of urine; it was the dry, acid taste in my mouth that told me something terrible had happened to my father. In the chaos of the assault I never saw him. He must have escaped. Perhaps he was hiding in the hills or had gone back to the sheds to look after Grace.

It hadn't taken long for the soldiers to herd all the miners back to Banda Hill and force us to sit on the ground in three lines. In front of me, Kamba was sobbing quietly. Behind, Arves was humming and Chipo had pulled her cap down and was curled up with her arms around her knees and her head bent low. If there was anything to be grateful for, it was that in the confusion of the occupation, the soldiers hadn't noticed she was a girl. Jamu was nowhere to be seen. Lucky for him he hadn't come to the mines that day.

Sometime later, two army trucks bounced over the veldt, bringing even more soldiers. One by one they jumped down from the truck, and it seemed as if the earth shook with the size of them in their full battle fatigues, heavy black boots, and gun-gray rifles. They strolled through the mine, paying us no attention. Some of them smoked; others talked in loud voices, with their ever-present rifles slung carelessly on their backs. One of them ordered the soldiers guarding us to off-load crates from the trucks. Instead, the guards kicked some of the miners from the lines and laughed as the men struggled to lift the heavy boxes to the ground.

"I want to pee," I said loudly, trying to catch the attention of one of the soldiers.

He ignored me.

"Just do it," whispered Arves behind me. "You'll dry quickly."

I shuffled away from where I had wet the ground.

"What will they do to us?" Kamba whispered.

No one answered.

Later, more men were pulled from our line to roll barbed wire around Banda Hill. Soon there were two fences around the mine. Others dug post holes for large tents, and through the course of the day, an army camp grew around us. Tables and chairs were laid out; boxes of ammunition, food, water, and kitchen supplies were off-loaded from the trucks. While the miners worked on building the camp, a few of the soldiers strolled through the mine, scuffing at the ground and inspecting our mining tools. One of them picked up an abandoned sieve still filled with ore and started shaking it so violently that the bottom fell out, and the ore spilled to the ground. A few of the soldiers laughed at his clumsy efforts. He swore at them and threw the sieve at some of the miners seated nearby.

We watched silently as the army took possession of Banda Hill. Where was Uncle James in all of this? I wondered. Surely he must have known something about this invasion.

A jeep pulled up and skidded to a stop at the entrance. The driver jumped out, opened the door, and stood at attention, waiting for the passenger. From where I sat, all I could see was a pair of military boots resting on the dashboard. Then, as if he had come to some decision, the owner of the boots sprang out of the jeep and strode purposefully toward us. He wore a red beret and silver sunglasses. Attached to his black belt was a knife sheath, and strapped around his leg was a revolver in a leather holster. His mouth was a hard line of power and distaste. Soldiers stamped out their cigarettes, unhitched their rifles, and stiffened to attention as he approached.

"Here comes the Big Cheese," whispered Arves. "Full of himself, ripe and smelly."

"Shut up, Arves," hissed Chipo.

The soldier in the red beret stopped before the miners huddled on the ground. He looked slowly up and down our lines as if searching for someone. His smooth jet-black face was a grim mask.

"I am Commander Jesus," he said, his voice rising above the noise of the camp.

The miners erecting the tents and unloading crates were ordered to stop working and join us. They scurried to where we were sitting and were pushed to the ground. All eyes were on Commander Jesus.

"Who has a permit to mine here?" he demanded, once there was silence.

No one answered.

"Permits," he screamed. "Can any of you miner-dogs show me a permit?"

He scanned the lines of the seated men shrinking before his glare.

"Just as I thought. You have all been stealing from the government, our government, the government of Zimbabwe. The president has sent me to get back what you miner-dogs, criminals, and thieves have stolen. Today is the beginning of Operation No Return. There will be no more illegal mining in Marange. There will be no more stealing from President Mugabe. This mine now belongs to the people of Zimbabwe."

He turned to the driver. "Bring them here," he ordered.

A pair of soldiers moved to the back of the jeep and hauled out two men. I wriggled up on my haunches to peer over the heads of the men sitting in front of me to see who it was being dragged before us.

Uncle James and Musi were thrown down in the dirt at Commander Jesus's feet. Uncle James's face was crusted in blood. Musi's hands were tied behind his back and his head was lying at a funny angle on the ground. He seemed unconscious.

Arves whistled softly behind me. "Now the paw-paw's hit the fan."

"This is James Banda. He and I have come to an arrangement," announced Commander Jesus. "Banda Hill will now be called Mai Mujuru, after the wife of our glorious General Mujuru, who fought in the liberation war to free the people of Zimbabwe from the white imperialists. Banda has also handed over the state property that he regretfully possessed illegally."

Commander Jesus pulled something from his pocket and held it up for all to see. It was Uncle James's small black velvet bag.

"This is only a fraction of what this mine is capable of producing. Banda knows who among you has stolen state property. Now would be a good time to give it back. Tell them, Banda," he commanded. "As you can see, I have forgiven him, and I will forgive you too."

Uncle James's face was twisted in agony and he looked around in terror and confusion. One of his eyes was puffed up and closed; his jaw seemed crooked. The blood on the side of his head had seeped into his shirt. He stared blankly, trying to rise to his knees. Something seemed wrong with one of his legs. Musi lay beside him, still not moving.

"Commander Jesus is in charge of Banda Hill and—" he croaked.

"Mai Mujuru," Commander Jesus corrected.

"Mujuru," repeated Uncle James. "We will be working together to pay back what we owe the government." His voice was hoarse and cracked, and his words were hard to hear. "Give him all the stones you have found."

Uncle James collapsed onto his hands, gripping his leg in pain. Arves and I glanced at each other.

"Do you think he knows about the *gwejana* syndicate?" whispered Kamba.

"Shhh," hissed Chipo, staring angrily at Kamba.

"Everybody steals *ngodas*," said Arves, loud enough for others sitting around us to hear. "But not us kids, we're not that stupid."

We didn't know who among the miners at Banda Hill knew about the *gwejana* syndicate. Every miner understood the danger of informers, people who believed they could make extra money by selling a secret.

"So who wants to be forgiven first?" asked Commander

Jesus as he stepped over Uncle James and nodded to the soldiers. They moved forward and grabbed Uncle James and Musi and threw them into the front line of cowering men.

"I am waiting," Commander Jesus said, strolling among the miners, his hands on his hips, his head swiveling from side to side as he studied us through his reflective sunglasses. Men shuffled out of the way of his shiny black army boots. He stopped close to where I was sitting and waited. Nobody moved but I felt a tremor of fear rippling through the miners. The stench of someone losing control of his bowels spread over us. Musi groaned as he tried to rise to his feet, but was quickly pulled down by Uncle James.

"No. Enough. Please," Uncle James choked. "We don't have any more. We gave them all to you."

"I will wait no longer," Commander Jesus said finally when no one offered up any *ngodas*. Slowly, he raised his hand, pointing a finger at a group of soldiers, who reacted immediately. They barked instructions and four more soldiers appeared from behind one of the tents, dragging two large branches hacked from a thorn tree. They laid the branches, thick with long white thorns, on the ground. The miners, who had been silent until now, started protesting, pleading, and lifting their hands as if in prayer toward Commander Jesus. The soldiers dragged another large thorn branch and threw it onto the pile. From one of the trucks, soldiers produced thick sticks, which prompted the men sitting on the ground to start shouting in fear.

"Keep your head down," Arves whispered. "Tell Kamba."

Kamba's shaking intensified. "Don't let them take me, Patson," he pleaded, his face lined with tears.

Commander Jesus gave the smallest of nods and the soldiers fell upon the miners. They pulled several to their feet, dragging them to the front, and threw them facedown onto the pile of branches. Thorns as long as needles pierced their flesh.

Then, without any further orders given, two soldiers ran across their backs. The men screamed and writhed in pain, trying to free themselves from the spikes embedded in their skin. The watching soldiers shouted and hooted as if cheering at a football match. And the bizarre game of miner-hopscotch continued.

Then the beatings began.

The soldiers surrounded the men impaled upon the branches and beat them with thick sticks. I dropped my head into my hands, trying to block out the screaming and the thud of wood against flesh, grateful that my father was not one of them.

The night brought no relief. More trucks arrived, their headlights bouncing off military tents, lighting up the razor-wire fence and the faces of soldiers. Miners jumped off the trucks and stumbled through the camp, herded by men with dogs on leashes. Many were injured; all were bewildered and frightened. Our group swelled as miners from Mafukose and PaMbada joined the lines behind us.

I tried to sleep but every muscle ached; my mouth was dry, my body shuddering at the blasts of rifle fire echoing across the plains. Arves lay with his head on his arm, not hearing the groans from the men trying to extract thorns from their flesh. He hadn't eaten all day and had missed his daily antiretroviral medication. Slowly he was growing weaker. By the time the sun set he had gone quiet and fallen into a deep sleep. He seemed to have shrunk and his face was a peculiar gray color. Chipo was curled up with her hat pulled over her eyes, her back against Kamba's. I dozed while fragments of conversation tugged me back from the borders of sleep.

"I thank the spirits I escaped…It's a war zone out there… They kill us like flies."

"The dogs were biting me…they say Air Marshal Shiri ordered the helicopters."

"They killed ten people at PaMbada. I saw it with my own eyes."

"Tear gas was fired into the holes and they shot the men as they came out…even those injured were finished off."

"I asked if we could bury those who had died in the holes; they said they were buried already."

"There are bodies everywhere."

Those words jolted me awake. All day I had looked for my father's face in the lines of miners around me, and watched for his tall figure among the men getting off the back of the trucks, but he was not in the camp. At first I'd thought this was a good sign, but now, in the middle of the night, I was no longer so sure.

Uncle James might know.

I crawled toward Uncle James and Musi, stopping only to

pretend sleep when a guard looked in my direction. My father must have gone back to the farm. Perhaps Uncle James even had a message for me. After what seemed like hours, I reached the men of the Banda family, who were sleeping some distance from the miners. Uncle James was a messy heap on the ground, snoring through his broken nose, his face twitching every time he breathed. Musi was lying on his back, his arm thrown over his eyes.

"Musi, Musi," I whispered, shaking him.

He jerked awake and stared at me through bleary, bloodshot eyes.

"What do you want?" he asked, his lip turning nasty when he recognized me.

"My father. Have you seen my father?"

He shook his head. "Leave me alone."

"Musi, were you at the house? Did you see my father there?" I shook him again.

He sat up and glared at me. "The army took over Kondozi Farm. It's the new headquarters for Commander Jesus. My mother and Kuda are at the tobacco sheds," he said bitterly. "They kicked us all out."

"And Grace?"

"She is with Kuda and Jamu. Now leave me alone."

Uncle James shifted, snored, and rolled away from me. "Uncle James," I whispered loudly.

His eyes opened and stared straight ahead of him.

"Uncle James, it's Patson. Where is my father?" I asked. "Have you seen him?"

He coughed, and spat onto the ground. His shirt was caked with blood and he smelled of vomit. There was a large bruise on his chest and his face flinched with pain as he turned to me, focusing for the first time.

"Joseph Moyo. My father," I urged, as loud as I dared.

"Patson?" he said, his voice faltering. "You saw my *girazi*, didn't you? I had it in my hands."

"Yes, Uncle James, I saw it." He gripped my wrist, frightening me with the wild look in his eyes.

"Commander Jesus took it from me. And now he's taken my mine and wants me to work for him. My *shavi* has left me. My ancestors are angry. I have to ask for forgiveness, there has to be a way—"

"Uncle James, I'm worried about my father. Did he come to the farmhouse? Is he with Grace?"

"I don't have a house anymore. Commander Jesus took Kondozi Farm."

"My father, Uncle James. Have you seen him?"

"I don't know. He's out there somewhere," he said, waving his hand vaguely in the direction of the hills.

17

My second *girazi* came to me because of rain.

It was our fourth day in the military camp and there was still no sign of my father. I knew he would not leave me here. He had plenty of money to buy my freedom from the soldiers. I had to believe that he had escaped when the soldiers attacked the mine and that he was not buried in a mass grave, that he was safe with Grace and working out a way of getting me out of the military camp.

Everything here had become very confusing. First, Commander Jesus said that we could not return to the mines, but then three days later he changed his mind. Now he said we should work together, soldiers and miners, for the good of Zimbabwe. If a *ngoda* or *girazi* was found by a miner, he would receive payment from the army paymaster. I didn't understand what was going on any better than the adults when they heard Commander Jesus's change of heart.

"You need not run away from us anymore," he had said, addressing the hundred captured miners. "Tell us how and where to find diamonds and we will share whatever you find."

First we had worked for the Banda syndicate and now we would be working for the army. Their words were hard to believe until they gave us plates of *sadza* and gravy, and handed out bottles of water and boxes of medical supplies. We ate their food, patched up our wounds, and stared blankly at our new masters. Mostly, we were still in shock at what Commander Jesus had done to us. One moment we were being fired on by helicopters, beaten by soldiers; the next we were in some weird partnership with him. Uncle James never gave his miners food or medicine, but then Uncle James never kept his miners prisoners in a camp.

"We are here to discuss a business proposition with you," Commander Jesus said to us the following day, in the manner of a reasonable manager. The miners glanced uneasily at one another, bewildered by his new approach. "We want the names of diamond dealers. We know about the dealers at the Dairy Den, and those men who come from Mutare wanting to buy the diamonds you find. We want their names."

I had a bad feeling about his business proposition. I would never betray Boubacar or the Baron to Commander Jesus.

"If you give me a name I'll pay you with more food and money." With a smile as taut as razor wire, he added, "And now we will sing a Chimurenga song."

Commander Jesus started singing and his powerful voice stirred some of the miners seated before him to join in. Others stared in stunned silence as he sang, but when the soldiers moved threateningly toward them, they quickly started singing too. Soon we all sang the old liberation song as loudly as we could.

> *Mothers, don't be afraid to send your sons to war.*
>
> *Keep disillusion at bay, keep fighting to have your say.*
>
> *These are the ways of good revolutionary soldiers;*
>
> *Don't take riches from the masses, return them to the*
>   *rightful owners.*
>
> *Hide in the mountains to free Zimbabwe!*

When the song ended, I felt strangely rejuvenated. I noticed that some of the other miners were even smiling, as if they had forgotten where they were and what they had been put through. Commander Jesus clapped his hands, slow and steady, exactly four times.

"Excellent. We shall sing every night after our work. It is good for the spirit," he announced, nodding approvingly. "Now, you boy miners, come here, all of you. I want to speak to you. Alone," he said, dismissing the rest, who by this time had learned to break ranks swiftly.

At first, none of us dared move. Kamba glanced over to where I was sitting. I could see he didn't want to get up. Chipo sat next to him, keeping her arms tightly folded across her chest.

"Come. Don't be frightened. I won't hurt you," Commander

Jesus said, with the warmth of a favorite uncle, but I still felt the menace radiating from his mirrored sunglasses. A few boys stood and moved forward; more followed. I woke up Arves and helped him to his feet. I hoped that if Commander Jesus saw how ill he was, he might allow him to go home.

"What does the Big Cheese want from us kids?" asked Arves weakly, coughing, as he stumbled toward Commander Jesus. "He's the devil, Patson, you watch out for the man with no eyes."

"Can you keep your big mouth shut for once, Arves?" I whispered, squeezing his arm tightly. He flinched in pain. I had forgotten how thin he was.

Kamba slipped in front of Chipo, blocking her from Commander Jesus's view. He was still trembling, but that was a brave thing for him to do. Chipo, meanwhile, hung at the back of the boys, her head still down. None of us could bear to think what was in store for her if even one soldier saw she was a girl.

"So, you are the boy miners of Marange," said Commander Jesus. Up close he was cleanly shaven and every feature of his face was hard and angular. There was something hypnotic about the glint coming off his sunglasses. I couldn't keep my eyes off the image of us in their reflection: a ragged group of mud-splattered boys, staring stupidly up at him. "James Banda says your hands and eyes are quicker than that of any man on this mine. Would you like to work for me? I will teach you boys about the meaning of community service and give you lessons in patriotism. Bring them more food," he ordered the soldiers. Then, as he leaned toward us again, his voice became low and smooth. "You will now be my eyes and ears on Mai Mujuru. If you bring me stones,

I will give you lots and lots of money. You can also help me in other ways. People shouldn't steal from the state. It's not only dishonest, it's unpatriotic. If you tell me who takes what does not belong to them, I will give you even more money. Do we understand each other?"

We listened to him intently; a few heads nodded.

"Arsehole," said Arves and for a moment I thought Commander Jesus had heard him. He jerked his head up—a black snake came to mind—and his head swiveled in our direction.

"You at the back, what's your name?" he asked.

The boys all turned around.

"Me?" I squeaked.

"Yes, you."

"Patson," I said.

"Did you say something, Patson?"

"No, sir, nothing, sir."

"What's wrong with that boy next to you?"

"I got diarrhea since I started eating your shitty food," said Arves loudly enough for all to hear. There were a few gasps before everyone turned back to Commander Jesus to see his reaction.

Commander Jesus choked three short coughs, but actually he was laughing. "Give that boy some Imodium," he ordered, and one of the soldiers tossed a box in my direction. It fell at my feet but I didn't pick it up.

Still smiling, he said, "I will look after you boys, if you look after me. Commander Jesus does not hurt children. You are our country's future."

I felt his gaze lock directly on me and I realized, no matter what he said, my situation was now worse than ever before.

Commander Jesus knew who I was.

The following day all the miners were ordered to return to work in the pits, but nobody was allowed to leave the camp. The soldiers patrolled the perimeter of the fence and walked through the mines, their rifles slung low over their backs, watching us silently. I noticed several pairs of soldiers working in the field beyond the fence. They appeared to be digging holes and covering them with sand. They would never find diamonds by digging such shallow holes. No wonder Commander Jesus wanted us to keep working the mines; the soldiers were useless at diamond mining. We worked harder than usual, with no breaks, no talking, only the lifting of heavy ore sacks and the backbreaking work of sieving, sieving, and more sieving.

At the end of the day we returned to the tents, but before we got our food all the boys had to report to Commander Jesus. He asked each of us what we had seen, who had found *ngodas*, and where we had worked. Once he was satisfied with our answers we were separated from the older miners and given the same food that was cooked and served to the soldiers. A pile of *sadza* with a meat stew and vegetables. The food was good and it didn't take us long to clean our plates.

Arves was feeling a little better but still couldn't work a full day. He was now five days without his medication and although he didn't say anything I knew his situation was serious. His face remained gray; dark rings grew under his eyes and he could barely lift even a half-full sieve.

The helicopters had not returned and the sky remained empty, except for the large black clouds that rolled over the far-away Bvumba Mountains, gathering strength above Marange. Each day had been marked by rounds of gunshots from the nearby hills. None of the miners looked up from their work any-more; gunshots had become routine. I overheard men speaking about it late at night: The soldiers were hunting down more miners, capturing them to work the fields, and killing those who tried to escape.

"We came to Chiadzwa Dam and there were bodies every-where," one man said quietly, his voice dark with sadness. "The soldiers made us dig a grave and bury the bodies. We put seventy-two people into that one hole."

"Do you know who they were?" asked another. "I am miss-ing my brother's son."

"I did not know any of them," he replied, and spoke about the military camps, similar to this one, that had been set up at PaMbada and how the diamond fields of Mafukose Munda had been closed down. The Mafukose eye had even been filled to cover the bodies of the people who died there on the first day the soldiers came. And there was talk of a torture camp up behind the hills for all those who refused to support President Mugabe. The men listening only shook their heads and none of them talked about running away.

Every day I worked at the far end of the mine, where I had a clear view of the entrance. I knew my father would come for me.

I would not allow myself to think that anything bad had happened to him, but at night, when the camp was quiet and I lay on my back looking up at the canvas, I wanted to weep for my lost father. In the morning, however, I would wake up with the reassuring thought that he was too clever to be shot by soldiers. Somehow he would have escaped. He had to be alive.

Chipo and Kamba were planning how they would escape from the camp, but I had to stay and wait for my father. Also, I was worried about Arves; his spark had been stubbed out. He slept most of the day, complaining of stomach cramps. The blisters on his tongue made it difficult for him to eat and he grew weaker every day. I promised that I would get him his medication as soon as possible. But in the meantime, if Chipo and Kamba did escape, I couldn't leave Arves alone in the camp.

"It looks like it might rain this afternoon," Chipo whispered to me as we worked close to one another in the shallow water. "Kamba and I are going tonight."

"They won't waste their bullets on kids trying to escape," said Kamba in a low voice. "And if it does rain, that will only help us."

Chipo nodded. "It's too dangerous for me here, Patson," she said. "I've seen the soldiers looking at me. I've got to get out of here before it's too late."

"I hate it here," murmured Kamba. "Living in my boring village in the mountains doesn't seem such a bad idea anymore."

"I want to go with you, but I have to come back," I said. "I need to see if Grace and my father are all right at the sheds. I also have to get Arves's medication from his grandmother at the school. He's getting sicker every day."

It was decided. Later that night we would slip under the razor wire behind the long-drop toilets. I hoped Kamba was right about the soldiers not worrying about kids escaping. There was no way to know what Commander Jesus would do if we were caught. So, for better or worse, we were all agreed. Tonight.

We returned to our work, the soldiers silently watching us, patrolling every corner of the mine. Their heavy boots and automatic rifles always close by; oppressive and threatening. As often as we dared, we looked up at the darkening sky as the clouds gathered, promising rain. Another truck arrived in the afternoon and off-loaded more men but my father was not among them. Everyone stopped working to stare at the familiar figure stumbling off the back of the truck. There, standing in the dirt, was the disheveled Prophet Ubert Angel and some of his followers still in their white robes. They were shunted through the main gates, handed mining tools, and set to work in one of the troughs close by the Banda men. Uncle James hardly greeted the prophet. He and Musi now seemed no different from any of the other miners—beaten, muddy, and exhausted.

Then the gray sky was shot open by bolts of lightning and the hills reverberated with claps of thunder that always came at this season. Rain fell in blinding sheets, and one by one the soldiers sought shelter under the tents. A few miners threw down their tools, but when rifles were pointed at them, they returned to their work.

The roar of the rainfall was deafening; air turned into water. I lifted my face to the stinging downpour, cupped my hands before my mouth, and drank from heaven's water. I had just finished sifting a bag of ore and laid my sieve down to fill it again, when I noticed a black rock sticking out from the river-bank. I picked up a shovel and started digging. The force of the rain had loosened the earth around it, but before I could grab it, the rock fell with a large *plop* into the water puddling at my feet. I groped blindly for it beneath the water, lifted it up, and, as I did so, a piece of it fell away into my hand as the rest of it slipped back into the water.

A *girazi* lay in the palm of my hand.

It was the size of a dove's egg and, unlike my first *girazi*, this one was smooth and clear. I plunged my tightened fist back underwater, while my brain raced back to what Arves had told me when I first came to the mines. What good had I done in my life that two *girazis* should come to me? In what way did I deserve them, or was finding them pure chance? I had been cleansed by Prophet Ubert Angel, who now worked knee-high in the mud, but then so had so many other miners. I couldn't work out what it meant, but I knew I had to get my *girazi* off the mine to a safer place.

Despite the heavy rain, I made the pretense of splashing my face with water—it made no sense to anyone watching, but it gave me the excuse I needed. Then I wiped my muddy hands on my pants and slid the rain-stone into my pocket. It was rain-ing so hard it was unlikely anyone could have seen what I did. The stone's hardness against my thigh felt good and I carried on working, my mind spinning. My anger-stone was bigger than this rain-stone, but this one was as clear as the rainwater that delivered it. A true *girazi*. The diamond must be at least eighteen carats. I imagined Farouk Abdullah staring at its multifacets for hours through his loupe. How much would he give me for this stone?

The rain poured down for the remainder of the day, presenting me with the perfect opportunity to get the diamond off the field. As we finished our shift we entered the tented area soaked and shivering, desperate to get warm and dry. In the rush to get under cover the soldiers weren't searching everyone as carefully as they normally did. It was easy to slip into the crush of adults heading straight for the hot food. I was careful to lose myself in the crowd, as standing anywhere alone meant someone would surely see the lump in my pocket. But everyone was exhausted, too wet and hungry to pay much attention to anyone else.

Once I finished eating, I ran back out through the rain to the long-drop toilet. I slipped my pants down to my ankles, retrieved the rain-stone, pulled the plug out of the sole of my running shoe, and worked the stone into the secret cavity. My two *girazis* fit snugly together, like the first had been waiting for its mate. I returned to the tents, feeling Arves's eyes on me as I took up my place in the line for an extra helping of food.

After the singing, everyone settled down for the night, and I lay on my back listening to raindrops falling on the canvas, waiting for the signal from Kamba and Chipo, and dreaming about all the things I could buy with the diamonds in the sole of my shoe.

"You shouldn't come back," whispered Arves, lying next to

me. "There's no reason to come back to the camp. You should run as far away from this place as you can. Bad things are going to happen here, I can feel it." Then, almost as if an afterthought, he pitched his voice low, looked me straight in the eyes, and said, "You've found your *girazi*, haven't you, Patson?"

I rolled over on my elbow, wondering how he knew. "Arves, I'm going to get your meds, check in on Grace, and see if my father is at the sheds," I replied. "But no matter what happens, I will come back. I'm not leaving you here."

"You've found one. I know you have."

This time I couldn't avoid answering him.

I nodded.

"How big?"

I showed him my thumb and he whistled softly. "You're set for the good times, Patson."

"We can share it, Arves," I said.

He smiled the sort of weak smile a condemned man offers his hangman. "I won't be around long enough to be driving any sports cars, Patson. I'll leave living the high life to you. The doctors at the clinic in Mutare said a long time ago that I was a walking miracle, but that doesn't make me feel any better."

I could have said a hundred things to Arves—about staying hopeful and being positive; about praying to God, eating the right food, making an offering to his ancestors—but it would have all sounded so hollow. I knew what having full-blown HIV/AIDS meant. If Arves was so honest about his own condition, how could I not be too?

"That's not going to happen tomorrow, Arves, nor next month or even next year, so we have plenty of time to spend a whole lot of money," I said.

He shrugged. "I suppose if I had my own *girazi* I'd give it to the doctors at the clinic. I miss them," he said. "If only you can get it out of here. What's your plan?"

"Not sure yet."

Then Arves spoke in a way that crushed my heart. "You know, Patson, your father has been gone for a week now and what everyone is saying—"

"I heard, Arves."

"About the mass graves. So many people were killed that first day."

"He's alive," I said, louder than I meant to, afraid at how huge my cave of doubt had grown. I couldn't think that my father was dead. He had to be alive, and by saying it aloud, it made it real somehow. "I know he is alive, Arves, I just know it. He's with Grace."

"I'm just saying. We all heard what the soldiers did out there."

"My father's at the tobacco sheds. I'll find out tonight. Okay?" I said, laying my hand on his arm. I noticed Kamba jerking his head in my direction. It was time to go. "See you later, Arves. I'll be back."

"Yah-yah, just like in the movies, right?" he said. "Now listen, don't let my granny scare you. She might speak funny but she knows a lot of stuff. Don't get her talking about your ancestors and shit. She'll keep you there for hours. Remember, she lives in the photocopying room. At the end of the corridor. My meds are in a little red tin. They're underneath my mattress. There's enough there to last a month. Tell her I'm fine and as soon as I can I'll bring her Chinese sweets."

"Chinese sweets?"

"Footy Pops. That's all she likes. She hasn't got many teeth but one of them is a real sweet tooth. She's obsessed with Footy Pops," he answered, smiling.

Chipo was up and moving silently through the tent toward the toilets. "Okay, Arves, I'll see you tomorrow morning," I whispered, and moved out into the pouring rain.

When I got to the toilet, I glanced over my shoulder. A soldier stood under the tarpaulin smoking a cigarette, looking in my direction. I opened the makeshift door to the corrugated lean-to, closed it, and crawled through to the back of the toilet where Kamba and Chipo were digging furiously through the mud.

"Come on, help us," whispered Chipo as she scooped handfuls of mud from under the fence.

Kamba pulled out a pair of oven gloves and slipped them on. "Standard issue for army chefs and easy to steal," he said with a grin, grabbing the razor wire and hauling it out of the earth.

Chipo wriggled into the channel she had dug and carefully made her way under the wire. Once she was through, she knelt down and kept her eyes trained on the camp.

"Keep your back down, Patson," she whispered as I made my way under the fence. Kamba passed me the gloves, which I slipped on, and I lifted the razor wire while he wriggled through.

We were outside the camp for the first time in a week, crouching in the mud, waiting for any sign that our escape had been noticed. The camp was quiet, except for the rain splashing in puddles, pounding down on the tents, and beating out a rhythm on the iron roof of the toilet. I slipped off the oven gloves and laid them next to the channel, held down with a rock to keep them from floating away. I would have to get back through here by myself later on tonight.

"See you later, Chipo," said Kamba.

"You know I'm not coming back," she answered. "From here on, you boys will have to look after yourselves."

"Bye, Chipo. I'll see you around, Kamba," I said.

He nodded to me and then we each ran our separate ways, knowing how unlikely it was that we would ever see each other again.

18

The door to number six tobacco shed was ajar. The lightbulb above the door flickered and all was quiet at the sheds. I crept up to the entrance and peered inside. Loud snoring came from the first mattress and I recognized the bulk of Prisca. I slipped past Kuda and there was Jamu sleeping next to his mother. Had he been here the whole time? I looked around the shed once more. There was no sleeping body that looked like my father, or the Wife, for that matter.

I walked slowly, deeper into the shed, the dim blue light of my phone creating a halo in the darkness, afraid that I might trip over my sister. And there, at the end of the shed, in the darkest corner, where the damp tobacco smell was at its worst, I found Grace lying asleep on the ground. The small things of her life—her toys, my father's briefcase, the book I had given him—were packed neatly around her, as if guarding her from the world. The Banda family must have taken her mattress. She was lying on a grass mat, with one of her soft toys as a pillow, and hanging above her was Boubacar's white tie.

I crouched beside her and gently stroked her arm.

"Grace," I whispered. "Wake up. It's Patson."

Her eyes opened slowly.

"It's me."

"Patson," she said, rubbing her eyes. "Where's Baba?"

Disappointment overwhelmed me as the tiny hope that I would find my father safely here with Grace turned first to dismay and then dissolved completely into nothingness. I needed him so much, in ways I couldn't even tell Grace. But the truth of his absence was inescapable and crushing: If my father were still alive he would have come back for Grace.

"He's hiding from the soldiers," I said. "I'm sure he'll come soon."

She sat up and threw her arms around my neck. "They told me such horrible stories about the soldiers," she said. "They beat Uncle James and Musi and took them away. Auntie Prisca said Baba was killed by the soldiers. Is it true, Patson?" Her voice trembled and I hugged her back, pressing down my urge to cry. That would come later, when I was alone.

"Shhh. We don't want to wake anybody. No, it's not true. Baba is alive. I'm sure he must be hiding but I came to tell you some good news," I said, gently taking her arms away from my neck.

"What is it, Patson?"

I glanced behind me. The shed remained quiet and dark. The rain must have stopped. There was no pounding on the roof.

"Look, Grace, I've found two," I said, taking off my shoe, and slipping out the plug to shine the light from my phone into the cavity. The rain-stone twinkled white and blue.

"Is it a diamond?" asked Grace, her voice rising.

"Shhh. Not so loud," I said, quickly replacing the plug and putting my shoe back on. "Two diamonds, Grace, but you mustn't tell anyone. Once Baba comes back we will leave. Go back to Bulawayo, maybe Harare—"

"Or maybe South Africa," said Grace, excited, her eyes bright. "Look, Patson." She pulled down the dress that hung from a hook. "It's my Girl Guide uniform. Determine said there's a jamboree in South Africa. He wants to take us all there."

"Where did you get this from?"

"Determine bought it for me," she said, biting the bottom of her lip. "I used some of Baba's money. It wasn't a lot. We're all going. Sidi and No Matter and Maka."

I flicked through the pages of the book. Most of the money was still there. Quickly I counted out thirty dollars and stuffed the rest of my money deep into my pocket.

"How much did you give him?"

"Only twenty dollars, Patson. It was very cheap."

It was a fortune. Grace didn't understand that these American dollars were worth thousands of times more than Zimbabwean dollars.

"And he gave me a packet of sweets," she said, pulling out a bag of Footy Pops.

"No matter what he tells you, don't give him any more money. Okay? Did you hear me?"

"Okay, Patson. But we'll need money for the bus—"

"No more money to Determine, Grace."

"I heard you, Patson. Have a sweetie," she said.

I took a handful and stuffed them into my other pocket. Arves would be pleased to hear about the Footy Pops. I pulled down Boubacar's lucky tie and slid the three ten-dollar bills inside its widest part. "Now listen, Grace, there is over a billion Zim dollars in there. Promise me you will only use it in an emergency. And that you won't tell anyone about it."

Her eyes widened as I handed her back the tie. "A billion Zim dollars," she said.

"Do you promise?"

"Yes, I promise, Patson. And look, I know how to use my phone now. I'm not a child anymore," she said. "Didn't you get any of my Mxit messages?"

"There's no reception on the mines," I said, pulling out my phone and checking the screen. The yellow low-battery light blinked. I had mail. Grace had sent me a string of messages. There were several from Sheena, too, but they would have to wait for later. "Are they treating you okay?"

She paused, looked over my shoulder, and dropped her head.

"Grace?"

"I miss Baba, Patson. And you. I don't like it here anymore.

Everyone's frightened of the soldiers and they hate living in the sheds.

"Auntie Prisca's mean. She makes me work all the time and she pinches me. She says I'm a nuisance. Kuda's kind to me, but she's afraid of Auntie Prisca now that Uncle James is on the mines. Auntie Prisca calls her the has-been second wife," she said, in a way that suggested that the two women's bickering had escalated now that Uncle James was not around.

"Where's Sylvia?"

Grace rolled her eyes, leaning forward, as if imparting secret information. "Auntie Sylvia was allowed to stay at the farm-house," she whispered. "When the soldiers moved in, she didn't come to the sheds. Kuda and Prisca talk about her all the time. They don't say very nice things about her. I think they're jealous."

"Patson?"

I spun around at the voice behind me.

"What are you doing here?" Jamu asked.

"I've come to see Grace. I thought my father might be here."

"You don't know?" he said. "They didn't tell you?"

"My father's hiding." I gripped his arm and pulled him away from my sister. "He's not dead. Meet me outside. I'm coming now." I waited for him to leave before turning back to Grace.

"Now, listen carefully, Grace, I have to go back to the mines for a while—"

"But why, Patson, you've found your diam—"

I put my hand over her mouth. "You can't tell anyone about that, Grace. It has to be our secret. You're good at secrets, aren't you?" I said sternly. "It won't be long and I'll come back for you. We'll find Baba together and then leave Marange. You keep Mxiting me, okay?"

She nodded and I saw tears brimming, but she hurriedly wiped them away. "And keep what's in Boubacar's tie only for an emergency. There's a lot of money there. You'll be fine."

She nodded, her head on her chest. "I don't like it here, Patson. I want to leave. I don't like to be alone," she said, her voice trembling. "Can't I come with you now?"

"No. Not tonight. But soon. I promise. And remember, you're not a little girl anymore. You can wait for me. It won't be long."

A tear rolled down her cheek. I hugged her again and she held on to me fiercely with strength I didn't know she had.

"I miss Baba, Patson, I miss him so much," she whispered.

And before she could see my tears, I turned away and left her to the dark and the damp, stale smell of the tobacco shed.

Jamu was waiting for me outside. He was full of questions but I was worried he would wake up Prisca and Kuda, so we walked down the muddy path. Without the rain, the earth was singing with the sound of crickets and frogs.

"You're going back to the mines, Patson? But why?"

"Arves is sick. I have to bring him his meds. I can't leave him there. What do you know about my father, Jamu?"

He shook his head. "They say he was shot, Patson. On the first day."

"Who said that?" My voice cracked with anger.

"Musi. He said he saw him fall. Later, they took the bodies away in trucks and dug a mass grave."

"Have you told Grace?"

"No. But I think Prisca did. I'm so sorry, Patson."

I would not hear it. "It's not true. I asked Musi. He said he didn't see my father. He was not on the mines the day the helicopters came. He's lying, Jamu. He's lying!"

"So many people were killed, Patson—"

"Not my father," I said, staring intently at him. "You understand, Jamu, not my father."

"Okay, okay," he said, shaken by the anger in my voice. "What are you going to do now?"

"Get Arves his meds and look for my father, and then I'll come back for Grace. We're leaving Marange," I answered, realizing how much I desperately wanted to get away from this place.

But one step at a time, I thought. First the meds.

"Arves says you've found a *girazi*. Is it true?"

I shook my head. "Arves is wrong."

"You can tell me, Patson. I can help you sell it."

"I haven't found anything, Jamu."

He didn't believe me. "You know you can't trust the soldiers. Look what they did to my father and he's James Banda."

"How come you weren't on the mines the day the soldiers came, Jamu?"

"I . . . um . . . I can't remember," he stuttered. "I don't think I was feeling very well—"

"Don't talk crap, Jamu. Your father knew the soldiers were coming. He kept you home that day. You could have warned us."

He raised his hands helplessly. "I wanted to, Patson. Honestly. But the soldiers were here already and—"

"I've got to go. I need you to keep an eye on Grace." It was no use talking to Jamu, and I didn't have any more time to waste on him. "Don't let the warthog bully her. Promise me, you can at least do that?"

"Yah-yah. She's safe with us. Don't worry. But listen, Patson, about your *girazi*—"

"I'll see you later, Jamu." I turned away and ran down the path.

As I ran past Kondozi Farm loud music blasted away the after-rain stillness of the night. I stopped and looked up at the farmhouse. Lights were on in the lounge and two army jeeps were parked in the driveway. I don't know what made me do it, but I slipped through the fence and darted across the front lawn, looking out for any guards that might be on the veranda. Once I had worked my way behind the large bougainvillea, I climbed up onto a ledge and peered through the window.

The Wife was dancing for Commander Jesus.

She wore an unbuttoned army shirt, a pair of high heels, and a red bra that barely contained her breasts. She swayed from side to side, turning slowly around in time with the music, sipping occasionally from a glass. Commander Jesus lay sprawled on the couch in shorts and a white sleeveless shirt, a bottle of whisky between his legs. He looked no less dangerous without his mirrored glasses as he drank from the bottle, his eyes fixed on every sensual movement of the Wife dancing for him in his army fatigues.

I wasn't surprised to see her with Commander Jesus. Once again the Wife got what she always wanted: a powerful man who could give her everything. She couldn't change who she was and the Wife always knew how to make the best out of any situation. It was obvious that when the soldiers came, the Wife would find a way of looking after herself. My father must have known that their marriage was over when she had chosen to stay at the farmhouse. The Wife had replaced him for the favors of her brother, and now Uncle James had been replaced by Commander Jesus. It all made perfect sense and it sickened me.

I jumped off the ledge to search the ground. My brain screamed at me to put down the large rock I found at my feet. But without hesitating, and with all the force and anger I could marshal, I stepped back and hurled the rock through the window.

The noise of glass shattering was impressive.

I did not hang around to see its effect on their party, but sprinted across the lawn without looking back. I might have heard some shouting, but it was quickly drowned out by the noise of gunfire. Whoever it was who was shooting was firing blindly into the night.

I ran through the veldt, long, wet grass licking my legs, thankful for the darkness provided by the low-hanging clouds and grimly satisfied with my small gesture of defiance.

◆◆◆

Once I was far away from Kondozi Farm, I checked my phone. Two bars. Not great reception but just enough for texts to come through. The low-battery light blinked. I hadn't been able to charge the phone, so I would have to be quick. I flicked through Grace's messages about her life in the sheds and shot off a quick text to remind her to keep our secret. She pinged me back with a smiley face with a halo and I grinned at her messaging skills. She was growing up fast.

I scrolled down to what I really wanted to read, Sheena's messages:

> U mean a lot to me, too. xxx ☺ I was worried
> now that u've gone, u would forget me … I miss
> u. ☹ Not just our running. But you. It's not
> the same here. That afternoon was special. I
> liked it … A lot. ☺☺☺ I never did that before.
> You must know that? Will u ever come back to
> Milton? On holiday?

And:

> R u there? We must talk! I told my dad about the
> ◆◆◆ in Marange. He wants to come and bring
> the whole family. Says he'll make more $$$ in
> Marange. Everyone is talking about ◆◆◆ fields.
> Sooo EXCITED to see u! ◆◆◆ for everyone,
> right? ☺

Sheena's message stopped me short. I read it again, just to be sure, and then stared up at the night sky in disbelief.

"Crap," I said aloud. They didn't know about the soldiers. About Commander Jesus, the torture camps, and the bodies in mass graves. Did anyone beyond the Bvumba Mountains know what the army had done here? I had to tell them. They couldn't come. It would be the worst mistake of their lives.

I scrolled to the next message:

> Can we talk? I want to know about the school, where u staying etc. Dad is planning our trip. ☺ We're coming to look for ♦♦♦! I'm coming to look for only one ♦ - you! ☺ x

And:

> Wake up! Where r u? We are coming to Marange! We'll be there soon!! Can't WAIT to see u. xxx

I couldn't believe what I was reading. Sheena was coming to Marange. She could be here already. I checked the dates of the messages. The last one was three days ago. Sheena had texted me every day and then stopped. I knew the reception on the road was patchy. No messages for two days could only mean they were traveling. I had to tell them to turn around.

With all that had happened in the last ten days, I had forgotten about the outside world. Her messages felt as if they had come from another planet, where life was safe, sane, and ordinary. I hadn't been honest with her about my life in Marange. I had lied about going to school and had made Patson-looking-for-diamonds sound like a game. If the army's Operation No Return had been enforced in the whole Marange area, wouldn't

Sheena's family have been stopped at one of the checkpoints on the highway? But what if they were dropped in the bush, like we were? I had to warn her. They had to know the truth.

> Army taken over mine. VERY dangerous tell ur
> dad 2 GO HOME no school here. DO NOT walk
> through the bush.

The low-battery light blinked red. I had to hurry. I was running out of battery.

> NOT safe here. Soldiers r everywhere.

I pressed Send and waited for the tick that meant my message had been sent.

The screen went black. My battery was dead.

19

From the shadows I watched the soldier rebuckling his belt and sauntering out of one of the classrooms at Junction Gate High School. It hadn't taken long for the army to find the working women from Harare. One of the washerwomen, as Baba had called them, appeared at the doorway and called to another soldier leaning against the wall smoking with yet a third soldier. He threw his cigarette down, made a comment to his companion, who laughed, and disappeared inside. The washerwomen were in business; night school was in session.

I moved slowly through the shadows, cautiously keeping the soldier in my sight, and headed toward the administration office. The front door was closed but with a little pressure I was able to force it open. The foyer was dark and quiet. At the end of the corridor I saw a glimmer of light leaking from under the door. I walked quietly down the corridor toward the photocopying room, aware that I was not the only person inside this building; behind each of the closed doors, people had made the offices their homes.

I softly knocked on the door of the photocopying room, realizing that I didn't know what to call Arves's granny. "Mrs. Makupe," I whispered. "I'm a friend of Tendekai."

There was no response, but I was sure I heard the faint sound of a metal plate being placed on a table.

"*Magogo*," I whispered again. "My name is Patson. Tendekai sent me to get his medication."

I knocked again, this time a little louder.

The door opened partially and a small figure stood in the crack of the doorway staring up at me. "Go 'way. It's late. This no time," she said, closing the door.

"Wait," I said, sliding my foot across the threshold and digging my hands into my pockets. "Tendekai said you liked Footy Pops. I brought some for you."

The old woman hesitated. I couldn't quite see her face, but in a flash her hand darted out, took one of the sweets, and popped it into her mouth. The door opened wider and I walked into the room, which was unlike any photocopying room I had ever seen at school.

The room was dimly lit by several flickering candles: One burned upon a pile of rusted bolts, nails, and animal bones; another seemed as if it were being swallowed by a black mamba. Another was on top of the school's safe, impaled upon one of the quills of a porcupine. Its eyes twinkled in the candlelight and it took me a moment to realize that, like the buck on the walls of the Kondozi farmhouse, the eyes of the snake and porcupine were also made of glass, the work of a talented taxidermist.

Against one wall was a set of shelves, where once reams of paper must have been stored. Now it was filled with all the colors and textures of life itself, swept up and waiting to be bottled and bundled for her patients. Small and large jars lined the shelves filled with a rainbow of remedies: bundles of roots, piles of bulbs, heaps of sticks and bark, packs of bones, parcels of dried plants, all ready to be treated, scraped, boiled, and then swallowed or applied. In another corner, above a mattress, the shimmering brown ribbon from old tape cassettes had been strung like a tangle of music seaweed over the skull of a small animal. The room was permeated with the bitter scent of smoldering *impepo*, a veldt bush often burned by *sangomas* to appease the spirits. The contents of a black oil pot bubbled on a gas burner at the center of the room, giving off an odious smell.

Once the old woman slammed the door shut she studied me with a pair of pinprick black eyes set deep in her wrinkled face. I recognized her immediately—she was the liver-chopping crone we met when my father came looking for Headmaster Ngoko. My stomach turned at the memory of her boiling liver and at the sight of my father collapsing against the wall. I remembered Jamu talking about a powerful spirit medium who lived at Junction Gate. This spirit medium must be Arves's grandmother. No wonder he had easy access to marijuana. She had shelves full of the stuff. All the hair on the back of my neck stood up at the thought of being here alone with her in the dead of night. I would get Arves his meds and leave as soon as I could.

"Tendekai is sick. He needs his medication," I said.

"The sickness. No good for nobody. Sit. Sit. I know you. I seen you before. Your father came here. Sit!"

I jumped at her command as she pulled up a stool and patted it with her hand. I sat down and she leaned over me, holding out her other hand and wagging it at me. I fished around in my pocket and gave her all the Footy Pops I had.

"These soldiers say I am witch. Their words make me angry, hah! Well, I'm sitting and suffering through the war of liberation! Years and years I work in the bush with the boys who fight the white man. I heal them. Dr. Muti fix them up. Hoh! They say, 'You're casting spells!' No way. Mm-mm. I say, 'Ah! And yet all these problems, they're coming from greed. Your greed,' I say. 'You kill the people of the soil. Why? For the stone that shines.' Hoh-hoh," she exclaimed, clicking her tongue and shaking her head.

I tried to interrupt her but she moved around the room still chattering, never looking in my direction.

"It's better if I go to a tree and hang myself. I die! In shame! Forget everything of those days. Forget all the voices that visit me. When you hear suffering all night, all day. I'm these years old, and I'm eating tears. Aah! I say, 'I want to be at peace, but you soldiers bring trouble.' Mmm. Well, my heart is angry."

I didn't understand half of what she was saying. It was

clear where Arves got his motormouth from. All the while she sucked on her Footy Pops, stirring her oil pot, tearing up bits of bark, grabbing stuff from the shelves, smelling it, discarding it, finding something else, and then, as if realizing there was a stranger in the room, she turned and pointed a stick at me.

"You. The Moyo boy. I remember now. T'kai told me you found a *girazi*. Hoh-hoh. Big trouble now for you. Bad and good together," she said, walking up to me and laying her hand upon my head. "But your totem is strong." Her fingers felt like the claw of a bird that perched upon my head. I shifted uncomfortably at her proximity, her body odor, and the pressure of her hand.

"Mmm. Hoh-hoh," she muttered, her voice now almost a whisper, and then, as if her breath had suddenly been drawn from her, she went very still.

I couldn't see her face, but felt the nails of her fingers lightly pressing into my skull. The candle on the pile of rusted bolts and nails sizzled; its flame fluttered and died. A wisp of smoke twirled upward into the darkness. My chest tightened at the sudden change of atmosphere. It was as if there were another being in the room, unseen, but unmistakably present.

"Your *shavi* is strong too. She watches. Mmm. Shuumbaa," she said, her voice clear now, and strangely altered, somehow younger. "Mmm. My half-and-half, my little lion. Now is the time to be strong."

I went cold; the voice sounded familiar. A tingling sensation rippled down my neck, right through to the core of my body. Only one person ever called me "half-and-half" and "little lion."

"You must look to Grace," she said, her voice light, almost lyrical. "You are the best thing that ever happened. Mmm. You will need to have the heart of a lion."

I wanted to reach out, to see the face of my mother, but I was afraid that if I moved, the moment might be broken and the sense of calm would be lost. I felt the bird lightly release its grip as the old woman stepped back, exhaled forcefully, and drew in a long, slow, shuddering breath.

"Hoh-hoh," she exclaimed, turning back to her pot and shelves as if nothing had happened. "They come when I not ask. Heh-heh. You are lucky, boy. Mmm. T'kai he was brought up by me. Not so lucky. Well, at first, he stays with his mother and father. They die; I stay and I raise him. Mmm. He was still a little child. I carry him on my back. He grows up. His uncle bring him here. I grow corn, I buy clothes for him, and I wash him. He grows a little. His uncle goes away. Mmm. I send him to school, but the sickness. They not want him. Mmm. Indeed, he grew up here, he was raised by me. But he will leave soon. He will not grow more. The doctor gives him medicine. We both try. You came for this?"

She handed me a red tin. Still dazed, I took it without a word and stood up. She laid her wrinkled hand on my arm gently.

"You be careful, boy," she said, looking into my eyes. "These soldiers are dangerous. Tell T'kai to come home. The camps are no good."

I nodded and, for no reason I could think of, I hugged her.

20

The third *girazi* came to me because of a dream.

My mother was sitting in the sun, carving a stick in the shape of the letter Y. While she whittled, shavings flying from her blade, she sang a song I hadn't heard since I was small. In the dream, the song was as clear a memory as I could have wished for. Her voice true and pure.

> *Pretty baby, where are you going?*
> *Come here, come here, let's play.*
> *I'm going to the clouds, Mama,*
> *To sleep and dream with my friends.*

She sang the song over and over, occasionally looking up at me and smiling. Once she was satisfied with her work, she lifted up the Y-shaped stick and planted it into the ground. I walked over to her and she took me by the hand.

"What are you doing, Mama?" I asked.

"Watch, little lion-heart," was all she said.

Green leaves started shooting from the stick, and a vine slowly curled around the Y-shape. Simultaneously, the stick grew into a baobab tree, which turned into a house, which became a building, which transformed into a gleaming skyscraper that soared through the clouds. I gazed in wonder at what had once been a simple Y-shaped stick but was now a towering edifice, breathtaking and radiant.

"This is all for you," she said, and then, while I gazed up at the mighty building, she floated away. I didn't mind her disappearing as the large skyscraper's doors swung open. Inside were many brightly lit rooms. I walked slowly toward the entrance, exhilarated by what I would discover inside. Then I woke up and Arves was shaking me.

"Hey, Patson, get up! Come on, wake up! Sorry I ate your breakfast," he said, without sounding the least bit sorry. "But you didn't miss much. It was last night's *sadza* fried up with tomatoes and onions. I took my meds as soon as I woke up and, man, did they make me hungry again. I'm feeling great! Why do you sleep with your shoes on, Patson? I like to let my toes breathe, otherwise I have bad toe-jam dreams. You should take them off at least once a week. You might get fungi-foot and that really stinks."

I groaned. "Arves, did anyone ever tell you that you sound

exactly like your granny?" I sat up, looking around for the gleaming skyscraper that had seemed so real.

"As long as you don't think I look like her. I hope *Magogo* didn't give you a hard time. No, don't answer that. She probably did. We got to go. Look," he said, hauling me to my feet, and pointing at soldiers herding miners onto the diamond fields. We were the only ones left in the tent and it wouldn't be long before we were noticed.

"I got so much to tell you," I said to Arves. "Grace is fine, and I saw Jamu. He was at the sheds the whole time. I think he knew the soldiers were coming. He told me my father had been killed."

Arves looked away. "Yah, I know."

"What do you know?"

"A lot happened around here last night after you were gone."

"What are you talking about?"

"After the rain stopped, soldiers went out into the fields beyond the fence and were digging. It made no sense to me."

"Why would they dig for stones in the dark?"

"Because they're stupid enough to think that *girazis* float." He laughed, and I was amazed at how pills in a small red tin had revived my friend's sense of humor. Then he reached into his pocket and handed me a shattered pair of glasses.

"Where did you get these?"

At first I didn't want to touch them. There was no mistaking their familiar shape.

"Musi. Last night. He came looking for you."

"How did he get them?" I took the glasses from Arves, my hands trembling. "What did he say?"

"He said I should give you your father's glasses."

I had no words. No tears. Only dull helplessness. I had held on to the idea that I would somehow *feel* in my heart the moment of my father's death. Now these broken glasses mocked that idea. Was I still so much a child that I was unable to even think about the possibility that my father had been killed on the first day the soldiers came? Everyone had been talking about the miners who had been shot trying to escape and how their bodies were buried in mass graves. Yet I had blindly believed that he was still alive. The memory of him polishing these glasses, pushing them up his nose, overwhelmed me in pain and confusion.

If my father was dead, my *girazi* dreams were worth nothing now.

I would have to tell Grace.

"Patson, come on," urged Arves, shaking me gently. "We've got to go. The soldiers are coming. Don't think about it. Not now."

Dazed, I allowed Arves to lead me back onto the diamond fields of Marange.

All morning I labored in the pits, tormented by the thought of the Wife dancing for Commander Jesus. Did she really care so little for my father that she could dance while her husband was shot dead by Commander Jesus's soldiers and thrown into a pit? I knew the Wife was selfish but this was heartless and cruel. I lashed out at the earth with my pickax, blaming the Wife with every blow for my father's death. She had forced us to come to Marange. Diamonds for everyone, she had said. If it weren't for her, he would still be alive. We would still be in Bulawayo. Grace and I would be going to school and we'd still have our father.

The Wife wanted, the Wife got—to the death of my father.

I slashed and hacked away at the soil, tearing up the bank with my sorrow, losing all sense of time and place, grieving for my father. The doubt that I had lived with the past week turned now into a black pit that swallowed me whole as I tried to imagine a future without Baba. My father was dead and I would never see him again. My anger turned slowly into tears as I imagined him shot by the soldiers, his body thrown into one of the mass graves and the earth covering him, without any ceremony to mark his passing.

And then, as I tore into the bank, pounding the earth with my pickax, I saw the exact same Y-shaped stick from my dream. I dropped the pickax, gripped the two ends of the root, and pulled as hard as I could. A part of the sand bank gave way, and a sky-blue *girazi* sparkled into the sunlight.

My *shavi* must be the shade of my mother, and she brought me here to find this stone. But why today, Mama, why on the day that I learned of Baba's death? What happened in the photocopying room last night hardly seemed real this morning. Nothing seemed real anymore. Had I heard the voice of my mother coming from the old woman? But she had called me "half-and-half." She could not have known my mother's pet name for me. And then she had called me "little lion." That was even stranger still. Using one of the pet names might be a coincidence but her knowing two was just plain creepy.

And she had said, "You must look to Grace." What was my mother trying to tell me? I hated to think of Aunt Prisca pinching Grace and her sleeping at the back of the shed, with only her soft toys to comfort her and Boubacar's tie to protect her. Had my mother led me to this diamond so that I could take Grace away from this place? With my father dead I was the only one who could look after my sister. I had to get her out of the sheds and away from Marange. I had three *girazis* now. That had to be enough.

The more I thought about my mother's presence in that photocopying room, the more bewildered I became, but I was certain that last night I had carried her back with me to the camp, under the wire and into my dreams. I shook off the rippling sensation down the back of my neck, quickly pressed the stone back into the soil, and tossed the root aside. I glanced around to see if anyone had seen what I had done and continued my work: thrust pickax into ground, wriggle it free, pick up shovel, scrape ore into pile, load sack, carry it to sieve. And the whole time, I had to be sure not to lose sight of where I'd reburied the dream-stone.

When I felt calm enough and ready to think about getting the *girazi* out of the mine, I knew I would have to plan it carefully, one step at a time, not let any of my tangled emotions get in the way. It might be small enough to slip inside my shoe, but with three in there I'd be sure to walk with a limp that would attract attention. Putting it into my pocket or under my tongue was out of the question, and I didn't have any chewing gum to stick it to the inside of my clothes. The *girazi* was so close at hand, and yet so far from being mine. I scanned the mines, looking for inspiration, and saw Arves watching me.

Our eyes locked.

I tilted my head at him, and without acknowledging anything, he casually lifted a sack onto his small, bony back and headed toward me. He crouched down and emptied his sack into my sieve, and whispered, "Where?"

"One hand-width up from your right foot," I said, carefully watching the soldiers strolling along the mound directly above us and pretending to work.

"How big?"

"A large raisin. A sky-blue *girazi*," I said, wiping sweat from my brow, and speaking to Arves as if we were talking about nothing more important than who was going to take the next break.

He whistled softly. "You've been a miner for two months, Patson, and you've found two *girazis*. What do you have that all these other miners don't have?"

"I've found three, Arves. Three *girazis*." There didn't seem any point in lying to Arves now. "And I don't know why I'm the one to find them."

"I feel the most amazing sick coming on. You'll have two seconds to get it out. Will that be enough?"

"Yah, but Arves—"

"Then you give it to me and help me back to the tent."

Before I could say anything, Arves slipped his finger down his throat and vomited. He coughed and groaned loudly, clutched his stomach, as a second plume of *sadza*-onion-tomato-vomit landed exactly where I had indicated, and Arves collapsed right on top of it. All eyes turned to the vomiting boy, and as I reached down to help him, the blue-sky *girazi* found its way into my hand. Arves looked up at me, winked, and then, never one to let the perfect moment pass, he puked once more into my hands.

"He's sick," I called out to the nearest soldier. "Help me. He's the HIV boy."

The soldier winced. "Not me," he said. "You get him out of here yourself."

I slipped the *girazi* into Arves's hand and together we stumbled toward the soldiers guarding the mine entrance. They patted me down, looked once at Arves, and the bits of *sadza* and tomato on his shirt and legs, and let him pass. Everyone knew about HIV and bodily fluids. When we got to our tent, I brought him a basin of water and Arves stripped off his shirt.

"Pretty spectacular performance, hey?" he said, grinning, then he rinsed out his mouth and splashed his face clean. There was no *girazi* in either of his hands.

"Oscar-winning, but where did you put it?"

"Time will tell," he said, tapping the wristwatch on his skinny arm.

How was it that I didn't know Arves had his own secret place for diamonds?

"We've got to go," I said. Now that I knew for certain my father would never come for me, there was no point in staying. It was time to leave this place. Arves and I would slip out of the mine, fetch Grace from the sheds, find Boubacar, and get the three stones to the Baron and leave Marange. "Tonight. We'll go the same way Chipo and Kamba went."

"Yah. Let's do it. You're going to be rich, Patson," he said. "I can't wait to see the Baron's face when he sees your stones."

I turned away so Arves would not see my tears. My *girazis* meant nothing to me now without my father. Searching the soil for stones had been for him, to prove that I could do a man's work, and help look after our family. My diamonds had meant my father could be a teacher again, and fulfill his dream of seeing Grace and me back in school. Now there was no purpose to any of it and I no longer had anyone to prove anything to.

We heard a jeep skid to a stop outside and the soldiers hurriedly ordering everyone back into lines in front of the tents. Outside, Commander Jesus stood in the jeep yelling. His soldiers barked orders at the miners, who quickly dropped their tools and were herded at gunpoint before the jeep. Commander Jesus stood over us, with one foot up on the dashboard, scanning the crowd as we shuffled closer.

"Oh no, not more campfire singing," quipped Arves.

The silver lenses of Commander Jesus's reflective glasses zeroed in on me and Arves and a sliver of fear ran down my spine.

"I thought we had come to an agreement," he shouted, his voice booming over us. "You work Mai Mujuru, and we pay you for what you find. We give you good food, water, medicine, and a dry place to sleep. But this is not good enough for you." His words were chillingly sarcastic, his voice deadly calm. "People run away. They are unpatriotic. They are not loyal to our president. They are not men. They are traitors. We must now put an end to people leaving Mai Mujuru without permission."

A fearful mumbling went through the crowd. Some miners protested, others shook their heads. A few brave ones called out that as they had not run away, they should not be punished.

Commander Jesus raised his hand and the men fell silent.

"I do not punish loyal workers. But some of you have thought of running away. Such thoughts must be reconsidered," he said, reaching down to a soldier who handed him up the oven glove Kamba had stolen. "However," he went on almost casually, "I have decided to let one of you go." The mitt came flying through the air and landed in the dirt at my feet.

"Patson! Come here," he said.

The miners backed slowly away as if I were suddenly toxic. I was alone, except for Arves's small hand curling around mine and squeezing it tight.

"Show him no fear," he whispered. "Bullies hate that."

"Come here, boy. Don't be frightened," Commander Jesus said pleasantly. "I know about you and your family." An image of the scarlet-lipped Wife dancing in an army shirt flashed into my head.

"You want to leave these mines? Well, you can go. I will not stop you."

Confused, I glanced at Arves. He shook his head.

"Come closer, boy."

I hesitated while Commander Jesus jumped down from the jeep and waited for me. I stopped before him and he laid his hand on my shoulder. He turned me slightly away from the miners and spoke in a voice only I could hear.

"Did you like what you saw last night, Patson? Your stepmother dancing in her bra and panties. Did it turn you on?"

I was too stunned to answer. My throat dried up and I couldn't stop trembling. I shook my head, not daring to look at him.

"That's okay." He chuckled, squeezing my shoulder painfully. "Sylvia told me all about you, and how you like looking at her breasts. I don't blame you. I was once a boy in love with an older woman. And Sylvia is a real woman. I know, I've tasted her."

He jerked my shoulder, forcing me to look up at him, and gave me the smile of a man whose mind was not smiling. I had nowhere to look but at the reflection of my terrified self in his mirrored glasses. Commander Jesus turned me around to face the company of miners and stood behind me, his hands resting lightly on my shoulders. "I have decided that this boy can leave Mai Mujuru. We only want men who wish to work here. Men who serve our president. So you are free to leave, boy," he announced, pushing me forward. "Go!"

I jumped at his command, looking desperately at the miners who viewed me now with pity instead of fear. I spotted Uncle James and Musi and stared hard at them, willing them to do something, but they shrunk back, dropping their eyes to the ground. Arves met my gaze and forced a smile. I was waiting for the branches with thorns and the soldiers with their sticks, but none of the soldiers moved. They stood watching me, their rifles slung limply across their backs. I felt small and pathetic, too scared to do anything.

"I said you can go," insisted Commander Jesus. "Go, the same way you went last night."

Totally confused, I looked up at him, hoping it would be for the last time.

"Leave. Now! Before I change my mind."

I turned toward the gate and saw that a jeep had blocked the road. I walked slowly out of the mine, feeling all eyes on my back. My head was spinning. How did he know it was me at Kondozi Farm last night? He seemed so sure. Could Jamu have told him? Or did the Wife somehow get something out of Grace?

I headed out past the barbed-wire fence, behind the toilets, and glanced back at the mine. Nobody had moved. Commander

Jesus had climbed back into the jeep for a better view of my departure.

"Run!" he shouted, drawing his pistol and firing it twice into the sky.

I started jogging across the field, my heart beating in my chest. Was he planning to shoot me as I ran? I picked up speed, my heart now thumping, my body darting from side to side, making sure not to run in a straight line. I expected the sound of gunfire, bullets hitting the ground around me until one smashed into my back.

I ran harder.

No gunshots. No bullets.

I was elated with every stride that took me away from the mine. I had managed to escape. With my diamonds. I'd fetch Grace. We'd be free.

And then I felt a metallic click under my left foot. There was searing heat and a flash of bright white. A crack of thunder; a cloud of dust.

I was airborne. A violent force from within the earth propelled me off the ground. My breath was sucked from me as if I had been splashed with freezing water. My ears stopped working. In slow motion I saw myself falling back to earth and landing on my side with an enormous thud.

I tried to get up but couldn't.

As I looked down, I saw a bloody tangle of white bones where my left foot should have been. The skin of my leg was smoldering. Some distance away lay a running shoe that looked very much like my own.

I lay there thinking how strange all this was, until pain roared through me like a blast of furnace wind, blowing away my thoughts and replacing them with an uncontrollable, raw scream that went on and on and on.

And then I went away.

21

"Wake up, Patson!"

Sunlight. Blue sky. A face.

Why was Arves slapping me? He was shouting at me, but I could barely hear him. He lifted my shoulders from the ground. I was upright.

Dizzy.

The world was zooming in at me from every angle. The ground was the sky. The hills were the tents; the soldiers were the miners. Commander Jesus was Uncle James running toward me.

"I was flying, Arves. Running and then flying." I was gasping for words, wondering why I couldn't move my legs, why I was so cold when the sun was so hot.

"You stepped on a land mine," came his voice from far away.

Arves was dragging me back toward the mine.

"The mine is in the land," I said. "No time for jokes now, Arves."

"Stay awake, Patson."

"My leg hurts," I said, aware I was crying. "There's something wrong with my leg."

Many hands were on me now. People shouting. A man with a belt, twisting it tightly below my knee. The back of a jeep, hard metal ridges. My head banging against the door handle. That should have hurt, but somehow it didn't, the furnace of pain coming from somewhere else.

"Careful!" someone shouted. "Slow down."

"Look at me, Patson!" shouted Arves.

Now my head was cradled in his lap and I saw his upside-down face. I was being rocked from side to side, inside a cacophony of white noise: Arves shouting, rushing wind, wheels humming over gravel, the scream of a motor, at times far away, and then thundering through me. I wished it could be quiet; I wanted so much to close my eyes. But Arves glared down at me, his eyes drilling into my own.

"I see you, Arves," I said. "Make them turn off the noise."

And somebody did.

I awoke with a porcupine staring at me. A black snake rose up with a flame in its mouth. From nowhere the old woman appeared and handed a jar to someone kneeling behind me on the floor.

"Drink, boy, drink," she ordered.

The noise was gone. I lay in a balm of quiet shadows, candles flickering. Someone poured a foul-tasting milky liquid into my mouth. Why couldn't I drink by myself? My arms wouldn't move. I gagged, trying to spit it out, but it was too late. I swallowed and more words passed over me.

"Talk to him, T'kai. Tell him what happened. He needs to know everything," said the old woman, forcing something different down my throat. "Keep him awake. Long as possible. Talk, boy. Talk to your friend, and hold him still."

"Patson, can you hear me?"

I nodded, choking down more bitter brew.

"You stepped on a land mine. Your leg is badly injured. But my granny can fix you. She has done this before, many times. In the liberation war. She traveled with the soldiers in the bush. They called her Dr. Muti. Can you hear me?"

"My leg?" It was as if, by mentioning my leg out loud, I had roused a sleeping monster with razor-sharp teeth that began feeding upon my lower limb. I heard myself gasp as pain spiked through me.

"It was nearly blown off. She needs to clean it." Arves's voice broke through. "She'll stretch your skin to close the wound, cauterize it to stop the bleeding. You have to stay awake." He pried open my clenched hand and forced something into it. "It's a lion's tooth. It will give you strength."

"How did you know?" I asked the old woman. "I never told you about my mother."

"You stay awake, boy," said the old woman, sharpening her

liver knife beside me. "This is going to hurt. Hoh-hoh. Hold him tight, T'kai."

"Arves, you take my stones. They're in my shoe. Give the biggest to Grace. You keep the other two."

The old woman's knife pierced the monster that had become my leg. It growled as she cut into its flesh, and my body jerked upward, fighting against the sharp blade. I saw the mangled beast then, its swollen stump-head wreathed in blood, devouring my leg. The beast roared pain that ripped through my body, delivering me into blackness.

The old woman showed me the oil pot. Why was she cooking my *girazis*? The anger-stone, rain-stone, and dream-stone were boiling away. They rattled around as she stirred them, steam rising from the pot on a gas stove. She was talking to me but her words made no sense. They were as obscure as the glass eyes in the porcupine, the flickering of a candle on an animal skull, and the fearful expression on Arves's face.

The old woman took up a heavy, red-hot flatiron off the flames. She continued talking but now I could not hear her. I was too scared of the iron, so hot, so close to me.

Why did she need to do her ironing now?

Seared flesh; burning blood.

The monster screamed at the sudden heat; its jagged teeth tore into my body.

I floated away through the ceiling, leaving my body on the floor of the photocopying room. I watched the old woman pressing the iron against a leg, Arves trying desperately to hold down a body that writhed and jerked as it waged a losing battle with a bloodthirsty monster.

I didn't care anymore.

Let them get on with it, I thought, and so I left.

Familiar voices pulled me back from the darkness.

"—and he knows a doctor in Mutare. My father will help you, Patson. He knows about the *girazis*. You give them to him and he will take care of you, get you a new leg."

This was Jamu talking, talking.

"Grace told me about your diamonds. My dad said he will take you to a hospital. He'll get the best doctor there is to make you better. He just has to wait for Commander Jesus to come back to the mine."

Jamu's words passed through me.

"The soldiers say he will be back in a week. Then my dad will ask permission to leave the mine and he will come for you. It won't be long now. My dad will help you, Patson. It will be okay. We're family. You give him the diamonds and he'll get you everything you need."

I wished Jamu would stop talking.

"Does he understand what I am saying?"

My head was too heavy to nod.

"Patson, can you hear me? Where are the diamonds?"

"You told your father about our syndicate?"

That must be Arves, but his voice was hard, unfriendly.

"Does Musi also know?"

"It's over, Arves, there is no more *gwejana*. Chipo and Kamba are gone. It's just you and me."

"You told them about our *gwejana* syndicate. You told your father everything."

"I had to, Arves, I had to." Jamu sounded frightened. "Things have changed. You have to understand, the soldiers are in control now. We have to be clever to get any diamonds past them. My father told me to come here. We've got to help Patson. My father promised to help him."

"Yah. I'm sure he will," said Arves. "Just like he helped me when I was sick."

Why was Arves so angry? I tried opening my eyes, but my eyelids seemed glued closed. I forced them open, peering with difficulty into the shadows, and saw only the shape of Jamu's mouth, crooked in his round and sweating face. Why was he sweating? Had he been running? His eyes glistened in the candlelight, darting around the room, searching, searching. I could not see Arves, but his hands rested light and cool on my shoulders.

And always the pain, pain that keeps my brain from fully understanding.

"Give them the diamonds," I muttered. "I don't care about them."

I don't know if anyone heard me.

Jamu was no longer there. The room was lighter. More words floated in the air.

"Hoh-hoh. Now trouble makes more trouble." The old lady's face appeared out of the shadows. Jars and potions flew off the shelf and were stuffed into a canvas bag. "Storm coming now. Mm-mm. When one knows, they all know. Hoh-hoh. Big-big trouble now. Quick, T'kai, move. Hoh-hoh. We have much to do."

◆ ◆ ◆

Who cares where I am
or what day it is.

Why?

That's all I want to know.

Why did this happen to me?

Somewhere in the room the old woman snores.
Arves sleeps. I'm awake alone in the night
and darkness presses down on me. Awake. Eyes
wide open. Sleep just out of reach. Brain
working overtime. My thoughts feeding on
themselves.

A single candle is all that keeps me from
crawling out of this room and into the
yard and into the bush and into a hole to
crawl up and die and let this sentence never
end because if it does I will end up crying
and crying until my insides turn into slush
and I don't know why I want to write in my
diary when I can't understand why this is

236

happening to me and the candle flickers and reminds me of people and warmth and light and now I have to find the place for a full stop because my hand aches as I write this and so it has to be somewhere round about now.

Baba help me. God help me. I think I am dying. The pain is too much. I can't think straight. I just want this to be over.

Please let it be the end...

◆ ◆ ◆

PATSON'S GAME

22

The boy tossed the ball into the air, bouncing it from knee to knee, and then, as if by magic, he caught it with his foot. He stood on one leg, the ball poised in the crook of his right foot, the embodiment of perfect physical balance. The next moment, he flicked the ball into the air, headed it twice, allowed it to fall to the ground and, with a flourish worthy of a magician, trapped the ball neatly under his foot. He looked up as if expecting applause from the crowd gathered before the Beitbridge Border Post.

But I hated him.

I hated the way he stood so effortlessly on one leg. Hated the casual way he transferred his weight from one foot to the other. Despised how he took for granted his talent to make that soccer ball do his bidding.

Most of all, I hated his wholeness.

And Stumpy, always in step with my mood, mocked both me and my hatred. He stung my no-longer-there foot with a sharp reminder not to compare who I once was with who I was now. I gasped at the phantom pain, as familiar now as my breathing. It was too soon for a nip of *ganja*. Besides, Boubacar wouldn't give me any of the magic herb until it was dark and the evening shadows brought back the nightmares. I took out my diary and turned to write on a new page.

Beitbridge

Zimbabwe–South African Border Post

Saturday, 12 April

All around me the border is jammed with people leaving Zimbabwe. The whole country has packed up their belongings on trucks and trailers and is getting out. No money, they say. No food, they say. No freedom, too. In South Africa, there's plenty of money and food. And Nelson Mandela fought for freedom and won. Mandela should educate Prez Mugabe about what freedom means.

While I waited for Boubacar some guys came around and offered to take me across with them. If you pay us a R150, we'll take you over the border, they said. I told them I was waiting for somebody. One of them asked me what happened to my leg. I told him to mind his own business. He laughed—and called me Crappy Crutches.

Boubacar said that in order to get to the other side everyone would expect to be paid something. On the Zim side the police, and the soldiers at the border gate; on the South African side, the soldiers there. Money makes things happen. That's what I once believed about diamonds and look where that got me! My stones are gone. Every single one. The girazis I cared so much about are lost. The last time I saw them was the day I got blown up. I thought they would change my life, but without Grace I have no life. I left her alone in the tobacco shed, thinking that she would be safe with the Banda family, but they made her their slave. It was so easy for Determine to get her to go with him to South Africa. Of course she wanted to get away from the sheds, and I wasn't around to look after her. I should never have trusted them, never have left her there...

Thinking about what had happened to Grace made it impossible to write any more. I checked the screen of my phone but there was still no Mxit message from her. Perhaps her battery was low? Or she was in a place with poor reception. I worried constantly that her phone might be taken away and I would lose contact with her. I thought about the last time I saw her—that night in the sheds when I woke her up and showed her my *girazi*—and she told me how she wanted to go to South Africa with Determine. I hadn't listened carefully enough to her; I was too busy thinking about myself. If only I had taken her with me that night; if only I hadn't gone back to the mine with Arves's meds. "If only" didn't help anyone, I thought bitterly.

I scanned the crush of people outside the immigration offices in a line that wasn't moving. No one seemed to know how long the border would stay closed. And still no sign of Boubacar. It had been more than an hour since he left me sitting on the pavement beside a line that wound around the huge courtyard, down beyond a stream of cars and trucks parked one behind the other. Boubacar had joined the hundreds of people who clutched their green passports and papers, all waiting to be processed and stamped before they would be allowed to cross over the Limpopo River into South Africa. I had no passport, no papers of any kind.

"They may not give you emergency travel papers, Patson, but I will try," Boubacar had told me as he helped me down onto the pavement.

"We've got to get over the border."

"There are other ways into South Africa, Patson. Now, don't go anywhere, okay?"

His last instruction was a cruel joke. It was not as if it was the easiest thing in the world for me to go anywhere. Sometimes Boubacar could be as sensitive as a brick. Mostly I'd be happy never to move again. If it weren't for Grace, well, I wouldn't have moved at all.

I unwrapped the black tire tubing that held the bamboo peg to my stump. I gently eased off the lattice fitting, trying not to annoy Stumpy, and dropped my handmade prosthesis to the ground. Relief was instantaneous. After I took off the bandaging, I fumbled around in my Amputee Survivor kitbag for the smelly ointment that Stumpy loved. He was red and angry, crying out for attention. If I didn't focus on him soon, I would pay for it with spikes of pain that would leave me sweating.

"Okay, okay," I muttered, rubbing the yellow ointment over Stumpy, gently massaging the wound. "Easy now, easy. You're going to be all right." The familiar tingling sensation spread through my leg and Stumpy was happy—for the moment. I slipped the specially adapted sock-with-no-toes over the stump, repositioning the holes that allowed Stumpy to breathe. It's always give and take with Stumpy. I give him attention, and he takes away pain. A fair enough trade and I sighed with relief as the pain transformed into a dull, familiar throb.

The boy kicked the ball and it sailed through the air toward another boy who had stepped out of the crowd. He laughed in delight as the odd-shaped soccer ball headed toward him, and he stuck out his chest and bumped the ball to the ground. Without looking up, he kicked it straight back. One by one, other boys left the line and hovered in the vicinity of the two boys kicking the ball to each other, awkwardly waiting and obviously eager to join in. The two boys walked toward each other.

I knew what was coming: the Choosing. Each captain would assess the physical attributes of those standing in the circle and one by one the fastest, strongest, and tallest would line up behind their captain. I watched as the two teams formed, and felt a different, more intense pain: the heartbreaking realization that I would never run again. What did I have to offer these two-footed boys and their extraordinary ability to play soccer? My pathetic bamboo peg leg was a joke and my shiny aluminum crutches were no match for my missing ankle and foot. I was neither fit nor able to join them. Besides, they would never see me, and yet they would stare themselves blind looking at Stumpy. He had taken over both my life and my body. Stumpy was now the star of the show, dangling uselessly in the air, no longer connected to the earth. Nobody saw Patson Moyo anymore; they only saw the half limb, flopping about in a space of its own, ignoring its owner as if he never existed. I watched as their expressions of curiosity changed to fascination, then revulsion and, finally, pity. Only then would they raise their eyes to look at the person who owned this calamity, but by then it would be too late. The book had been judged by its cover, and the cover shouted "Stumpy" to the world. I would never be chosen again. I was disabled and no good for anything; a useless boy, worthy only of their sympathy.

But sympathy can be useful, I thought.

That unbidden phrase popped into my mind. Where had I heard it before? And then I remembered. Arves had said it that day in Mutare, just before he darted through the traffic to do business with the diamond dealers opposite Dairy Den. The HIV/AIDS-positive boy who carried death on his shoulder and feared nothing in this world. The boy who called Commander Jesus an arsehole and who talked me through the pain of losing my foot. Arves, the best friend I'd ever had.

My hand instinctively reached for the lion-tooth that hung around my neck as I wondered what Arves would do if he were me now. The answer hit me with the force of a ten-ton truck hurtling down Uggy's Hill: If Arves had one leg, he would play soccer.

Before I could dismiss this mad idea, I picked up my crutches, struggled to my knees, and hauled myself upright. I hooked my arms over my crutches and dug them into the ground, lurching forward. Stumpy reacted immediately and bit me with a painful warning not to go any farther. "Not now," I muttered as thirteen pairs of eyes turned toward me.

The boys stared at Stumpy. I saw their predictable range of expressions as I took another step forward. I stared back, daring any one of those able-bodied boys to refuse to let me join in their game. I would not go away, and to make my point, I jerked my head at the boy holding the ball, lifted my crutch, and signaled for him to throw it at me.

The ball flew through the air and I watched it carefully as it bounced on the ground close to my good foot. I planted my crutches, swung my right leg, and kicked with all the force I could muster. The connection was perfect and the ball sailed over their heads.

"I'll take you," said the owner of the ball.

You had no choice, I thought, moving forward to join his team. We stood in a huddle while our captain gave everyone his position. He was a small boy, maybe thirteen or fourteen, but with a charisma that was hard to resist. He knew his soccer and his eyes blazed with passion as he organized us into a team. A few of the boys were from Zimbabwe, but others were from Senegal, Democratic Republic of Congo, and Angola. Their names—Fantan, Sinbaba, and Aziz—sounded to my ears like exotic foreign fruits.

"And you, what's your name?" asked Deo, my captain.

"Patson," I answered. "I play goalie."

"Where you from, Patson?" asked Deo.

I hadn't joined them to tell them my life story, so I kept it short. "Masvingo Province." I turned toward the goal that I was now prepared to defend with my life.

The game didn't start well. I let in two quick goals and noticed the exchange of eye-rolling glances between some of the players. I was struggling to find my balance on the uneven ground and the game was played at a furious pace. Older men gathered on the sidelines and cheered on the boys they knew, clapping and shouting instructions. I was sweating buckets, the crutches were bruising my armpits, and Stumpy was bawling tears of pain, but I had never felt more alive.

Our captain was everywhere. He encouraged the others to

stay in their positions and mark their opposing player. "Don't run after the ball. Wait for it to come to you," he shouted, intercepting a pass and then losing the ball to the skill of the talented Aziz.

"That's a foul," cried Aziz as Deo brought him to the ground with a bone-crunching tackle. "That's a penalty, Deo."

Fantan ran over and got between the two boys, pushing them apart. "Who cares? Let's play on."

"No!" said Aziz. "That's a penalty and he knows it."

The standoff lasted only a moment until Deo, who knew he was in the wrong, backed down.

"Penalty," he said, striding toward me as if he intended to replace me as goalie. I jerked my crutch at him to move away, and squared myself in the goal, my eyes locked on Aziz. He marked out the distance and casually placed the ball on the ground. There was some argument about where the penalty should be taken from, but once it was agreed, everyone gathered to watch the shot at goal. Aziz paced out a few steps backward and regarded me with a grin. I knew what he was thinking: This would be like stealing a lollipop from a baby.

I balanced on one leg and lifted my arms, extending my crutches to almost cover the entire goal. You'll have to get past me *and* my appendages, I thought, staring him down with fire in my eyes.

There was no way I'd let Aziz score. He just didn't know it yet.

Out of the corner of my eye, I noticed more people gathering to watch the outcome of this contest between the abled and disabled. All the players watched me swaying unsteadily on one leg. I knew they gave me no chance against the opposing captain. I longed for the natural balance that a two-footed connection with the earth would give me, and at that moment I knew I would never experience that connection again. Now I only had one good leg. It would have to be enough.

Aziz ran up to make the kick. He feinted left but I wasn't buying it. The ball flew to the right, heading for the top corner. Instinct took over as I used all the power I had in my one leg to launch myself into the air, dive to the right and jab at the ball with the end of my crutch. It fell to the ground and, somehow, as if it was supposed to happen just like this, it rolled right in front of me. With one painful hop I was upright again. I quickly planted the crutches and kicked the ball to Fantan, who passed it swiftly to Deo, who dribbled it past Sinbaba, sprinted toward the opposite goal, and scored.

"Goooaaal!"

Our team went crazy as a man sitting with his ear pressed to his radio jumped up, spread out his arms like wings, and ran up and down the sideline shouting *"Goooaaal!"*

The watching crowd applauded, and a few of them yelled to me, "Good save, Goalie!" and "Well done, boy!"

Deo ran up and looked at me, really looked at me for the first time. Not at Stumpy but at me, Patson.

"Good save!" he said, grinning with admiration.

I held back my tears and smiled instead.

We played until the insects buzzed around the tall lights of the courtyard and the night crept up on the Beitbridge Border Post. All was forgotten as the ball moved from player to player, foot to head, head to goal. I ignored Stumpy's protests, knowing he would take his revenge for my moment of madness later. I didn't care. All I wanted was to be part of this soccer game, not thinking about Grace somewhere in South Africa or how I would find her. I had lost myself in the rhythm of this beautiful game, shouting encouragement to my new friends, and reveling at how, in this moment at least, I was their equal. I was a normal boy, playing with other normal boys, not worrying about tomorrow or what the days after tomorrow would bring.

We played for another hour but soon the magic passed and our game disintegrated as, one by one, the boys were called away. Someone somewhere must have given an instruction for the border to reopen. The air filled with diesel fumes as truck drivers started up their engines and inched closer to Beitbridge. There was a stirring in the crowd as word passed down the line that the offices had reopened. People picked up their luggage, rounded up their children, and shuffled forward. Deo grabbed his ball and ran off in the direction of the line of slowly moving trucks.

The game was over. The magic was gone.

I stood alone, exhausted, thirsty, and in pain. The soccer field was now nothing more than a dusty patch of dirt. I was no longer a star goalie. Once again I was a crippled boy on crutches with a tired aching body. I hobbled away from the goal to where I had left my Amputee Survival kitbag.

Boubacar stood scowling at me with my kitbag in his hand. Don't go anywhere, he had told me. Well, I wasn't sorry that that instruction hadn't worked for me.

"Patson," he said as I approached. "What are you hiding?"

His question stunned me. I hung my head and leaned heavily on my crutches. "Nothing, Boubacar. What are you talking about?"

"Commander Jesus is here," he said. "And he's looking for you."

23

Old Mutare Mission Station

Brumba Mountains. Day 8

Tuesday, 8 April

After my leg was blown off by Commander Jesus's land mine, I became aware of what my body really meant to me. Before I lost my leg, my body always did my bidding. It served me well in everything I demanded: Run hard up Uggy's Hill and it would run hard; walk ten kilometers through the forest at night and it would walk; dig for hours in the sun and it would dig. If I told it to jump, climb, hop, crawl, or skip, my body obeyed. I didn't care if I hurt it, because it would always heal. If it occasionally complained, I ignored it. I was the master; my body the slave.

But now everything is reversed. I can no longer do the things I once did and I will never do them again. The memory of who I was once is fading fast. Even though I still think the same thoughts and feel like the old two-legged Patson, there is one big difference: I no longer live in a body that obeys my every command. Now, Patson is a slave to the needs of a body without balance, a body that has a crucial part cut away. A useless body that can't jump, climb, walk, or run. I would give this half body away if I could, but I can't. I am trapped, a prisoner in a half-functioning bag of blood and bones. I will be hauling this stump around with me for the rest of my life.

And that is why I am angry all the time, Nurse Godi. That is why I cannot think about the future, Dr. T. That is why I

don't want to do your stupid exercises,
because what's the point? My lower leg isn't
going to grow back just because I'm bending
my knee. It's gone. Blown into hundreds of
pieces, cut up by the liver knife of Dr. Muti.
And no, I will not be fine, Dr. T. I will never
be fine again. I will be half-fine. And that's
not fine at all...

Some days I wrote myself into such a rage that I had to stop. The pen gouged out words with so much fury they passed through the paper and could be read all over again on the following page. I had taken to writing in the diary my father gave me out of boredom but also as a way of avoiding talking to people. To make matters worse, there was no cell phone reception at the Old Mutare Mission Station. For the last eight days I'd had no contact with Grace or Boubacar. I had no idea what happened to Sheena and her family and their trip to Marange or where Arves and his grandmother were. I was truly alone.

When I wrote in my diary, however, it kept away the ever-present cloud of gloom that hovered over me. It was also a connection to my father; every time I took up his present he hovered in the periphery of my mind. Why could no one understand that I would rather write than talk to people I didn't know? It was even an effort to smile and nod at Dr. T.'s optimistic observations of my progress, let alone my future.

When I did smile he would write "Good Progress" on the

clipboard that hung at the end of my bed at the mission station hospital. He would touch me lightly on the arm and instruct Nurse Godi to give me an extra helping of sweet green jelly and yellow custard after dinner. The other patients at the mission station would clap their hands and shout, "Good job, Patson, good job."

But that was not the end of it. I had to be grateful for their encouragement. I had to smile and nod like a proud boy displaying some debating medal he'd won. And all I really wanted to do was scream: *How do I get rid of this thing that lies at the end of the bed attached to me and swollen like an elephant's foot? This does not belong to me. Somebody take it away, please, take it away. I never deserved this.*

Of course Dr. Theodore Jackson always had a ready answer to my mouthful of complaints. He would step into the ward in his immaculate white coat and stethoscope wreathed around his neck, and walk from bed to bed dispensing encouragement. Those of us who were able to sit up did so proudly, to make a good impression on Dr. T. He was, after all, the African-American pastor of the United Methodist Church and citizen of Charlottesville, Virginia, USA. And the others, unable to rise, would lift their heads, smile bravely, and provide him with the latest news from the country of the Diseased and Disabled, where now we were all miserable citizens.

"You have to remember, Patson, you're dealing with the basic dilemma of every amputee," he said to me in his American accent. "No matter how well-fitting the prosthesis may be, the residual limb doesn't stay the same. It swells and shrinks. It also gets muscle cramps, calluses, blisters, and all the other maladies that afflict normal human skin. Even pimples." He smiled at that and then went on as if he were talking about the care of an untrained puppy dog. "You have to listen carefully to what your wound is saying and pay close attention to it. Especially when it needs a bit of TLC."

The words *amputee*, *prosthesis*, and *residual limb* rolled easily off his tongue but I heard only a foreign language I could never learn. I stared into his sympathetic eyes, unable to comprehend what these strange words actually meant. My hands gripped the sheets as I held his gaze, too afraid to look at the bottom of the bed at the space where my foot should have been.

I wanted to shout at him, *This is not happening to me! I am a normal boy, with a normal life. There has been some terrible mistake. Make it right, Dr. T., please make it right!* But my jaw stayed clenched and I said nothing.

"It will take some getting used to, Patson, but you'll get the hang of it," he said, in his good-humored twang, so similar to the actors in American television comedies. "To compound matters, the skin of your stump is most often in a warm, moist, and dark environment. It's also under pressures that it was never designed to withstand. So it will be up to you, young man, to look after your stump at all times."

I nodded in agreement only because remaining positive was expected from residents of the country of the Diseased and Disabled.

"Are we in good spirits?" He touched me on the shoulder, causing me to flinch. "You're still in shock, Patson, but you'll get better. You're going to heal. Whoever worked on you did a real fine job. In about two weeks' time we will move you to another hospital, for more surgery, but in the meantime you need to rest. Mr. Boubacar will be back for you before long. You're going to be just fine, kid. Remember, you're not disabled by the disability you have, you are enabled by the abilities you have."

I nodded again at his broad row of white teeth and attempted a similar smile. Anything less than a cheery attitude displeased Dr. T., even though it was rage that burned through me, and tears brimmed in my eyes at the injustice of all this.

It had been eight days since Arves had phoned Boubacar to tell him what had happened to me. Boubacar had come immediately and swept me up off the floor of the photocopying room, loaded me into the front seat of his truck, and drove into the Bvumba Mountains as if chased by the devil. We had left so suddenly, it had the feel of a dream: the old woman muttering instructions while she gathered potions and stuffed them into my canvas bag; Arves wrapping my cell phone and charger in newspaper and slipping a chain with his lion's tooth around my neck; the lip-sticked lips of the blue-eye-shadowed washerwomen chattering with questions as Boubacar laid me down in the front seat of his cab. And Boubacar rolling down his window to swear at them that he'd be back to burn down their classroom if they told any-one he had taken me away.

Arves stood outside my window of the truck staring at me as if he would never see me again. His face was pale gray and the dark shadows under his eyes formed deep rings that made him look like an old man. I thought it odd that he should be so worried about me when he was the one who looked so gaunt and ill. I tried to wind the window down to talk to him, to tell him to keep eating and taking his meds, but my hand kept slipping off the handle. He placed his right hand on the glass, his fingers spread out in a silent high five, and smiled at me. His lips moved slowly and I thought I caught the word *diamonds* but I couldn't be sure.

"Thank you, Arves, thank you so much," I mouthed slowly, hoping he would understand. There were a hundred things I wanted to tell him. But I only had time to raise my hand against the glass, mirroring his, before Boubacar threw the truck into gear and hurriedly reversed.

"He must come with me," I said to Boubacar. "We must take him with us."

Boubacar gripped the steering wheel and gunned us forward across the veldt.

"Not possible, Patson," he said, shaking his head, keeping his eyes on the track.

I looked back over my shoulder as we sped away, but all I caught was a glimpse of Arves standing alone in the courtyard of Junction Gate High School, waving good-bye.

Boubacar explained that it wasn't safe for me in Marange anymore. He didn't tell me why, only that I had to get away as quickly as possible. He was taking me into the Bvumba Mountains to a mission station run by an American he knew.

I remember little of that journey; only that it seemed to last forever. I was so tired I gave over to the bumpy road, the rush of passing trees in green forests, the gray mist over high mountains, and later, the bright headlights coming at us and flashing past.

Then I was lying in a quiet bed with clean sheets, in a room that smelled of straw, disinfectant, and freshly made tea. When I opened my eyes I was in the small, eight-bed ward of the mission station hospital, sun streaming through the window. A tall man in a white coat was examining my leg, murmuring to himself as if he had made an important discovery. There was no sign of Boubacar anywhere.

"Excellent, Patson," Dr. T. chirped. "Everything looks just fine and dandy. You will be up and about in no time."

What do you say in the face of such enthusiasm for a leg lost? I had no answer and so fumbled for my pen, opened my diary, and wrote a story about how a one-legged boy climbed onto the thatch roof of the mission station in his hospital gown, his bare arse displayed for all to see, clutching a stolen bag of condoms. In my story Nurse Godi and Dr. T. tried to get the difficult, wild, rude boy down from the roof, but he pelted them with condoms and then, just as they were about to reach him, he set the thatch roof alight and burned down the mission station and himself in the process.

The only urgent question I had for the staff they couldn't answer: When would Boubacar return? I counted every day that he had left me there. Eight days and eight very long nights. I had lost the ability to sleep. My mind seemed to feed upon itself and sleep was a bridge I walked along without ever reaching the other side. The pain in my phantom foot insisted I stay awake and the itch in my toe-no-longer-there remained unscratched. I could not roll over to lie comfortably on my side while my good foot mourned its missing twin. Outside my window, the crickets chirped the night away, and I would stare into the oblivion of the dark ceiling, listening with envy to the other snoring patients. I couldn't stay away from random thoughts of my father's broken glasses, the voice of my mother coming from an old woman's mouth, and a glowing white tie in a dark tobacco shed hanging over Grace. I gave up the idea of sleep and turned on the bedside lamp and wrote in my diary:

Old Mutare Mission Station

After midnight

Wednesday, 9 April

Sheena and I once had an argument about who was the tallest. So we turned bottom to bottom to settle the issue, but we still couldn't tell for certain. I turned her around to face me. We were so close to each other our noses almost touched and I remembered being fascinated at how her pupils enlarged as I looked into her eyes. The back of my hand glanced her arm, and she smiled. She decided that for the moment we were the same height, but that I would be taller by next year. Sheena. Nut-brown eyes and skin as soft as caramel, with a smile I could feel all the way to my toes.

I don't know where she is. If her family made it to Marange. And if I ever decide to talk to her again, what do I tell her?

It's all fun and games, until someone loses a foot....

On my ninth day at the mission station, Nurse Godi refused to help me to the toilet or provide me with the cold metal bedpan I hated.

"Not today, young man, and not ever again," she said, placing a pair of crutches beside my bed. "Today you go to the toilet yourself."

"I don't want them," I said, glaring at the offensive giraffe-leg crutches that represented far too much to me.

"You may find them useful."

"I'm too sore," I whined, amazed at her cruelty, aware of the other patients watching while pretending not to. "I don't want to walk today."

She folded her arms and looked at me with the indifference

reserved for the efforts of a struggling dung beetle rolling its ball of shit up a hill.

"I can't do it," I said, smoldering with anger and frustration.

"Yes, you can, Patson." She picked up my chart and made a mark, as if my reaction was normal and noteworthy.

"Give me a few more days," I pleaded. "I promise I will try tomorrow."

"Today is the day." She smiled like a boxer just before he knocks out his opponent.

Under her pitiless gaze, rage bloomed in my chest. I gripped the bedsheets and shook my head from side to side. I would not look at her. *Do you have any idea how I feel? No, because you are standing upright on both your legs. If I could end my life, I would do it right now.*

"And I would start early, Patson, unless you want to wet yourself on the way. Then you'll have to clean that up too." With that she turned on her heel and left me to reconsider my choices.

I swore under my breath, refusing to give her or any of the other patients the pleasure of seeing me give in too easily. I lay in the bed fuming, but also aware of the pressure building in my bladder. After a while I yelled for Nurse Godi, in one last effort, not really believing she would leave me to wet my bed. Then I tried bribing the woman on my left with the promise of my evening slice of bread and jam. But she only waved her hand at me and rolled over. When I looked to the man on my right, he feigned sleep. Obviously no one wanted to help me and then find themselves on the bad side of Nurse Godi.

Cursing the unfairness of a full bladder and a leg and a half, I threw off the sheets and viewed the *thing* hanging below my knee. I didn't know what to name it. It was no longer possible to not think about it as my own. For the first time, I felt the humiliation at seeing my foot-no-longer-there, in front of everyone. And when I finally glanced up, every head in the room quickly turned away.

I lifted the stump and gingerly maneuvered myself to the edge of the bed, swinging my good leg onto the floor. I hopped toward the end of the bed and, using one of the crutches, I attempted to stand. I'd seen people maneuver on crutches before and I was surprised by the power in my right leg. It felt familiar and comfortable. Encouraged, I gripped the second crutch. The other patients in the ward became strangely quiet, while I focused on getting around to the far corner of the bed.

"Staring at me is not helping," I growled.

"You can do it—"

"I don't need anyone to tell me what I can or cannot do," I snapped at the woman who had declined my bribe.

I planted the crutches a few feet in front of me and swung my good leg forward. The stump followed, almost knocking me off balance. The trick was not to put the crutches too far forward and to take smaller steps. Beads of perspiration rolled down the side of my face but I had no free hand to wipe them away. My arms had never felt the full weight of my body before, but with the next step I figured out what the handles halfway down were actually for. I looked down the length of the ward.

The toilet seemed a mile away and the pressure to pee intensified. I lurched from the security of the bed and started down the central aisle, ignoring the patients' stares as I slowly passed one bed after another. My new way of walking was like a three-legged giraffe crossing the muddy banks of a watering hole: lift crutches, balance on one leg, plant crutches in front, shift my weight to lift good leg off the ground, and swing it one step forward, and the stump at least seemed to know enough to follow along. This complicated procedure of taking just one step at a time meant that the toilet, almost thirty steps away, seemed unreachable.

I wobbled my way slowly forward, with my stump aching and my frustration building. I was in no-man's-land—too far from my bed and still too far from the toilet to make it in time. I placed my crutches farther and farther ahead of me, in an attempt to cover more ground, and then, with only, say, ten paces more to go, one of the crutches slipped from under me and I fell. Trying to break my fall, I hurled the other crutch into the air, onto a cabinet stacked with drinking glasses that shattered on impact.

I felt the warm release spread across my thighs, the floor, and over my hospital gown.

Somebody hovered over me to help me up, but I kicked them away. "Leave me alone," I screamed. "Just leave me alone."

I lay in my puddle of piss, crying, lashing out with my crutch at anyone who came near me. "Don't touch me! Fuck you. Fuck you all."

♦ ♦ ♦

The following morning, I woke up from a groggy, double-dose sedative sleep to a voice saying, "You ready to travel?"

It sounded like Boubacar, but I might have been dreaming.

"We have a long way to go, Patson," he said. "Or do you want to stay here?"

I opened my eyes and Boubacar was standing at the foot of my bed. "No. I don't want to stay here." I swallowed the sob that threatened to bring tears. I would not cry in front of him.

"Good. I don't think the hospital can afford any more broken crockery."

I offered him a weak smile as an apology, ashamed that he knew about my meltdown.

"I slipped. It was an accident."

Boubacar's mouth twitched maybe in a smile, but I wasn't sure. "There's something else," he said, moving to my bedside cabinet and stuffing all that I owned into the old woman's sack, which was now my Amputee Survival kitbag. "Grace is not at the sheds. She and a few of the other kids have gone to South Africa with Determine."

I struggled to sit up. "Grace has gone to South Africa?"

Boubacar nodded. "Yes. I went to pick her up but she was not there. The Banda women let her go to a scout jamboree in Cape Town. They said you knew about it."

"No, I don't—"

And then I remembered Grace proudly showing me her uniform, telling me about the money she had given Determine. She had mentioned going to South Africa. I just hadn't listened to her properly.

"I told the Banda wives if anything happened to Grace, they would have to answer to me," Boubacar said, his voice edged with anger. "I will find her and get you far away from Marange and into a proper hospital in South Africa."

I was so pleased to see Boubacar, I wanted to hug him. "And take Arves with us," I said, suddenly filled with hope. "He has to come with us."

"Arves and the *magogo* have disappeared from the school. I don't know where they are."

"I do." I sat up, swinging my good leg off the bed. "I know just where Arves would have gone."

24

I clung to Boubacar's neck, wrapping my good leg around his waist, as we moved rapidly through the crowds at Beitbridge. Commander Jesus was here somewhere. Looking for me. My leg had buckled at the mention of his name but Boubacar caught me before I fell, and swung me onto his back. I couldn't stop the trembling, and pressed myself against Boubacar. I was sure he could feel the pounding of my heart.

Commander Jesus would find me. There was no escape. I was going to die.

"Take it easy, Patson. You're going to be all right, but not if you strangle me," Boubacar said, tapping my arms wrapped tightly around his throat.

"Why's he here? How did he know…" I stammered, trying to catch my breath.

"I thought you could tell me that," said Boubacar, sidestepping a family loaded down with luggage, and moving into the shadows outside the brightness cast by the heavy floodlights above the immigration offices and courtyard. He glanced over his shoulder.

"Can you see him?"

"No, but I know he's here," he said, moving steadily away from the crowd, in the direction of the surrounding bush.

"What happened at the border office?"

"When I finally got to the counter and showed my passport, the official asked me to wait. I didn't like the way he looked at me and then I saw him making a phone call. I ran back to the truck, but the soldiers were already there. They had broken into my cab and were searching it. I asked a girl what was going on. She said someone had told her that the commander from Fifth Brigade was looking for a man and a one-legged boy."

"But why? What does he want from me?"

"Your diamonds, Patson. What else? They will make him a very rich man."

"But I don't have them. I gave them to Arves—in the photocopying room. Jamu came. Maybe he took them. I don't know where they are, Boubacar. I swear."

"Who did you tell about your *girazis*, Patson?"

I couldn't think straight or control the rush of fear. I had no idea what happened to my stones. All I remembered was seeing them boiling in an oil pot; telling Arves to take them; and Jamu asking for them. The only thing I knew for certain was that the hole in my shoe was empty.

"Grace. I told my sister. And Jamu was around when I told her. Maybe he overheard me? Maybe he got it out of Grace the next day? Jamu came to the photocopying room and asked me about the diamonds. He told his father about the *gwejana*." I remembered how angry Arves had been with Jamu for betraying the *gwejana*. "And my father," I said, suddenly remembering his reaction when I had told him. "I told my father the night you had food with us. And of course I told Arves. But he wouldn't have told anyone. And his grandmother too."

"So enough people knew about them that it was only a matter of time before Commander Jesus would find out," he said, jogging into the darkness, moving away from the border post. "We're not going to be able to cross the border tonight. We'll have to spend all of tomorrow hiding and then try again when it's dark. I've got to find the River Woman. She'll get us across the Limpopo River. Once we're in South Africa, you'll be safe."

We followed a path that led to a barbed-wire fence. It was dark there. The noise of the border was replaced by the steady sound of the unseen Limpopo River. Boubacar eased me to the ground and we both looked back at the brightly lit border post against a dark night sky. Commander Jesus's soldiers were still walking up and down the lines of people, pulling truck drivers from their cabs, opening the doors and trunks of every car and van. We were looking at them looking for us and, somewhere in that brightly lit oasis, Commander Jesus was giving orders.

"Come on, move," said Boubacar as he lifted the barbed-wire

fence. I crawled into a shallow trench dug by hundreds of hands before me and worked my way to the other side. Boubacar followed and scooped me up, and we headed down the banks, stumbling along the uneven pathway. Powerful searchlights from Beitbridge moved slowly over the bushes, probing, searching for us. At one point we fell to the ground and lay in a hollow as a beam of light passed over us. Loud voices floated up from the banks of the river. More soldiers were patrolling the Zimbabwean side of the Limpopo River.

"We're going to have to hide," Boubacar said. "Lie on top of your crutches. Keep as low as you can and wait here."

"No, don't leave me, Boubacar. I'm coming with you."

Boubacar dashed quickly from bush to bush, looking for a better place to hide. I tried to shuffle forward on my stomach, but keeping the crutches out of the spotlight made progress impossible.

The voices drew nearer. The soldiers were coming in our direction.

"Over here, Patson. Come quickly," whispered Boubacar as he disappeared over a small rise. I crawled forward, shuffling on my knees, dragging my crutches, dropping down each time the white light swept over my head. I flopped down into a small space, protected on one side by a sandbank and on the other by the leaves and branches of thick bushes. And then I felt Boubacar's big hands dragging me the rest of the way through the undergrowth into a deep burrow.

Someone had been here before us. Cardboard from packing

cases covered the ground; empty tins lay scattered in one corner with a plastic bottle half full of water. A cloth hung from a branch above a single baby shoe. Boubacar quickly covered our tracks and rearranged some of the branches over the entrance, just as the searchlight drifted over the bush. The soldiers' voices were closer now, and as their heavy footsteps approached, Boubacar laid a hand on my arm. He was breathing calmly beside me but his knife was drawn and ready.

Three men walked along the path only a few meters away. One carried a powerful flashlight, sweeping the ground in front of them.

"This is a waste of time," he grumbled.

"And you want to tell the commander that?"

"They'll never cross the river at night. It's too dangerous," said one of the other soldiers as they stomped past us.

Boubacar stared hard into the darkness after the men. He waited, listening intently for at least another ten minutes. Then he peered through the branches and whispered, "Relax. They've gone."

I was still too afraid to relax, and between Stumpy, the cramps in my good leg, and the crutches jutting into my chest, I had to shift my position.

He crawled out of our burrow. "I need to go—"

"Don't leave me, Boubacar!" I pleaded, grabbing his arm.

"Patson, listen to me. I'm not leaving you. I'll be right back. Stay calm and you'll be fine."

I was ashamed of how afraid I was of being left alone. Before my leg was blown off, I had been fearless, to the point of reck-lessness. Now everything frightened me. I nodded reluctantly, biting my lower lip, and slowly released my grip on his arm.

"If you're in pain, chew on this. You've earned a double dose tonight."

He handed me a nub of *ganja* and I gratefully popped it into my mouth. My panic at being left alone was equal to my shame at how afraid I was. As I chewed the soft substance, I began to believe that everything would be fine.

"I'll be back soon," he promised. "Don't move. And sleep if you can."

This time I would do exactly as I was told. Boubacar slipped out of the burrow, repositioned the branches to hide the entrance, and disappeared. I listened until I could no longer hear his footsteps. I was alone with the soothing sound of the river as the warm glow and bright flashing colors of the *ganja* flowed through me. I could lie here for days. No one would find me. Then my flesh would be peeled off by giant termites and my bones would be crushed and carried away to be eaten by small animals until nothing was left but the horrible crutches of the boy once called Patson. I chewed on the last of the bitter *ganja*, took a sip of water, and gazed through the patches of the bush at the night sky. A star sparkled, sending me an image of my sister, Grace.

I sighed deeply, trying desperately to hold on to her, as my exhausted body sank deeper into the sand. Stumpy was still mad at me for the soccer game and spiked me a couple of times before the *ganja* made him finally go quiet. With my eyes closed, I saw the ashen figure leaning on a pair of crutches and its dust-gray arm pointing me in a direction I didn't want to go. My eyes flickered open at the memory. Moonlight, spilling through the branches, covered me like a quilt of silver light. If that figure with the shimmering halo was trying to tell me something, I still couldn't understand. But the more I thought of it, the more it looked like Arves.

25

I was elated the day Boubacar and I drove away from the Old Mutare Mission Station hospital. For the first time since the land mine took off my leg I had a real purpose beyond feeling sorry for myself. Instead of lying in the hospital bed with my dismal thoughts, I would be doing something positive. Boubacar was driving me away from the country of the Diseased and Disabled, to fetch Arves and take him with us to get the best HIV treatment in South Africa. There we would find Grace and with the money still left from the Baron for our *ngodas*, everything would be possible.

It was late afternoon when we arrived on the outskirts of Mutare, and after charging my cell phone in the pickup truck, it buzzed alive as message after message downloaded. It felt good to be connected again. I skimmed past Grace's texts from before she left the tobacco shed to her new ones.

"Listen to this, Boubacar," I said, reading her messages aloud.

Wed 4/9/08 10.16am

Big Brother, I want to go with Scoutmaster
Determine to jamboree in SA. Be back in a
week. Lot of fun!!! ☺ Please say yes, BB. ☹
Okay? xxx

Wed 4/9/08 11.23am

Can I go? Where r u BB?! xxx

Wed 4/9/08 04.32pm

I hate the sheds. ☹ Auntie Prisca is mean. ☹
She makes me work all day. ☹ Determine is
taking No Matter, Maka + Sidi. Can I go? Dad
would let me. BB u there??? xxx

Wed 4/9/08 08.19pm

Kuda says I can go. ☺ Jamboree in Cape Town.
Yayyy!!! Back in a week. Don't worry. Text me.
Plzzzz! xxx

"And the last message came from her this morning, Boubacar. She's at the border already," I said, realizing that she had
probably crossed into South Africa by now.

At the border now. We hide in a truck. Sidi hates
the dark. Determine has no travel papers. I'm
scared. xxx

"We should be at the border tomorrow and in Musina the
day after," he said, overtaking another truck heading south. "If
all goes well."

"You don't think she's in any danger, do you?"

"The border's a dangerous place, Patson. The sooner we get
there the better."

"What shall I text her?"

"Tell her we're coming to fetch her and she should go to the
police in Musina," he replied flatly.

I wrote the Mxit and pressed Send. I imagined these words
flying through space to a satellite and bouncing back to a tower
in South Africa. She would open my message and know that she
was not alone; her big brother was on his way to find her.

"Grace doesn't know what happened to me, does she,
Boubacar?"

"No, Patson."

"Are you sure?"

"Nobody told her about your accident."

"It wasn't an accident," I muttered, lost in the stream of messages Sheena had sent while I was off-line. She had received my
last Mxit warning her about the soldiers. Her family had been
stopped at an army checkpoint on the highway to Marange and

277

had been forced to return to Bulawayo. There were several messages about her not getting to see me again; how worried she was about me; and how sad they were to be back in Bulawayo. Then the tone of her messages changed. She must have become irritated with my nonresponse and pinged me with a few angry faces and a string of question marks. Her last Mxit was now four days old:

> I can't do this anymore. Why don't you answer?
> What happened to us? Patson speak to me!!!

A great sadness swallowed me. How could I describe what had happened to me? Up at the mission station I had attempted several draft messages to her in my diary, but they were all pathetic. It was better if she thought I was dead. She was part of my old life, the two-legged-Patson's life. Of course I could pretend that nothing had happened and lie to her again, but that had backfired spectacularly. I had put her and her family at great risk, and surely it was now better just to end it. Our relationship was over. I would never run with her again and she would never want a boyfriend with one leg. There was nothing left to say to her.

Boubacar drove the truck across the open veldt and past the familiar hills of Marange. We approached Gwejana Rock from the west, well out of sight of the mine and army checkpoints. Once we reached the foot of the hill, Boubacar turned off the ignition and the cab filled with the silence of the veldt.

"So you think he's up there?" he said, looking up at the hill.

I nodded. "Do you see that flat-shaped rock halfway? Our campsite is just behind it. He'll be there and then we can go straight to the border."

278

Boubacar had made it clear that the longer we stayed in Zimbabwe, the harder it would be to find Grace. I watched as he climbed out of the truck and headed up the hill to the meeting place of the *gwejana* syndicate. Soon he was out of sight, and I waited as patiently as I could to see the smiling face of my friend.

The time before the soldiers now seemed an idyll. I missed my friends and the way we had worked together on the fields. That part of my life had also been cut away. Poor people becoming rich overnight had drawn the attention of people more powerful than miners. Diamonds for everyone had been the dream but Operation No Return had become the truth. I waited anxiously, keeping an eye on the hill, until finally Boubacar reappeared, standing on a rock, alone, looking down at me. He came slowly back to the truck, wiping perspiration from his brow.

"He's not there?"

"Yes, he's there, Patson, waiting for you."

My heart soared. "But why didn't he come down?"

"You need to go and see him."

"But how can I climb that hill, Boubacar?"

"You can for your friend."

"I can't. Even if I wanted to, I can't get up there. You know I can't. Don't look at me like that. You're no better than Nurse Godi," I said, spitting out angry words, and feeling their sting of self-pity.

"Have you forgotten, Patson, what I told you when I found you and your family in the forest?"

"What are you talking about?" I snapped.

"I warned you that when you have worked the mines you are

no longer a boy. Once you have come through the eye you are a man. Stop behaving like a boy, Patson. No diamond is a true diamond until it has been cut and polished. The same is true for a man. Not one of us becomes a man without the pain of being tested, or without the polish of suffering. So you've lost something. So you've suffered. So have we all.

"You want to be a Stumpy all your life? Don't look so shocked. I will call you Stumpy but that's not who you are, Patson. *That* is Stumpy," he said, pointing at my half leg. "You are a man now, but if you are going to make the rest of this journey with me, you'd better start believing it. You owe it to your friend to climb that hill." He turned his back on me, walking far enough away that I would not follow.

I was stunned by his words, the tone of his voice, and the choices before me. I looked up at the hill that I had bounded up so many times and down at my missing foot. "Are we going to do this, Stumpy?" I felt his spike of a reply. "Okay. I heard you, but I'm not listening. We're going, and it will be just the two of us," I added as I climbed out of the truck without my crutches.

The day I climbed up to Gwejana Rock on one leg, I learned that pain could be controlled, managed, and even ignored. I learned, too, that being slow and steady was one way of achieving the impossible. I also made friends with Stumpy as I climbed over one rock at a time toward our secret camp. I never stopped talking to him the whole way up. I cajoled, encouraged, berated, swore, and praised him with every painful step. I refused to give in to his uselessness, or his outrage at being hauled over rocks.

He had to learn who was boss, and although it was a painful lesson for both of us, this time, I was not going to back down. I dragged myself up the hill, and found that having one good leg was all I needed to make it to the top. All the way up I knew that Arves was waiting for me. When I lost my balance and fell to the ground, I got up, reminding myself how Arves had run through a minefield to fetch me. When I grazed my knee and cut my palms crawling over loose rocks, I remembered Arves cradling my head in his lap, assuring me I would survive.

With each step I took up that hill, I knew I could not fail. I had to reclaim, even if only briefly, some part of the old Patson. Boubacar was right: I owed it to Arves. When I finally reached Gwejana Rock, my T-shirt was soaked with sweat, and every muscle in my body trembled and ached, but none of that mattered. Stumpy and I had made it together.

"Arves," I shouted, looking about the camp, half expecting him to leap out from behind the rock where Kamba had produced his *ngodas*, armed with some outrageous joke. "Arves!" I crawled into the open space that was covered with the ashes of a recent fire, and saw evidence of his gran's parcels of herbs and puddles of melted candle wax on the rocks around me.

"Arves?"

I pivoted around, looking up to the top of the hill and then down onto the familiar view of Mai Mujuru mine. There was no sign of anyone at our secret camp. A gust of wind scattered the ashes from the dead fire. And then I saw the mound of earth, the length and width of a boy, covered with small stones, carefully placed. Sorrow swept over me. Boubacar was right when he said that Arves was waiting for me. All the way up the hill, our friendship had been the reality that dragged me forward, and now the unmistakable shape and size of that pile of stones brought me the reality of his death.

In all the moments Arves and I shared, in the back of my mind I knew that there would be a day when the sun would rise, and the sky would be as blue as it was today, and Arves would not be there to see it. He knew all along what the outcome of his illness would be. A walking miracle, the doctors had told him, and yet I only saw the spark of his life; I was only partially aware of the weight of mortality he carried on his shoulders.

I knelt beside the mound. A stick had been wedged between the rocks, and hanging from it was an ironic comment only Arves could have made: his broken watch. Time will tell, he had said, and remembering that ever-present lilt in his voice, I shed tears for my friend, Tendekai Makupe. I realized that when someone dies so young it is not so much the past that is buried but all the things of the future. I wept for what we would never do together, for the loss of a friendship that would only grow as a memory. I wept for myself and for my father and the future I would have without both of them.

From deep in my pocket I took out my father's broken glasses and hooked them through the loop of Arves's watch and hung them from the stick. Let him rest here too. Let me remember Joseph Moyo, my father, resting with my best friend at Gwejana Rock, overlooking the diamond fields of Marange. Sitting there alone, I realized that a friend and a father were not that different from each other. Both of them had loved me, wanted only what was best for me, and, more than that, I thought with tears streaming down my face, they had wanted and encouraged what was best inside me.

When I had no more tears, and Stumpy began to intrude on my grief, I felt the presence of someone nearby. Boubacar was standing over me.

He offered me his hand. "Are you ready now to find Grace? We must leave this terrible place. The eye will take nothing more from us."

26

"Time to get up, Patson."

I awoke from my *ganja* dreams to find Boubacar preparing to leave our burrow to search for the River Woman who
would take us across the river.

"You'll be safe here. I'm going to get some food," he said,
crawling through the bushes.

The sun was already high; cicada beetles trilled.

I was hungry but rested enough to now feel okay with being
alone. Nobody, not even Commander Jesus, would find me
here. Stumpy was hungry, too, so I fed him with the ointments
from my kitbag and got on to washing his sock and dressings
with some of the water still in the plastic bottle. Time passed more
quickly when my hands were busy, so I rewove and strengthened
the lattice of my peg leg with twigs, and scraped away some of the

chipped bamboo from the base. Then, pulling my diary from my kitbag, I wrote about my *ganja* dreams while I waited for Boubacar to return. At one point, I heard voices down by the river, and later a man and a woman carrying a baby walked right past my hideout without seeing me. After that, I heard only the wail of a faraway police van. I checked my phone as often as I dared. Once again the battery was low and I had no idea when I'd be able to recharge it. Around midmorning, it buzzed.

> Sun 4/13/08 11.02am
>
> Musina is a bad place. So many people. Det wants my money! Sidi and No Matter gone. Det's changed. Where r u BB??? xxx

She obviously hadn't got my last message. But then the phone buzzed again.

> Sun 4/13/08 11.06am
>
> Hey, BB!!! So plzzzzd to hear from u!!!! ☺☺ Where r u now? xxx

My thumbs darted over the keypad.

> At border. Coming to Musina. Go to the police. Where r u? Battery low. XXX
>
> Sun 4/13/08 11.10am
>
> @Showgrounds. Can't go to police. Come soon. ☹ xxx

Grace was all that mattered now. Every step I took was for her. Stumpy could protest all he liked but I could not give up on my sister. "Look to Grace" was what Arves's granny had said in her trance. I owed it to my parents to find her. I could not ignore my *shavi*.

Around midday Boubacar returned with some food and news about our crossing into South Africa. I wolfed down the bread, atchar, and barbecued chicken he had brought for me and showed him the texts I had received from Grace.

"She's at the Showgrounds in Musina."

"Ah yes, I know the place. All the refugees that make it to Musina are sent there."

"Do you really think Determine's taking her to a stupid jamboree?"

"Some people take children to South Africa and sell them as domestic workers."

It was obvious Boubacar was not telling me everything. I had heard the stories about young girls sold to truckers who kept them in their cabs as they rode the highways of Africa. "But it could be worse than that, Boubacar, isn't that right?"

"It also could be innocent, Patson. There's no point in guessing. How does that help us? We will find Grace. It is as simple as that. Yes?" And he quickly changed the subject to the River Woman. "I know where she is, but we will have to wait here until it is dark before we can move. The soldiers are everywhere and the border was closed all morning. They're still searching for us. The sooner we get across the river into South Africa, the safer we will be."

"Do you think Commander Jesus really knows about the *girazis* I found?"

"Yes, I'm afraid so. I've been thinking a lot about all the people you told about your *girazis*. James Banda might have told the commander to bribe his way out of the mine. Also, the wives of Banda could have forced it out of Gracie and then told Sylvia and she would surely have told Commander Jesus. There were many different ways he could have found out about the diamonds."

"When I was in the photocopying room I told Arves to give them to Grace, but I don't think she has them. Maybe Arves hid them somewhere before he died? I don't know where they are, Boubacar. You have to believe me." Nothing that happened in the photocopy room was any clearer to me now than it was then. "What I really don't understand is why Commander Jesus wants them so much."

"You have no idea, do you?" he said with a hint of a smile. "From the way you've described them, just one of those stones is worth hundreds of thousands of US dollars. Commander Jesus knows that with those three stones he can retire from the army, buy his way anywhere in the world, and live the rest of his life in luxury."

As soon as it was dark, we crept out of the burrow and headed away from the searchlights. Boubacar had trouble finding the path to the River Woman, and as he struggled to walk in the dark I was more aware of the effort it took for him to carry me. An hour later we found the small clearing, hidden behind bushes and tall trees, where a man stepped out of the shadows and stopped us. Once Boubacar explained what we wanted with the River Woman, the man pointed us to a narrower pathway that led to a larger clearing, high above the Limpopo River. At its center a man was preparing food over a fire, and people moved in and out of the simple shelters nearby. Two other men were busily hacking down long bamboo poles, while a third was laying luggage in neat rows in preparation for the crossing.

"Welcome to the alternative border post," Boubacar said, lowering me to the ground. "There's no paperwork needed here, but to avoid any questions, I think we should say we are family. Perhaps I should be your uncle? Or maybe your father?"

"No, not my uncle," I said, struggling up onto my crutches.

"Very well then, I shall be your papa, but only for the crossing."

Together we stood at the edge of the clearing, unsure how to proceed, until a woman clapped her hands in delight at seeing us, and with a Congolese accent very similar to Boubacar's bellowed, "HOH-HOH. LOOK WHO'S HERE—THE ONE-LEGGED GOALIE I TOLD YOU ABOUT." Her physical size matched her booming voice and she had a nest of thick Rastafarian dreadlocks that hung to her shoulders. A scar ran from her forehead over her nose to the corner of her too-large mouth, which was open wide enough for me to see the glint of her gold teeth. This had to be the River Woman.

Boubacar greeted her like an old friend as she smothered him with her enormous embrace. "Mugabe's soldiers are still looking for us, Mai Maria," he said, disentangling himself from her and shaking his head with laughter. "Now they know exactly where we are."

288

"BY JAH! THOSE SOLDIER BOYS DO NOT DARE COME TO MAI MARIA'S BORDER LODGE. I WILL EAT THEM FOR BREAKFAST AND SPIT THEM OUT LIKE THE FOUL-TASTING PIPS THAT THEY ARE." Mai Maria had one loose eye that moved around in its socket as if it had a life of its own. I couldn't help but stare at her, and when she looked directly at me, I didn't know which eye to focus on.

"ARE YOU CATCHING FLIES, BOY? CLOSE YOUR MOUTH OR SPEAK."

"I need to charge my phone," I stammered.

Mai Maria shook her head, laughing, while her dreadlocks bounced around her shoulders as if alive. "Boubacar, you didn't tell this boy that Mai Maria's lodge has only one star? There's no electricity here. You will have to wait until you get to South Africa for that," she said, pointing across the river.

"Mai Maria, this is Patson," said Boubacar. "My son."

I felt a twinge when Boubacar called me his son. I was sure Baba wouldn't mind but it reminded me again of the hole in my life now that my father was gone. No one would ever call me son again. "I'm pleased to meet you, Mai Maria. When do we cross the river?"

"You will sleep here tonight. Anyone who can play soccer the way you can is my honored guest. Then in the early morning, when it is still dark and the crocodiles are sleeping, we will cross the river. Your friends are here, too, Goalie," she said, pointing to Deo standing beside a man in the doorway of one of the huts. "Why don't you say hello to them. Boubacar and I have some business to discuss."

I hobbled over to Deo.

"Hey," I said.

"Hey, Patson. What are you doing here?" he responded awkwardly.

"Same as you, I guess."

"What happened to your leg?" asked the man standing next to Deo.

"This is Innocent, my brother."

Innocent's question took me by surprise. Not because how obvious it was, but by the simple way he had asked it. People were usually either too embarrassed to ask straight-out or they preferred to pretend that Stumpy wasn't there. Innocent, however, had addressed the most noticeable thing about me, in a way that was intimate, even friendly. And he was looking right at *me* when he asked, as if I were the most important person in the world. For the first time, that question I always dreaded didn't feel oppressive.

"I stepped on a land mine."

"It must have been very sore." The back of Innocent's hand fluttered near my cheek, as if he wanted to stroke me, but then he pulled it back and smiled. "I watched you play soccer yesterday. You were brilliant. Deo says you are the best goalie he ever had."

I turned to Deo in surprise. "You said that?"

He shrugged. "My brother likes to exaggerate."

"Do you want to listen to my radio?" Innocent asked. "If we are lucky, there might be a soccer game on." He carried a Weet-Bix cereal box under his arm; he opened it and carefully withdrew a small transistor radio. He bent his head low, slowly turned the tuning dial, and shyly motioned for me to come closer. There was something childlike about this man, as if he hadn't quite grown up.

"You're lucky, Patson. Innocent doesn't share his radio with anyone."

"You can show me your made-up leg, Patson. The bamboo one. I want to know if you can run on it and—"

"Innocent, Patson doesn't want to show you his leg," snapped Deo.

"No, it's okay," I said, finding myself laughing at his honesty and refreshing curiosity. "But I can't run on one leg, Innocent."

"My brother's a bit special," said Deo, by way of an apology.

"That makes two of us," I said, taking Innocent's hand and moving to sit with him beside the fire to listen to his radio.

27

Stumpy jabbed me awake early on the morning we were to cross the Limpopo River. It was almost as if he knew the coming day would be long and difficult. All around me people were sleeping under the makeshift shelter, but with Stumpy's constant complaining, I couldn't lie still another moment. I smeared the yellow ointment over my stump, gently massaged away the night's stiffness, and tried to mentally prepare both of us for the crossing into South Africa.

I packed away my ointments and moved outside the shelter. The morning was still dark and quiet. I crutched my way toward the clearing where Innocent was sitting by the embers of last night's fire. He glanced up as I approached and made room for me on the log beside him.

"This is my Bix-box," he said. "In here I have everything I will ever need."

"Good morning, Innocent. Can't you sleep?"

He shook his head, his fingers lightly tapping the lid of his box, and then, as if he had suddenly thought of something, he turned toward the noise of the river. "Are there crocodiles in the water?"

"There might be a few, but none where we will cross."

"Patson, why do you have to go across the river?"

"I have to find my sister. She is somewhere in South Africa."

"How old?"

"Nine."

"What's her name?"

"Grace."

Innocent fluttered his hand above his head, as if he had caught a memory in midair. "The Ephesians said that you are saved by grace through faith," he stated, proudly. "That's what Amai taught me. She also said I have to look after Deo. He's my little brother. He's fourteen. I have a picture for you, Patson."

"For me?"

"Yes. In my Bix-box," he said, nodding his head and smiling shyly at me.

"Well, can I see it?"

"I collect things. I don't know why I wanted this picture, but now I know," he said. "It was meant for you."

He opened the cereal box and placed the lid on his lap. His long, slender fingers disappeared and I heard things rattling around inside the tin.

"You said you can't run on one leg. This man runs with no legs. You should ask him how he does it."

Innocent handed me a piece of newspaper folded into a tight square. It was a photograph of a man wearing a pair of orange sunglasses, a running shirt, and shorts. Both of his knees were connected to J-shaped, black space-age prosthetic blades. His whole body was clear off the ground, flying down a cinder track, and his face was a picture of perfect concentration.

"I bet you that one day you will run faster than him," said Innocent, closing the lid of his Bix-box. "Because you've got one good leg and he's got no legs."

There was something compelling about the man running with no legs. It didn't seem possible that he could be flying so effortlessly down the track and yet he was clearly running very fast. I couldn't argue with Innocent's reasoning; one leg had to be better than no legs at all. I had never imagined myself ever running again and yet here was someone more handicapped than I making it look so simple. "Thank you, Innocent, that's quite amazing," I said, handing him back the clipping.

"But that's your picture now. I gave it to you," he said, smiling. "You'll see. One day you'll run fast too. Just like that man."

I folded the photograph and slipped it between the lattice of my peg leg and Stumpy, hoping it might offer him a bit of encouragement.

"There will be no crocodiles where we cross," Innocent said to Deo as he walked over with mugs of tea and slices of buttered bread. "Patson says so."

Above the tallest trees in the clearing a glimmer of light hinted at sunrise. People moved out of the grass huts and made their final preparations. Other men lifted the bamboo poles onto their shoulders and disappeared down the path toward the river. I caught Deo looking at my leg.

"My father will have to carry me some of the way," I said, aware of his skeptical expression. "He promised Mai Maria that I would not hold up everyone."

"We leave in ten minutes," one of Mai Maria's helpers announced as Boubacar walked over to the fire carrying our bags. He looked tense and serious.

"You're ready, son?" he asked, putting out his hand to help me up.

"Ready," I replied, throwing the last of my tea into the fire.

We moved out of the clearing and down a steep path to the Limpopo River shrouded in early-morning mist. Every minute we were not moving forward gave Commander Jesus more time to find us, and Grace would be farther and farther away. In front of us thirty people walked single file, slowly toward the cold, gray river in the shadows below. The path was filled with loose rocks and I struggled silently on my crutches, until Boubacar swung his backpack in front of him and lifted me onto his back. We had figured out that if Boubacar held my crutches firmly and flat behind him, I could sit and balance on them without having my arms so tight around his neck. Mai Maria was sitting calmly on a rock beside the river when we arrived.

"Across the river is South Africa. On the other side there will be others who will lead you through the park. Listen to them carefully. Your life may depend on it. They have done this many times. You will need to do it only once."

The river was wide and fast moving; crossing it would not be easy.

"It looks deep, Deo," said Innocent nervously. He told me last night he didn't swim. "Where's the bridge that bites?"

Innocent made me smile, but I knew exactly how he felt. I didn't know how to swim either and suspected that neither did Deo. If only we could have walked across Beitbridge.

"There is no bridge here, Innocent. You'll be fine," Deo answered.

"Each of you will hold on to the stick with your right hand," Mai Maria instructed, as her helpers divided us into groups and demonstrated how we should grip the rope knots tied to the poles at regular intervals. "Do not let go of the pole!" she barked. "If you do, you will be swept away by the river toward the croco- diles you saw on your way here. Keep your feet on the riverbed and drag yourself through the water. If you lift your feet too high, the water will take you."

Deo, Innocent, Boubacar, two men who joined our group, and I stood back and watched the first border jumpers enter the river. Water splashed around their legs and one of the women cursed as she slipped and disappeared under the water.

"DON'T LET GO!" bellowed Mai Maria.

The last man on the pole pulled her out of the water, and she came up spluttering and coughing. They continued into the middle of the river, and one by one other groups entered the water and made their way to the other side.

"Give me your phone, Patson. I think we're going to get wet," Boubacar said as he stuffed my phone into a plastic bag in his backpack. Beside me Innocent was shivering violently.

"No, Deo, Innocent doesn't want to do this," he stammered. "Let's go home. This is no good. No good at all."

His panic was understandable, and I saw doubt on Deo's face as he looked from the swirling water to his brother and then back to the safety of the path.

"Innocent, will you help me?" I held out one of my crutches to him. "My father has to carry me on his back. It is the only way. I cannot get across without your help." I turned to Deo. "Deo, don't leave now. You can make it. I know you can. Look."

I pointed to the first group, which had almost made it to the other side. Innocent grabbed my crutches and stumbled forward. "I can help you, Patson. You must get across. You must find Grace."

"Come over here, Lennox!" Mai Maria shouted to the strongest of her helpers. "I want you to look after these three boys. No trouble for them, hey? The Ghuma-ghuma can take the first lot, but these three—you look after them."

Lennox quickly took my crutches from Innocent, lashed them to the bamboo pole, and held it out behind him and over the water. Boubacar lifted me onto his back, waded into the river, and gripped the knot on the bamboo pole. I wrapped my legs around his waist and clung to his neck and shoulders. Behind us, Innocent and Deo gripped their knots, and behind them, the two men did the same. The last of Mai Maria's helpers held the end of the pole until we were all in the shallow part of the river. Then the eight of us moved slowly forward into the deeper water.

"HEY, SOCCER BOY, WHEN YOU GET INTO THE PARK, DON'T STOP RUNNING. YOU HEAR ME? NOT FOR ANYTHING!" yelled Mai Maria, waving from her perch on the rock.

The water splashed up Boubacar's thighs, into my face, while I tried my best not to strangle him.

"Nobody must let go!" shouted Lennox from the front. "The water may pull you, but you must not let go of the pole."

The water clawed higher up Boubacar's body and I felt myself slipping from around his waist, but was determined not to let the river sweep either of us away. Then behind me Innocent went down into the fast-flowing water.

"Don't let go!" shouted Lennox.

"Let him go! He will take us all down!" bellowed the man at the back of our pole.

We stopped, and without thinking, I reached out to grab Innocent, who was trying to hold on to his Bix-box and the bamboo pole at the same time.

"No, Patson!" shouted Boubacar. "Hold on to me." Innocent was thrashing about, trying to grip the pole. Only his face broke the surface and then a wave covered him again. Even if I could grab him, I knew I was not strong enough to pull him upright, and if he held on to me, we would both go tumbling downstream toward the crocodiles. Lennox shouted at Boubacar to hold the pole as he moved around him and furiously jerked

Innocent to his feet. With one hand Boubacar held me, and with Lennox's help they kept the bamboo and the rest of us from being swept away.

"I've got him now," shouted Lennox. "Patson, hold on to the pole!"

I went under, and swallowed a mouthful of cold river that took my breath away. My hands groped for the slippery pole just as Boubacar pulled me back from the force of the water. Somehow I gripped his belt, coughing and spluttering, when my foot found solid ground in the shallower water. Unexpectedly, the river had released us. Together we scrambled up the bank, wet and exhausted. We had made it across the Limpopo; we were in South Africa.

"Hurry! No rest now," shouted Lennox. "The Ghuma-ghuma will come. The danger is not over."

Lennox ran up the riverbank, carrying our bamboo pole with my crutches toward the nearest bushes.

"Wait!" shouted Boubacar, pointing to my crutches. "My son needs them." He caught up to Lennox and struggled to untie the wet knots, leaving me collapsed on the riverbank. The two men who had crossed the river with us ran after Lennox, leaving me behind, and Mai Maria's other helper waded into the river back to Zimbabwe.

"In my Bix-box," Innocent shouted to Boubacar. "In my Bix-box."

Innocent stumbled over the rocks with Boubacar and handed him a pocketknife. Boubacar quickly cut my crutches free, and I somehow managed to get myself upright. Then with my crutches and peg leg sinking into the sand, and with the help of Boubacar and Innocent, I hopped my way to where Deo and the others were waiting in the bushes. Most of the groups that had crossed ahead of us had disappeared into the bush. The first group, however, rested beside the river, the men smoking cigarettes, the women wringing out their clothes as if they were having a picnic.

Then, with no warning, eight men broke through the bush dressed in thick coats and woolen hats, carrying heavy sticks and machetes. One was carrying a rifle.

"Ghuma-ghuma," whispered Lennox. "Hurry! They must not find us here. Big trouble. Come!"

"What do they want?"

"Everything you have," he replied.

"Come on, Patson," urged Boubacar, grabbing me from the other side and dragging me into a nearby thicket.

We scrambled through the bushes and ducked out of sight. Behind me I heard a woman scream. I bellied my way back to where Lennox and Boubacar lay, to see one man desperately trying to run away only to be caught and beaten. The others cowered on the ground as the two women stood shivering in their bras and panties, wailing and pleading for mercy.

"Who are they?"

"Robbers. They steal everything they can from border jumpers or anyone stupid enough to be found sitting on the riverbank," muttered Boubacar.

"Lie still! Not a word. Keep quiet or they will find us," hissed Lennox, pulling Boubacar deeper into the bushes. "And you," Lennox said, pointing at Innocent. "Shut up or I will cut off your balls."

A few of the Ghuma-ghuma were still searching the ground near where we had stood only a few moments ago. Behind them strolled the man holding the rifle, wearing the all-too-familiar pair of mirrored, silver sunglasses.

28

Commander Jesus studied our footprints in the sand. He stood up slowly, scanning the bushes that ran the length of the riverbank. He was so close I could see the hard line of his mouth twitch with displeasure. He wore jeans and a T-shirt with a pair of binoculars around his neck; only his army boots and rifle marked him as a soldier and not a robber.

The trembling began in my arms and quickly spread. As much as I wanted to blot him out of my memory, I couldn't keep my eyes off him. He tilted his head at an angle, as if listening for my heartbeat. His mirrored glasses mesmerized me, and I had to fight an urge to crawl out of the bush and kneel before him.

Then one of his men spotted the final group of border jumpers struggling ashore. Commander Jesus hitched his rifle onto his shoulder, raised the binoculars, and carefully studied the line of people as they made their way through the shallow waters onto the South African side. He glanced back in my direction, and, with only a slight hesitation, headed toward the Ghuma-ghuma's latest prey.

"Now!" whispered Lennox. "Let's go."

But I couldn't move, frozen by the sight of Commander Jesus.

"Patson! Come on." Boubacar grabbed my good leg and pulled me.

"It was him," I said. "Didn't you see him? He's here."

"Calm down, Patson."

"You said I would be safe in South Africa," I stammered, gasping for air, strangled by my panic. Boubacar squatted and I clambered onto his back, but my trembling grew worse. Those mirrored glasses...His hands on my shoulders...His snakelike smile..."You are free to go, boy. Run!" And then the explosion that followed.

"Patson, hold tight," Boubacar said, trying desperately to catch up with Lennox, who had headed toward a high fence laced with barbed wire.

I gulped for air.

He saw me. He's behind me. He's coming for me.

"He's following us, Boubacar."

"We're almost there. It's okay," he said, panting as we joined the others and I slipped off his back. Ahead of us was the empty veldt; behind us was Commander Jesus.

"This is the first park," Lennox said. "There is great danger beyond this fence. We must run now for two hours."

"A game reserve," said Boubacar. "It's a place with wild animals?"

"Or you can stay if you want to," replied Lennox, "and deal with them." He jerked his thumb back toward the river.

"No, we can't stay. Not here," I said, but nobody paid me any attention.

"Follow me." Lennox took off his shirt, rolled it up tightly, and stuffed it down the front of his trousers. Then, hand-over-knee, knee-over-hand, he worked his way through an opening that had been cut and concealed in the tangle of barbed wire. One by one we all took off our shirts and followed him. Once through, Lennox put his shirt back on.

"Now we run," he said. "There are animals here. Hyenas, wild dogs, buffalo, elephants, but the worst of all are the lions. We will run in a line. We must hold hands where we can. You might see some bad things. But you do not stop. If you stop running, I will leave you behind." Lennox's tone of voice made it clear that this was a dangerous part of our journey.

"What about Patson?" asked Innocent. "He can't run."

"I will carry him," replied Boubacar.

I saw the tension on Lennox's face and felt the others' fear, but none of them realized that the real danger was following us.

We ran through the park joined together, moving steadily away from the Limpopo River. Lennox led from the front, followed by Boubacar with me on his back and Innocent holding on to the crutch I carried, while Deo held his other hand and my other crutch. Behind him came the other two men; all of us jogging along, past a herd of impalas that leapt away from this strange thirteen-legged creature.

We ran, not fast but steadily, until Lennox raised his hand, signaling us to fall to the ground. We crouched in the long grass, happy to be off our feet, not too far from an unconcerned herd of grazing black buffalo.

"I'm tired, Deo," said Innocent.

"We're almost there," Deo answered. I remembered saying the same thing to Grace when I used to carry her on my back. But I was a lot heavier than Grace, and Boubacar was panting heavily in an exhausted heap beside me.

"Hyena!" shouted one of the men.

Behind us a hyena loped sideways, lifting his nose in the air, sniffing, and then dropping his head down. Lennox moved quickly to the back of the line as the hyena stopped and eyed the last man, who had raised the warning. His shirt was drenched with fresh blood.

"The hyena has smelled your blood," cursed Lennox. "Why didn't you tell me you were bleeding?"

Lennox ripped off the shirt and wrapped it tightly around the man's chest, his eyes never leaving the hyena, which bounded forward.

"Everyone lift your bags up in the air!" shouted Lennox. "Follow me." He ran directly at the oncoming hyena. "Come on!" he shouted. "It's the only way. Hyenas are scared of things higher than them."

Deo grabbed one of my crutches and turned to his brother. "Innocent, Operation Look After Patson, Operation Don't Move. Okay?"

"I'll look after Patson," he said, calmly nodding.

Deo raced after Lennox, waving my crutch in the air, shouting at the hyena. The other two men, momentarily stunned by Deo's bravery, followed with their bags high over their heads.

Then Lennox stumbled, and fell headfirst into the long grass. The two men stopped. The hyena growled, snapping its jaws at Deo, now in the lead.

Innocent sprang to his feet. "Operation Save Deo," he said to me, pulling a whistle from his Bix-box and starting to run toward the hyena. At the screeching sound of the referee's whistle the buffalo scattered and the hyena bolted away with its tail between its legs. From a distance, I watched Lennox tie the man's shirt to a thorn tree, before returning to Boubacar and me. "That will keep the other hyenas busy for a while. Now we must run. We still have far to go."

Once again I climbed onto Boubacar's back and we headed across the plain, this time past a herd of elephants feeding on the leaves of thorn trees shading a small pool.

"Hippos," said Boubacar, panting. But only their noses, eyes, and funny small ears showed above the water. The two men fell to their knees on the bank of the river and drank greedily.

"Not too fast," warned Lennox. "It will be painful to carry so much water inside you. We are not through the park yet."

I hopped off Boubacar's back and splashed my face, drinking

only a little of the water, even though I was thirsty. Stumpy stabbed me spitefully and I flinched with pain, but there was nothing I could do for him now. Deo pointed out a stack of bones and a skull lying on the opposite bank. He walked through the shallow water to study them up close.

"What do you think it is?" I called.

"I don't know," he replied.

"Probably a baboon, or even a monkey," Lennox said quickly.

Boubacar shot me a glance that suggested that the bones were not those of a baboon or a monkey.

"Leave them alone," Lennox said. "We cannot stop here."

The mud-tasting water gave us new energy, and the bones were a grim reminder that we were in a game reserve with wild animals. The sun moved steadily across the sky; the morning grew hotter, and soon we were running through the scorching midday heat. The men who had drunk so greedily had slowed down and one of them pleaded with Lennox to stop. But he paused only long enough to pick up a tiny pebble.

"Put this under your tongue, suck on it. It will help," he said.

Boubacar was moving slower too. He was obviously struggling under my weight, stumbling forward, trying to keep up with the others.

"Enough, Boubacar," I said. "This is useless." I slid to the ground and collapsed on my knees.

The men argued angrily with Lennox. "Why should we be in danger because of them?"

"We should leave them here," said the other.

"We stay together." Lennox was adamant. "Would you want me to leave you alone in the park?"

"Get up, Patson," commanded Boubacar. And then more gently: "We can't give up now."

All I could do was breathe in and out and nod to Boubacar as Stumpy fired missiles through my body. I was dizzy with pain. How stupid I had been to think I could get this useless body into South Africa. I drove into a tree, Baba. You were right. I lost control of my life, just like that man who found the first diamonds in Marange. You said that people would kill for a *girazi*. And you were right, Baba. There's no use now in my arguing with you. I remembered turning my back on my father when he called out my name in the darkness of the shed on the night before he died. I felt so ashamed at the memory. Forgive me, Baba, forgive me.

Now is the time for you to be strong, son.

"Come on, Patson. I'll help you." Innocent's gentle voice reached through the pain and haze of my confusion.

I felt hands lifting me onto Boubacar's back and the rhythm of his running return. Deo and Innocent ran on either side of Boubacar, helping him, holding me on his back. I wept at their kindness, at the strength of Boubacar's will to keep on running, and the voice of my father urging me on.

Be strong, son.

"Leave me, Daddy, leave me," I whispered.

Boubacar ran on, gripping me more tightly.

"The end of the park," shouted Lennox.

I lifted my head off Boubacar's shoulder. We had reached the top of a slight rise, and in the distance, the welcome sight of a fence. Boubacar sank to his knees, and I slid from his back. Was it possible that we had made it?

"Lennox! Look!" Deo exclaimed.

"Don't look!" shouted Lennox.

But it was too late. We had all seen what made Deo shout. Lying in the shade were the scattered parts of a human body.

Then we heard the low rumbling sound.

"Lion!" Lennox whispered, looking wildly about him, trying to locate where the sound came from. "Listen. Listen carefully. Nobody must run. If you run away, it is over." His voice was firm. The rumble was followed by a deep growl.

"They're feeding. Close by," Boubacar whispered to me, and when he gripped my shoulder, I felt his hand tremble.

"We must hold hands." Lennox's voice was tight with fear. "Walk slowly away. Toward the fence."

It was possible that the lions, who were busily gorging themselves, were unaware of us, but if we panicked and ran, they would be upon us. We reached for one another's hands and moved slowly and ever so silently away from the sound of the lions feeding.

I clung to Boubacar's back until all I heard was the wind in the grass and his heavy breathing. Then Lennox picked up the pace, allowing us to run freely. He threw Deo his bag, lifted me from Boubacar's back, and tossed me over his shoulder, running toward the metal fence. Boubacar ran alongside us, but the two other men in our party sprinted ahead, reached the fence, and hastily started climbing.

"No!" shouted Lennox, but his warning was too late. The wire fizzled, crackled, and the men fell to the ground shrieking in pain. "Not there—I'll show you."

He led us alongside the electrified fence until he pointed to a section that at first appeared no different from the rest, but here the wire had been carefully handwoven to only look as if it were whole and untouched. In a few minutes, we were all out of the park, exhausted, but standing safely beside a deserted dusty road.

"You can wait here," said Lennox. "It is safe here. Someone will come and pick you up. You just have to wait."

Boubacar and I fell to the ground in unspoken relief beside Innocent and Deo. They looked as bad as I felt. The other two men had recovered from their electrical shock and stayed on their feet, peering up and down the road that seemed to go nowhere in both directions. With only a whisper between them, and no word of thanks to Lennox, they began jogging down the road.

"Let them go," mumbled Lennox. "They're too stupid to know that the direction they are running won't take them anywhere they want to be. You wait here. You will be okay."

"Thank you, Monsieur Lennox," said Boubacar. "We would never have made it through the park without you. If you say we must wait here, that's what we will do."

"And you?" Deo asked Lennox.

He pointed back to the park where we had come from. "I go back."

For a moment Deo looked confused. "Thank you. Thank you for getting us to South Africa."

Lennox shook his head and walked over to Innocent. "Thank you for chasing the hyena away." Then, with a wave over his shoulder, he trotted back the way we had come, disappearing through the fence and into the grasslands beyond.

In the mottled shade of the only thorn tree in the middle of nowhere, Deo and Innocent quickly fell asleep, and I had no choice but to settle up with Stumpy. Boubacar walked a little way down the road, his eyes scanning the game reserve. When he returned, something about the tension in his body startled me.

"He won't give up, will he, Boubacar?"

"He wouldn't risk going through the game reserve, but he will be in Musina waiting for us. All the border jumpers have to go through the taxi ranks at Musina to get to Johannesburg," replied Boubacar. "We will have to find another way." He pulled out his cell phone. "I have some Congolese friends in Musina. They will help us."

As he made his call, my own cell phone buzzed in my kitbag. I checked the screen. Three bars. Two messages downloaded despite the battery light blinking red.

Mon 4/14/08 2.16pm

In taxi now to Joburg. Maka gone. Come to Joburg. Looking for a way to escape. R you close? What do I do?! xxx

Once Boubacar had finished his conversation I showed him her message.

"This Determine fellow is not who you thought he was."

That part I got on my own. "And he's not taking Grace to a Girl Guide jamboree in Cape Town, is he, Boubacar?"

"No, he's not. Tell her we are in South Africa now and that she must let us know when she gets to Johannesburg."

I texted her:

> We r in SA now. Send address when you get
> Jhb. We'll find you xxx

My message got through just as the battery died.

"I'm going to have to charge my phone, Boubacar."

"We'll do that later. Rest now. You deserve it."

Stumpy was still crying out for attention, so I massaged him with extra ointment, changed his dressings, and carefully wrapped him up again. The bamboo peg leg was falling apart and needed major repairs. While Boubacar tried to fix it, I lay down, looked up at the sky, and clutched my phone to my chest. I had made it across the Limpopo River and was in another country, but the South African sky looked no different from the one in Zimbabwe. For the first time in a long time, I remembered how blue the sky could actually be. A headache buzzed in the base of my neck, and it was hard to keep my eyes open. Slowly Stumpy dozed off and the painful throbbing receded. I closed my eyes, giving over to a memory of Grace playing in the sunshine outside the tobacco shed.

Look to Grace. I'll find you, Gracie, I'll find you.

And then Boubacar was shaking me awake. "Someone's coming," he said as I struggled to stand up, disorientated and dizzy from the too-short sleep and the now-pounding headache. I heard the truck barreling toward us before I saw it appear through the glare of the afternoon sun, dust billowing behind it. Brakes squeaked, and more dust rained down on us.

A white man leaned out the window. "You want work?"

Boubacar stood up. "Yes, but—"

"You want to work, you get in the back of the truck, otherwise I leave you here," he said, revving the engine.

Deo and Innocent hopped aboard, and with Boubacar's strong hands, they hauled me over the side. I had lost all my strength and felt weak and feverish. Stumpy roared at me with angry spikes for disturbing him; blood and pus seeped through the dressing.

Boubacar took a seat leaning against the cab and laid my crutches beside me.

"Are you all right, Patson?" he asked. "You don't look good."

"My leg is bleeding," I said quietly. "I need to change the dressing."

Above me, Deo and Innocent found room on top of the wooden boxes.

"Don't sit on the bloody boxes!" the white man shouted, turning the truck around and driving away, as the dust rose into the air behind us and I flinched at every painful bump along the dirt track and wondered why I was so cold.

◆ ◆ ◆

Flying Tomato Farm

South Africa

16 April

I met Boubacar under a huge baobab tree in
the middle of the forest. He was the ugliest
man I had ever seen, and Grace was afraid
of him. He took us around Elephant Skull
mountain, through a dangerous, dark forest,
and delivered us safely to Marange. He helped
me get a fortune from the Baron. He drove
me into the mountains so that I could heal.
He taught me what it means to be a man. He
hid me in a burrow, dragged me across a river,
carried me away from lions, and once we
made it into South Africa, he found a cow
doctor to take my fever away.

But most important of all, he is helping me
find my sister, the only person I have left
in the world.

Now Boubacar is no longer ugly to me. The
scars on his cheeks are stripes of courage,

his broken nose a mark of determination, and his bloodshot eyes are the kindest I have ever known. But there is one thing I don't understand. Why? Why is he doing this? Why is he so determined to help me?

♦♦♦

GRACE

29

The first morning I woke up at the Flying Tomato Farm, I was hot and sweating one moment, then cold and shivering the next. My stump was swollen; the skin was red and tender, and pus oozed from the wound. Obviously this was Stumpy's revenge for dousing him in the muddy Limpopo River and dragging him through the game reserve. For the next two days I drifted in and out of fever-sleep, thankful for the bed, the plates of freshly sliced and salted tomatoes, and the jugs of clean, cool water that Boubacar forced me to drink. I don't remember much about the Flying Tomato Farm, except that at one point I woke up to find a white woman with blue eyes and blond hair staring down at me. She looked both concerned and sympathetic as she cleaned my wound and rebandaged it, all the while mumbling something about sepsis. Then I felt a sharp prick in my arm and fell back to sleep.

Stumpy must have liked her attention, as the next day he stopped complaining and his swelling subsided. Later, Boubacar explained that she was actually a veterinarian called to the farm to attend to a cow in labor, and the shot in my arm had been an intramuscular antibiotic; the best she had to offer. She'd also given him five days' worth of antibiotic pills, but warned that gangrene could still happen if I didn't get to a proper hospital soon.

Gerber, the burly, well-tanned foreman of the Flying Tomato Farm, was less helpful. "I'm running a business, not a hospital," he said, stopping just inside the doorway to the workers' dormitory. "Benjamin," he called out to the old white-haired black man who managed all the farm's refugee workers. "I want these two gone, first thing tomorrow morning. Understood?"

"Yes, boss," Benjamin replied, and then turned to Boubacar as Gerber left the dormitory. "I'm sorry. You will have to go. These beds are for people who work here. Tomorrow more will come."

"We understand, *madala*," said Boubacar, using the respectful name for the older man. "You'll get no trouble from us."

Benjamin nodded, lifted his hands in apology, and left.

"You feeling better, Patson?"

"A little, and at least Stumpy's not so swollen."

"We have to leave tomorrow, Patson. I think early is best. My Congolese friends will pick us up and drive us to Johannesburg. The journey will take maybe six or seven hours."

"I'll be ready," I said, showing him Grace's latest Mxit.

Tues 4/15/08 3.16pm

Where r u BB?!!! I'm in Alexandra township
now. Det left me with old man in a shack. Tried
to escape but nowhere to go. Det found me.
Come soon. xxx

Wed 4/16/08 10.01am

Det took my money. He wants me to work for
him when we get to Cape Town. What do I do?
Plzzzz come!! xxx

"Tell her we'll be in Joburg tomorrow afternoon. Get an address. We're close now, Patson," he said, laying his hand on my shoulder.

I sent Grace the message, then turned to my last diary entry. "I wrote something, Boubacar. About you. Would you like to hear?"

"About me?" he said with an embarrassed chuckle. "You have me curious now. So what did you write about this fellow Boubacar?"

I opened my diary and started reading the passage I had written about him. When I had finished, Boubacar reached for the diary and flicked through its pages. "But she was at least a pretty cow doctor, yes?" he said with a smile. "Are all the words written here as good as those you just read to me?"

"Not all of them." I shrugged. "But why, Boubacar? I don't understand why you are helping me."

He ran his hand over his face and dropped his head to his chest, avoiding my eyes. Then he clasped his large hands, weaving his fingers together, and I watched them pulse in and out, in and out, like a beating heart beneath his chin.

"Boubacar?"

He shook his head, and, without looking at me, raised his hand, as if he were trying to work out a puzzle. I waited, and when he finally spoke, his voice was strained as he searched for words to explain what I could not understand.

"There is a war in my country. They may call the DRC the Democratic Republic of Congo, but it is not so democratic. Many people are being killed there. Rebel soldiers fight the government. They came to my village when I was fourteen and made me into a soldier. There were other boys who had been stolen from their families, but I went into the bush with the rebels because I hated the government. They had taken my father away and killed him. So I left my sister and my little brother with my mother and joined Reverend Lubango's Army of Assurance. It was a time of madness. Drugs, alcohol, and words. Dangerous words.

"The Reverend taught us how to fight and kill people. We would sit and smoke marijuana, drink, smoke some more, and listen to his words driven into our heads. We had rifles and bullets and became firing machines fueled by narcotics. We followed every order just to keep the drugs coming. The things I did...terrible things, Patson, I can never tell you. And I was a good soldier. Too good. They made me a leader and gave me my own boys so that I could turn them into soldiers as good as me.

"One day we were ordered to attack a village. It was always the same—words, alcohol, drugs, and more words until we were ready to kill. That night we hid in the bushes waiting for the storm to break. I led the way through the dark rain, firing and running, running and firing at anything that moved. The villagers stood no chance. We cut them down but then, as the sun rose, that village of dead people seemed strangely familiar to me.

"I recognized the tree my brother and I had climbed, the hut where my mother lived, and the toys my sister played with. When I found my family, they looked no different from the other dead bodies. I started crying only because I felt nothing. I was dead inside. After that day, my need for drugs, alcohol, and words to keep my life bearable, died.

"Somehow I found a way to stop taking the drugs. To only pretend to drink and later to understand that Reverend Lubango's words were lies. Slowly I found a way back to myself. And when I looked at the boys who followed me so blindly, I wanted to save them. One by one I got them off the drugs, and together we found the strength to resist Reverend Lubango's words. I led seven of them out of the forest until the UN soldiers found us and took us in. They changed my life except that I had nothing left to live for."

Boubacar paused to catch his breath while I tried to grasp the enormity of what he had told me, ashamed, too, at how selfishly I had been wrapped up only in my own story. When he finally looked up his face was streaked with tears.

"When you came to me in the forest, Patson, holding your sister's hand, I saw my own little brother and sister coming back to me." He paused, struggling to catch his breath. "You see, Pat-son, my sister's name was also Grace."

His shoulders started to shake then, as he gave way to his tears, and I leaned forward to clumsily embrace him.

"We will find her, Boubacar, I know we will," were the only words I could manage.

30

Early the next morning we stood outside the Flying Tomato Farm, searching the dust road for the minibus that would take us to Johannesburg. My head buzzed with a headache and, despite the warm sunshine, I shivered in another fever chill. I had taken one of the vet's pills, but it had made me nauseous and woozy. So much for her horse medicine, I thought, and threw the remaining pills away. We both knew I was not ready to travel, but Foreman Gerber's orders and the late-night Mxit message I got from Grace left us no choice: Determine had bought their Joburg to Cape Town tickets; they were leaving on the three o'clock train this afternoon. If all went well, Boubacar thought that we could be at the train station by two o'clock, and still be in good time to intercept them before they boarded for

Cape Town. There was no time for me to recover; we had to keep moving.

While we waited, I looked across field after field of tomato bushes stretched out toward the faraway mountains. Boubacar explained that the white plastic tents were protecting the young bushes, and I was amazed at the gleaming tractors, the cultivating machines, and the trucks coming and going with boxes all stamped with a red tomato with angel wings. I had never seen any Zimbabwean farm like this, and Boubacar remarked that here in South Africa, there were many farms that were even bigger than this one. How was it possible that across the Limpopo River, people were without work and starving, and yet here there was such wealth and opportunity? It was no wonder thousands of people were leaving Zimbabwe and risking their lives to get here.

In a nearby field, I saw Innocent's lanky frame moving up and down the bushes, picking tomatoes. He spotted me and waved furiously. I waved back, sorry not to have said good-bye properly to him and Deo. I had never met anyone quite like Innocent, so accepting, so kind, and yet in a world of his own. He was so convinced that I would run again one day that it was hard not to believe him.

"Here he comes," said Boubacar as a cloud of dust appeared over the horizon, but the vehicle that came into sight was a police van. As it approached the gate the van drove past us slowly, and a black policeman in the passenger seat glanced our way as they went by.

The brake lights flashed red; the van reversed and both doors flew open simultaneously. Two hefty officers got out and walked toward us. The white man was Sergeant Brandt, according to the brass badge pinned to the pocket above his huge stomach, which his belt could hardly contain. His partner, the owner of a pair of tree-trunk thighs, hitched up his trousers as he looked us up and down. Boubacar stepped in front of me, his hand slowly slipping into his backpack.

"ID," demanded the white man.

"Good day, Sergeant Brandt," said Boubacar pleasantly. "I'm afraid we do not have our passports with us at present. We were visiting friends here and—"

"You're from the Congo, aren't you, Frenchie?" Boubacar barely nodded. "And you, boy, you're from Zimbabwe, right?"

"Yes, sir."

"Get in the back of the van."

"You're both illegals. Let's go," shouted the black policeman, making a move toward me.

"Please, Corporal Mashau, there is no need to shout," soothed Boubacar. "We're all intelligent men. Perhaps we might come to some arrangement."

"We've already made our arrangement," said Mashau, chuckling.

Neither of them knew the danger they were in. Boubacar's beguiling French accent had lulled them into believing he was harmless, but the tension in his muscles and the softness of his words told me that at any moment he might pull his knife, and these overweight policemen wouldn't stand a chance.

"No, Boubacar," I said, hobbling between them. "Please, sir, my sister has been kidnapped and we have to find her." I attempted my most affecting voice, playing the cripple card as best I could, but, obviously hardened by the never-ending hard-luck stories of refugees, the policeman only shrugged.

"Yah, that's at least a new one. Now get in," ordered Brandt as he opened the back of the van. With only a slight hesitation, Boubacar freed his hand from his bag to help me into the van.

Mashau was laughing as he padlocked the rear door and walked back to the front. "Well, that was the easiest ten grand I ever made," he said.

"All in a day's work," grunted Brandt, heaving himself into the van, which dipped under his weight. We heard the doors slam, and felt the vehicle maneuver a three-point turn and barrel down the dirt road back the way they had come. Boubacar took out his cell phone and spoke rapidly in French as I tried to hold on while the van hurtled along the road.

"Please, sir, my sister has been kidnapped," I yelled through the hatch into the front seat. "We have to be at the train station in Johannesburg by two o'clock. Please. A bad man is taking her to Cape Town. She's only nine years old." The only thing I heard was Brandt talking on his cell phone, before Mashau slammed the dividing window shut.

I turned back to Boubacar, who stared grimly out the small window in the van's rear door. "Once we get to the police station, we can explain everything. I can show them Grace's Mxit messages—"

"Patson, they're not taking us to any police station."

The drive to Musina took almost two hours. We passed several men on the sides of the road, most of them looking like refugees, but we sped by them in a cloud of dust. Outside the town, more people, burdened with luggage, plastic containers, pots, children on their backs, were trying to get through the front gates into a large area beneath the sign: MUSINA SHOWGROUND.

"There's nowhere else to put the thousands of people coming over the border," explained Boubacar, and in the fields beyond I saw hundreds of makeshift shelters packed tightly together. On the pavement outside the Showground, families were camped out in the open, their clothes, blankets, and bags piled around them and hanging from the Showground fence. Women were cooking food on the pavement, and small children were being washed in open buckets. Grace had seen all this too. No wonder she was afraid in Musina.

Farther along we were stopped at an intersection where an army troop carrier and two police vans were parked. Out our small window I could see a large billboard:

WE KNOW WHY YOU ARE IN SOUTH AFRICA:

LIFE IN ZIMBABWE IS MURDER

BUT PLEASE GO BACK TO VOTE. WE CAN ALL BE FREE.

Two men were on a ladder scraping off the sign. Across the street a small crowd was shouting at them to leave it alone. They

held placards with slogans: FREE ZIMBABWE, ARREST WAR CRIMI-
NAL MUGABE, and WE WANT FREE ELECTIONS. The South African
soldiers stood silently watching, their rifles pointing casually to
the ground.

Boubacar's cell phone buzzed, and he answered in rapid
French. Then he nudged me aside to peer out through the window. "Come on, come on," he muttered.

"What is it?"

"My Congolese brothers," he said as our van picked up speed
and swung around a corner. I lost my balance, and fell hard
to the floor. "Hey!" shouted Boubacar, smacking his fist into
the side of the van. "Be careful. You have a sick boy here!"

His protest made no difference. Brandt switched on the
siren and we raced down the main road and drove right past the
Musina Police Station. Boubacar was right: Sergeant Brandt and
Corporal Mashau had another destination in mind for us. On
the way to Musina, Boubacar had described the network that
existed between the Zimbabwean military and rogue members
of the South African police open to bribery. Political refugees
crossing the border were easily identified by spies in their midst,
picked up by the South African police, and, for a substantial fee,
were handed straight back into the arms of the officers of the
Zimbabwean Central Intelligence Organisation.

"That's why I did not want us to come anywhere near
Musina," he had said. "There are many spies working for
Mugabe's soldiers."

Commander Jesus must have alerted his contacts on this side

of the border, and we had been so easy to find. Now even the dangers of the fast-flowing river and the game reserve seemed preferable to being trapped in this hot metal box bulleting through Musina with its sirens blaring, to an unknown destination where Commander Jesus would surely be waiting for us. I could hardly think straight. I was sweating and thirsty and my head felt as if it would burst. Escape seemed impossible; our journey had ended in the back of a police van. All I wanted to do was to lie down and give over to my exhaustion. This time Commander Jesus would never let me go, and I would never know what happened to Grace.

"Ah, there they are," said Boubacar. "Behind us."

I dragged myself back to look through the small window but saw only traffic weaving across the road.

"Two cars back. That yellow Bolt Safeguard security van."

"I see them, Boubacar, but how can they help us?"

"It's our last chance, Patson, and we're taking it."

9.45 AM

Sergeant Brandt turned off the main road and pulled over just before the palm-lined drive into the Blue Flamingo Hotel. I saw the yellow security van pass us by and turn into the hotel grounds. Another car, a small red hatchback taxi, followed close behind it.

"Brandt and Mashau are discussing how to hand us over," whispered Boubacar. "If the wrong people see them, they will be in big trouble."

We moved close to the hatch to listen.

"Let's just leave them here," Mashau said. "The cripple kid can't go far."

"And how do you suggest we get our money?" asked Brandt.

"He can leave an envelope at reception. I'll pick it up, and you turn them over to him here on the street."

"It's too open," said Sergeant Brandt. "We should have taken them to the military base."

"Too late now. Phone him."

"No, you stay here," decided Brandt. "Let me go to the hotel, find him, get the money, and arrange for a better place to hand them over. Then he can follow us, and once we've dropped them off, we leave and our hands are clean."

The van bounced as Brandt got out, slammed the door, and walked through the shade of a palm tree toward the hotel while making the call. Meanwhile, Mashau came around to the back, lit a cigarette, and checked up and down the road.

Boubacar was texting furiously. "Talk to him," he whispered.

I hiked myself up to the rear window and knocked on it. "Can you give me some water, Mr. Mashau? It's very hot in here," I said, smiling.

Mashau glanced up at me.

"It's true what I told you. My sister's name is Grace. A man took her from our home in Marange and now he's taking her to Cape Town. I have to go to a hospital, my leg is very sore. Please help me."

Corporal Mashau took another drag on his cigarette and threw the butt to the ground.

"I'm sorry for your trouble, boy, but there's nothing I can do," he said, turning at the sound of approaching footsteps.

"Corporal Mashau?" said a man in army fatigues coming around the side of the van.

"Yes," answered Mashau, taken by surprise at this stranger addressing him so familiarly.

"Sergeant Brandt sent me for them. You have to wait five minutes and then pick him up outside the lobby. The commander will pay him and your business will be done."

Mashau glanced inside at us, looked more closely at this man, and then up the winding road of the hotel grounds.

"Please, sir, do not give us to this man," yelled Boubacar suddenly, beating on the van door. "He is CIO. He will torture and then kill us! Please, sir, I beg you. Don't listen to him."

"Shut up," yelled Mashau as he quickly put the key into the padlock and opened the door. "Get out and shut up!"

Cool air swept inside the back of the van as Boubacar jumped out and turned back to help me out. "Act frightened," he whispered.

I didn't need to act; I was terrified. I shuffled through the door and climbed onto Boubacar's back. I clung awkwardly to his neck, clutching my crutches and kitbag.

"Five minutes," said the CIO officer. "Then you go to the hotel and pick up your sergeant. Understood?"

"I heard you the first time," said Mashau, glancing anxiously up and down the road as the CIO man gripped Boubacar's arm, dragging him forward.

"Get a move on, you two," he ordered. "The commander has waited long enough."

I gripped tightly to Boubacar's neck as he walked around the bend in the hotel road to where the Bolt van was parked out of Mashau's sight. Its driver was waiting for us and shouted, "I've got them now. Yes, sir. At once, sir." He made even more noise slamming the empty van shut.

"*Très bien*, Regis," Boubacar whispered, slapping the CIO man on his back as they ran toward the red hatchback parked behind a tall hedge. Regis tore off his fatigue jacket, threw it on the floor of the car, and jumped into the driver's seat as Boubacar heaved me onto the backseat.

"Stay down," he ordered, and wedged my crutches and his big body onto the floor before pulling the door shut. "What's happening? What do you see, Regis?"

"Nothing yet," came the answer from the front seat. "Here comes the sergeant. He's almost back to Mashau. Stay down. He looks pleased with himself. And there goes Patrice in our van. So we only have to wait to see if they take the bait."

I heard Brandt cursing Mashau, then the screech of their siren and the squeal of tires. Regis started the taxi and drove slowly back out onto the main road. The wailing of the police siren faded away in the opposite direction.

"It worked," said Boubacar, looking out the back window. "They are following him. Bravo, Regis!"

Regis only chuckled. "It was a good plan, Boubacar. When they do catch up and stop Patrice they'll find only an empty van, driven by a guard for Bolt Safeguard."

I struggled to sit up. It was hard to believe that moments ago I had given up and now we were free. "And we'll get out of Musina?" I asked, surprised at how quickly everything had changed.

"Yes, leaving Commander Jesus waiting for nothing at the Blue Flamingo," Boubacar added.

"You are a lucky boy to be traveling with this man," said Regis, grinning at me in his rearview mirror. "He is a hero among we Congolese—"

Boubacar cut him off. "We have wasted enough time already. We have to be at the Johannesburg train station no later than two thirty, Regis."

"Ah, Boubacar, you know that is impossible. It will take us at least—"

"You will drive like the wind, Regis. We will be there before three o'clock."

And I felt the engine surge.

12.02 PM

The landscape of South Africa flashed past my window: One-Stop petrol stations with jungle gyms and swings for children; gleaming fast-food shops alongside wide, double-lane pothole-free highways; cultivated fields dotted with tractors and crop sprayers with the wingspans of airplanes; luxury vehicles cruising past with white children staring out of closed-up windows; battered minibuses packed with people, pulling trailers piled high with furniture and luggage. Then came the walled suburbs with tall trees and fancy houses that offered only glimpses of their sapphire-blue swimming pools through iron gates. And on the faraway hills, smoke rose from shantytowns, their tin roofs glinting in the sun.

As fascinated as I was by this new country, I kept checking the time, willing the clock on my phone to go slower. In three hours the train would be pulling out of the station and heading for Cape Town. I sent Grace message after message about our progress along the N1 highway, through the towns of Mahoda, Louis Trichardt, and Polokwane, but she never responded. A sign flashed by—JOHANNESBURG 360 KM—and I leaned forward to check the speedometer. The needle hovered around the 130 mark.

"We'll never make it, Boubacar. At this speed it will take us more than three hours," I protested.

"Can't you go any faster, Regis?" asked Boubacar.

But Regis only smiled and swore back at him in French. "As long as you have enough money for the speeding fines."

Time collapsed into a feverish haze, punctuated by stabs from Stumpy. I checked my phone but the numbers on the screen no longer made any sense.

2.22 PM

I jerked awake. We had stopped. Traffic was rushing past. The front seats were empty. Disorientated, I opened the door.

"Don't get out," cursed Regis.

"What's going on?"

"Flat tire," said Boubacar. "Stay in the car. It's almost finished."

Boubacar rattled a string of French words to Regis, who responded angrily.

"I can only go as fast as I can go," he said, tightening the lug nuts, one after the other.

"Forget the hubcap," said Boubacar, tossing it through my open window.

My phone buzzed with a message from Grace:

Thurs 4/17/08 2.15pm

@ JHB Park Station. Platform 17. Where r u??
What must I do? xxx

"Tell her we are almost there—"

"No, we are not," snapped Regis. "We have at least another thirty minutes—"

"And that she must not get on that train," Boubacar added, moving quickly to the driving seat. "I'm driving, Regis. Get in!"

Boubacar pulled out onto the busy highway and swung across the fast lane to a chorus of hooting from angry drivers. I sat rigid, focused only on the screen of my phone and how rapidly the digits progressed.

2.52 PM

Boubacar pulled up to the front entrance of the train station, jumped out, and ran down the escalators two steps at a time.

"I'll park the car," shouted Regis as I stumbled out and hooked my crutches into my arms, looking around for an elevator. As I descended I gasped at the scale of the station: The Johannesburg Park train station was the size of two football fields, with huge metal rafters stretching out above forty-five platforms. The elevator doors opened on hundreds of people moving in every direction. I tried to decipher the signs that directed travelers to the different platforms but it was confusing and I had no idea where to go.

"Please, I have to go to Platform Seventeen. Which way?" I asked a woman passing by.

"You don't look very well, boy—" she said, pointing off to the left.

I threaded my way through the crowds as quickly as I could, using my crutch to clear my passage. I was covered in sweat, and when I looked up I was only at Platform 9.

2.58 PM

I crutched past Platform 15, when I heard the announcement. "The three o'clock train for Cape Town. Departing on Platform Seventeen. Departing now for Cape Town. Platform Seventeen. All aboard." There was still time. I swung the crutches forward, taking bigger and bigger strides, but the next platform had no train beside it. Platform 16. One more to go, and then there was the train, its engines already humming. Boubacar must have made it before me. He must be on board, I thought, as the train slid away from the platform, on its way out of the terminal.

3.01 PM

"No, no," I yelled.

Then I saw Boubacar farther down the platform, running alongside the train as it picked up speed.

"Get on board," I shouted, knowing deep down that he couldn't hear me.

Boubacar glanced back toward me and stopped running. The three o'clock train had left on time and was moving farther and farther away from both of us.

3.03 PM

I fumbled for the phone buzzing in my pocket:

Thurs 4/17/08 3.02pm

I'm on train. I saw Boubacar!!!

31

My father once told me, when the world was still a safe place of bedtime stories, soft baby sisters, and gentle mothers, that before people arose from the Pool of Life, the Great Spirit created the first goddess in human form. This goddess, the Great Mother Mai, was created so that she could make the stars, the sun, and the earth, he had explained as I sat at his feet, a small boy, eager for his stories.

"When she finished her task, the Great Mother Mai was lonely," my father said in his deep, serious voice. "And she wept so many tears that the stars trembled and fell from the sky."

"But how can stars fall from the sky, Baba?" I asked, imagining a black void in the heavens.

"Oh, but they can, Patson, and when they do they can cause great damage," my father replied. "So the Great Spirit commanded the goddess to stop her tears of loneliness, but she replied that she could not stop crying until she had a companion to comfort her. 'Who can I talk to in my lonely hours?' she asked the Great Spirit. 'I have only the barren plains, the silent mountains, and the stupid stars that twinkle foolishly at me,' she wailed. The Great Spirit took pity on Mai and agreed to grant her wish for a companion. 'But what manner of companion will you send me?' she asked. The Great Spirit replied that as she was a female her companion shall be her opposite, and thus be a male. Well, Mai was so happy with this news she grew four immense breasts, each with a sharp pointed nipple of emerald green—"

"Joseph, stop embroidering!" My mother laughed, holding Grace asleep in her arms. "Patson, don't listen to your father. Mai did not grow four breasts, as much as your father might like that to be true."

Like all good storytellers, my father paused to pour his tea, and debate the issue at length with my mother, while I waited at his feet ever so still. When he continued, it wasn't about breasts or nipples but rather about how curious Mai was about the companion promised to her by the Great Spirit.

"Well, being the only woman on earth, the Great Mother Mai was vain and wanted to know if her mysterious companion would be as beautiful as she was. The Great Spirit thought for a while and then said, 'In the boundless reaches of infinity nothing is ugly—nothing is beautiful.'"

I threw myself backward on the floor, and my father laughed at my puzzled expression. "That doesn't make sense, Baba."

"Of course it does, Patson. Remember, all that is created is equal in the eyes of the Great Spirit," he explained. "There is nothing ugly or beautiful. All that the Great Spirit created is good. Do you understand?"

I nodded, in part just to keep the story going, and sat up again.

"Well, the Great Spirit told her that the male would bring her contentment and that together they would bring forth life upon earth," he continued. "'But what will he look like?' Mai asked a second time. 'Will he be as lovely as I?' But the Great Spirit only insisted that she had to be patient.

"Oh, how the Great Mother Mai burned with curiosity, wondering what kind of contentment her companion would bring, and wishing, above all else, that he be as beautiful as she. And so she waited impatiently for the first rays of light," my father said, smiling over at my mother gently shaking her head at him. "As you know, Patson, women can be very impatient with men—"

"Only because men can be so difficult," retorted my mother.

"When Mai thought she could wait no longer, she heard an awful voice call out hoarsely to her. 'Come, oh, my mate, I await thee here,'" my father said in a low, gravelly voice, which made me shiver.

Fever chills dragged me back into the never-ending humming of the taxi's tires on tar, and the bright lights, rattle, and rush of a passing truck. Then foreign words from splintered conversations broke into the story and I heard my name over and over again.

"Patson? Patson, are you all right?"

"Let him sleep, Regis."

"The kid looks bad."

"But he is strong. Two more hours to Bloemfontein. There we fill up, have something to eat, and your shift begins."

"Relax, Boubacar, there is still time. We will be in Cape Town well before the train."

Their words melted into the droning of the engine and I willed my father's voice to return.

"She was so excited, Patson, that with a cry of joy she stretched out her arms to welcome her companion. Then, in a thundering cloud of dust, boulders began to move from beneath the mountainside, and hungry limbs reached out of the ground for her lithe, beautiful form. At first she called to him, 'My mate! My mate, I am here,' but then she grew silent seeing that the limbs that reached for her were not arms anything like her own."

"What was it, Baba? What came out of the mountain?"

"Must you excite the boy so just before he goes to bed, Joseph?" chided my mother, but I knew she listened as eagerly as I did.

"Well now, what do you think it might be, Patson?"

"I don't know, Baba, tell me."

"They were the arms of a creeping vine, whose bark was studded with jagged pieces of granite and diamonds. Those branches had sprung from the top of the biggest baobab tree that had ever grown on earth. And from the middle of the monstrous trunk emerged dozens of bulging, bloodshot eyes, burning with hunger for Mai—"

"Easy, Joseph," warned my mother.

"Beneath the eyes a wicked mouth grinned, and a long green tongue, like the hide of a crocodile, licked its granite lips. 'Come, my beloved, come to me!'" said my father in that same low voice. "Then the tree roared, and its vines drew Mai close. Its diamond-studded mouth bruised her silvery lips with a savage kiss. 'I am the Tree of Life, thy mate, and I desire thee!'"

I screamed in disgust, but my mother laughed. "Joseph, stop it. He'll wake up Grace."

But my father's story was in full flight, and his voice took on the panicked, breathy tones of the goddess. "'No,' cried Mai, 'you are not my mate. You are an ugly, monstrous thing, release me!' But the tree laughed and drew her ever closer. 'You are my heart's desire. I did not catch you only to release you,' he said as more branches held her even tighter to him, until the baobab towered over her and—"

"Okay, Joseph, that's enough," interrupted my mother. "I think Patson knows what happened next."

I looked from my father's twinkling eyes to the blush on my mother's cheeks. "I know, I know! They made *jiggy-jiggy*," I said proudly, and much to the delight of my parents.

"Well, in a manner of speaking, Patson, they did." He laughed. "But when the tree finally released Mai, she fled across the plains and complained bitterly to the Great Spirit about the horrible mate he had given her. 'You have had your wish—now what more do you want?' was his reply."

My mother shook her head, settled Grace on a blanket, and picked up the story, this time cradling me in her arms. She told me how the terrified goddess fled into a valley to get away from the hideous tree, but no matter how far or how fast she fled, the Tree of Life pursued her.

"You see, Patson, the tree was on fire with love. And like any young man," she said, looking at my father, "he had no wish to let his bride return home to her mother."

"Indeed," my father said, chuckling.

"After many years of flight and pursuit, the tree and the goddess plunged into the waters of the great Kariba lake. There Mai streaked through the water like a silvery fish and then soared like an owl into the night sky. Below, her mate lay stuck in mud until a desperate idea pierced his sluggish, wooden brain—"

"Not so sluggish," interrupted my father.

"He searched for a mighty round rock at the bottom of the lake, which he rolled into a ball, and in one lightning movement, with all his branches combined, he hurled it upward at the object of his love, now almost lost to him in the stars," she said.

"Straight and true went the soaring ball," continued my father, "and the goddess, feeling a great blow on her silvery head, plunged back through the stars, the clouds, and the air, limp and unconscious—"

"But to save her," cut in my mother, "the great, ugly tree caught her in his outstretched limbs. 'My dearest beloved,' he crooned, 'I do so love thee.'"

"Meanwhile," said my father, "the great ball that had

bounced off the goddess's head went into orbit and became our own shining moon."

I opened my eyes to see that moon moving rapidly through clouds, and the faraway sound of music from a radio pulled me back into the car. I didn't want to leave my father and mother or the warm embrace of their love. The story was not over yet, but my mouth was dry, and Stumpy was restless.

"Water. Can I have some water?"

A bottle was placed in my hand, and I drank mouthful after mouthful, not caring that some of it spilled down my shirt. It felt cool against my burning chest.

"How much farther?"

Boubacar listed the names of towns we had passed and others yet to come, but all meant nothing to me.

"Who's snoring so loudly?"

"Regis," he said. "We're taking turns driving. We've got the Karroo desert ahead of us, but as soon as we get to Cape Town, you're going to a hospital, Patson."

"But what about Grace? I can't—"

"I will find her."

I reached inside my kitbag and saw that there were no new messages from her, and not enough ointment left to make any difference in Stumpy's mood. I lay back again, searching for the moon racing through the clouds.

And my mother's arms encircled me while my father leaned forward and gently stroked her cheek.

"Then the Great Spirit, in his almighty wisdom, declared the moon the Guardian of Love," said my mother.

"And to this day the moon makes lovers seek each other's arms, and wives the comfort of their children's father," my father added, looking meaningfully into my mother's eyes.

"You see how romantic your father is becoming, little half-and-half," said my mother with a shy smile.

"Stop it, Baba, now you're looking silly," I squealed.

"Time for bed, young man," he said, picking me up and carrying me on his shoulders. "Your mother and I need time alone to work out some of the details of the story that were not fully told."

He laid me down in my bed, running his hand over my head. "One day you will tell this story to your own children, Patson. Think what a fine day that will be. And you must always remember, the story you tell makes you who you are."

32

"How did you get here, Patson?"

Sometimes the simplest questions take the longest time to answer. I had swum away from the place of love and safety, moving steadily back into the throbbing pain that still lived in my leg. My old companion had not left me. As I drifted to the surface of sensation, Stumpy was waiting, sharpening his teeth, as he always did whenever he craved my attention.

The man had a white mask over his face and a funny floral cap on his head. Yet his soft, brown eyes twinkled with good humor.

"It's a long story," I replied.

"And I'd love to hear it," he said, touching me gently. "I'm Dr. David Morris, and we're going to have a good, long look at that leg of yours. There's nothing for you to worry about. You'll be going to sleep for a while, and we'll speak again later. Everything's going to be all right, Patson."

I nodded, looking around at the other people in what had to be an operating room. All wore masks, caps, rubber gloves, and identical gowns, and they seemed alert and very busy. A great disk of light hovered over me, while another masked woman leaned over me.

"I'm Dr. Kaplan, Patson, and I'm going to put you to sleep with this," she said, showing me a plastic cup attached to a machine by a hose. "All I want you to do is breathe deeply, and count to ten."

That seemed easy enough until I forgot what came after six.

"Patson, your mother has come to see you."

It would be nice to see my mother again. I have so much to tell her.

Every day when I came home from school, we would sit at the kitchen table, drinking sweet tea and eating oranges cut into wedges. I would tell her about my lessons, the funny things I said in class, which always made her laugh. That was our best time to talk, and I loved having her completely to myself. Now there are days when I can't remember what she looked like.

"Wake up, Patson, your mother is here."

Floating upward seemed easier now. I remembered the coolness of the sheets, the size of the pillow, and the tall feeling of the bed. The flat Table Mountain of Cape Town. And the best part of it all was that Stumpy was numb, quiet, and still.

"I think he's awake, Mrs. Moyo. Just give him a moment. He's still a bit woozy from the anesthesia. Patson? Your mother is here."

How could my mother be here in this hospital in Cape Town? I opened my eyes, but the bright lights and the sun streaming in through a window forced them shut again.

"Oh, Patson, I'm so glad I found you. I've been looking everywhere for you. I've been so worried."

There was something familiar about that voice. I had heard it before, and it always made me angry. I opened my eyes and the Wife was standing at my bedside.

I swallowed hard, but something was wrong deep in my throat. I was unable to speak and could only stare at her, not believing my own eyes. But it was definitely her, in a tightly fitting sunflower-patterned dress, smiling at me from a perfectly made-up mouth, patting my hand as if it were the paw of some disease-infected animal.

And if the Wife was here, then Commander Jesus must be here too. I pulled my hand away and looked wildly around the room, silently imploring the nurse to do something.

"I'll be back in a minute, Mrs. Moyo. I'm sure you'd like a private moment with your son."

Don't leave, I wanted to scream, this woman is not my mother. But nothing came out of my mouth. I reached for my cell phone, only to realize that I had given it to Boubacar, who must still be looking for Grace. I thrashed around for the call button, but found only the TV remote. The Wife laughed at my feeble attempt. She had already casually swept it off the bed.

"Thank you, Nurse," she said. "Patson and I have so much catching up to do."

As the door closed, her pomegranate smile hardened.

"Where are they, Patson? I know you've got them," she said, opening the small cabinet next to the bed. Helplessly, I watched her rifle through my stuff. "You led us on a goose chase, you little bastard. But did you really think you could get away with them?"

At the sight of her frantically searching for something I no longer had, I realized how much I wanted to laugh. It started as a little bubble in my chest, and became a cough. You may have found me, I thought, but my *girazis* were lost in Marange a long time ago.

The Wife pulled the sheet off me and flung it to the floor. I lay helpless in my hospital gown with the drip in my arm attached to a pole beside my bed. Stumpy was swaddled in thick new bandages, my knee resting over a pillow. The Wife gazed at my leg.

"God, that's disgusting. But for someone with only one leg, you covered a lot of ground, Patson. Now, where are the diamonds?" She ran her hand under my pillow, the corners of my bed, even under Stumpy, before she turned out the drawers of my bedside table.

"I don't know where they are, and I don't care."

"He always gets what he wants, you know?" she said, her red nails ticking out a short message on her cell phone. "He wanted me, and I didn't have much choice in the matter. Not that I'm

351

complaining." She giggled. "You mustn't deny him what he wants, Patson, he can get very angry. You always were very stubborn. Just like your poor father."

With that, she shrugged and moved to look out the window into the parking lot. Moments later, the door opened, and a man backed into the room pulling a wheelchair. He kicked the door closed and rolled it next to my bed.

Commander Jesus smiled down at me.

"I've checked through everything. They're not here," she said.

"Pack it all up," he demanded. "We're taking everything."

Then he turned his full attention to me. "Had I known what you found on my mine, Patson, I would never have let you leave. Such a terrible accident, but all you had to do was bring me the *girazis*, and it would never have happened. If you had followed my rules, you would still have both your legs." He yanked the drip from my arm, nodded to the Wife, and, while she continued stuffing my few things into my kitbag, he placed his hand on my chest and pressed me hard into the bed.

"It's too late now to choose between the *girazis* and your leg. But I wonder what you would have chosen given the chance?"

He stank of sour beer and stale perspiration. I tried to wrestle my way free, but he lifted me off the bed, as if sweeping up a bag of laundry, and threw me into the wheelchair.

"I nearly had you in Musina. I should never have relied on those fools of the South African police force. But they did tell me your sad story, how poor little Gracie had been taken to Cape Town and how your Congolese friend was trying to get you to this hospital."

He grabbed the sheet from the floor and tucked it firmly around my legs, pinning my arms at my sides. He hooked my kitbag over the handle and leaned down close to my ear. "You and I are going to have a man-to-man talk. About mining. You're going to tell me how the *gwejana* syndicate steals my diamonds. And when we're finished talking, you will return the diamonds you stole from me."

"Remember what I told you, Patson," chirped the Wife as we moved toward the door. "You don't want to get him angry."

We left my room and headed down the corridor. If anyone had bothered to look at us, all they would have seen was a happy mother reunited with her son, who was being wheeled out of the hospital by a kind uncle.

33

I don't have them," I croaked, still finding it hard to speak, as Commander Jesus rolled me toward the hospital's front door. "You've been chasing me for nothing. I lost them in Marange a long time ago."

"That's not what Jamu told us," said the Wife.

"Jamu doesn't know anything, you stupid woman."

"What did you call me?"

"Stupid—"

"Did you hear this little brat?"

"Shut up, both of you," hissed Commander Jesus, walking rapidly toward the double glass doors. "You can have your family fight later."

"She is no family of mine," I retorted, feeling power return to my voice and clarity to my brain. Once they had me out of the hospital I would have no chance. I glanced anxiously around, trying to attract someone's attention.

"Stay right where you are," called out a familiar voice. The Wife and Commander Jesus stopped and looked around as Regis, Dr. Morris, and two burly hospital guards surrounded us. "You are not taking that boy anywhere," said Regis.

Commander Jesus's eyes shot toward the exit, as if he might try running for the door. However, outside, a South African police van pulled up with its tires screeching, and two policemen jumped out and dashed up the hospital steps toward us.

"I'm taking my boy home with me right now," blurted the Wife, standing behind me and placing her hands on my shoulders. "You can't stop me. I am Mrs. Moyo, and he is my son and I can prove it."

"Patson is still under my care, Mrs. Moyo, and no one can leave this hospital without properly signing the required release papers," added Dr. Morris calmly.

"I am not your son," I said, shaking her hands off me and trying to rise out of the wheelchair. "My father might have married you, but you were never my mother. You abandoned my family a long time ago." I snatched the crutches away from her, hooked them under my arms, and turned toward Commander Jesus, now full of the courage I needed to face him for the first time. "This is the man who blew off my leg and who killed my father," I said loudly, so that everyone in the room, everyone in the whole hospital for all I cared, could hear me. The two policemen stepped forward, blocking any possible escape. "He is the commander of the Fifth Brigade of the Zimbabwean army who took over the Marange mines and murdered hundreds of miners there. He has been chasing me ever since I left Zimbabwe, because he thinks I have diamonds. Well, all I own in the whole world are these crutches and what's in that bag. If you don't believe me, ask her," I said, and pointed straight at the Wife. "She searched everything in my room, and when she found nothing, they both tried to kidnap me."

But as powerful and angry as I felt, I was still too weak to stand for long. Regis caught me before I hit the floor, and helped me back into the wheelchair. As he rolled me back through the hospital lobby, I glanced over my shoulder to see the Wife arguing with Dr. Morris and a policeman holding her arm. But the best part was seeing the hospital security guards hand Commander Jesus over to the police with their handcuffs at the ready.

"What will happen to him?" I asked Regis.

"The police in Cape Town have their own ways of dealing with men from other countries who attempt a kidnapping from a state hospital."

"But how did they—"

"You mustn't forget that Boubacar is a great soldier. He ordered me to stay here and watch over you. When I saw them taking you from your room, I called the doctor, who called security, who called the police."

"Has he found Grace?"

"Not yet, but he will."

Regis took me back to my room, where the nurse couldn't stop apologizing as she reconnected my drip. "She told me she was your mother, and showed me her passport. I am so sorry, Patson."

"She can be quite convincing. It's not your fault," I said, pulling up the sheets and resting my head against the pillows and closing my eyes while she fussed over me; I wished that she would leave me alone.

"Rest now. We'll talk later," said Regis. "I'll be outside if you need me."

Once I was alone I opened my eyes, and felt the trembling that had started in my hands work its way up my arms. I took a deep breath, exhaled, and reminded myself that I was safe in the hospital. Commander Jesus was no longer chasing me. He'd been arrested, hauled away by the police. I had stood up to him and accused him of the death of my father, and nothing had happened to me. I let out another long, slow breath, and this time instead of fear, I felt relief. I had defeated him. There would be no more running from Commander Jesus.

When I opened my eyes again, Dr. Morris was closing the door behind him. "Well, it's been quite a morning, Patson," he said, placing a metal tray at the side of my bed. "How are you feeling?"

"Okay, I suppose, although my throat's sore, and I get a bit dizzy when I stand up."

"Those are the normal symptoms of the anesthetic wearing off," he said, checking my pulse and temperature. "By tomorrow you'll feel a lot better." And then he smiled as he sat down beside my bed. "I had a long conversation with Mrs. Moyo—"

"She's not my mother," I said abruptly.

"I know that, Patson, but you are still a minor and, legally speaking, she is responsible for you."

"But that's impossible! You don't understand, Doctor," I said, and all the reasons why the Wife was not fit to be my guardian poured out of me. "She abandoned us a long time ago. I don't want to have anything to do with her. I don't want to see her ever again." She danced for Commander Jesus while my father lay in an unmarked grave. I could never forgive her for that. I didn't realize how loud I was getting, until the doctor laid his hand on my arm.

"It's okay, Patson, I understand. Calm down. The hospital's security guards have removed her, and I don't think she'll be coming back. As far as I'm concerned, Boubacar brought you into the hospital, and he can be the one who signs you out. Is that all right?"

"Thank you, Doctor. Thank you so much."

"Now, I need to talk to you about your leg. The operation we performed early this morning is called debridement, and that means we cut away all the damaged tissue and infection around the wound so that it will heal properly. Thankfully, there was no sign of gangrene and I was able to stretch the skin around the wound to make a healthy stump that will hold your future prostheses nicely. You are a strong boy, Patson, and with physiotherapy and, later, regular exercise, I know you'll get your full strength back in your upper leg. How does it feel now?"

"Whatever you did, Doctor, Stumpy has gone all quiet. That horrible pain is gone."

"That's good news, and what I have here may make you

feel even better," he said, picking up the metal tray. "Part of the debridement procedure is to remove any foreign objects embedded in the wound. And as yours was caused by a land mine, it was possible that there were shards of metal, dirt, even pieces of your clothing or shoe still inside. So I did a meticulous cleaning of the wound, and, I have to say, I was quite surprised at what I found. In fact, no one in the operating theater had ever seen anything like it before."

He handed me the tray.

My three *girazis* sparkled up at me. The anger-stone, the rain-stone, and the dream-stone lay shining and bright in the corner of the tray. I picked them up one at a time, amazed to be holding them again. Their familiar size and shape hurtled me back to the mud between my toes, the water around my knees, the sun on my back, and the repeated action of sieving, sieving, and sieving.

"Your diamonds caused quite a stir around the operating table when they came out one after the other from your leg."

The doctor smiled at me, but I was too bewildered to respond. I was back in the photocopying room with Arves holding me down; his granny boiling my *girazis* in her pot; the red-hot iron glowing in the dark. She had hidden the stones in the wound of my leg, the one place she was sure no one would find them.

"You didn't know they were in your leg?"

"No, I didn't," I answered, and let them fall back into the tray.

"I thought so. I knew you were telling the truth in the foyer, Patson. Of course you didn't have the diamonds. They were with me," he said, smiling. "Whoever put them in your wound knew what they were doing."

"It was an old lady. People called her Dr. Muti. She worked with the soldiers in the bush war," I answered, stunned, staring down at the stones I had for so long prized above everything else, stones I believed were lost, and stones that caused me so much trouble. But now my *girazis* had come back to me. I didn't know why or whether I deserved them, but there they were, lying in the corner of the metal tray, each with its own history: the first because of the angry words of Banda, the second dislodged from the bank by a downpour, and the third, the most beautiful one of all, sent to me in a dream by my *shavi*. I remembered the flickering candles, the smell of herbs and burned blood, and the tinkle of diamonds boiling in an oil pot. "All you need is within you, Patson," the old woman had said, and now I understood. She was telling me, even as she was putting those stones inside me, that I would have to rely on something far deeper than anything diamonds could provide.

"Take them away," I said quietly, handing Dr. Morris the tray. "I don't want them. I don't want to see them ever again."

He looked surprised. "These are your stones, Patson. Didn't you find them?"

"Yes, they're my stones. My father and I worked together on Banda Hill until Commander Jesus took over the mine and called it Mai Mujuru. My father was shot by Commander Jesus's soldiers and I found these—" I stopped. My words were all wrong, as if finding the stones had been some sort of compensation for losing my father. "No. That's not what I meant. My father was shot by the soldiers simply because he was a miner. And all I have from my time at Marange are..." I couldn't go on, my voice had turned to stone in my throat.

"Then they do belong to you, Patson."

"But I don't want them," I said. "You take them. Use them for your hospital or something."

Dr. Morris looked down at me and waited. And even as I was wishing he would take them away, I felt the desire to hold them building up inside me again. In that very same instant, I hated them and prized them. I wanted nothing to do with them, but at the same time, I wanted everything they could do for me. I realized I had to make decisions about them, good decisions that would benefit other people and not just myself. Then I understood that owning these stones was a responsibility, and one that I was not yet strong enough to deal with.

"Please, Doctor, take them away."

"Okay, Patson. I will keep them in the hospital safe, and later, together, we can discuss the matter with Boubacar. You trust the man who brought you here?"

"With my life."

"Very well then, but now it's time for you to rest and grow stronger. I'll ask the nurse to give you a mild sedative, and I want you to sleep as much as you can," he said, pressing the nurse's call button. "And no more adventures for you for a while. Okay?"

"Yes, Doctor. And thank you."

"It's my pleasure, Patson. I want to see you up and about. That's all I care about."

The doctor left as the nurse came in to give me the pills. Once I was alone, I closed my eyes and felt my body sinking into the bed. My mind was racing, my thoughts spinning out like a spider's web. I lay there thinking about how I had carried the stones in my leg the whole time, completely unaware of their existence, and the pain they caused me on the journey each time they reasserted their presence. And as I closed my eyes I remembered the last words my father said to me.

Never let the stones become more than you, Patson.

"I won't, Baba. I promise you," I mumbled out loud, remembering again how I had turned my back on my father, pretending to be asleep, on the last night we were together.

Rest now, son. That's the most sensible thing to do in these circumstances. The body needs time to recover. You will be strong again, but first you must rest.

My father's presence in this room was overwhelming: You're right, Baba. You were always right.

34

"Wake up, Patson," Grace whispered into my ear. "You've been sleeping too long, big brother." I felt my eyelids gently prised open, and my sister's face came into focus. For a brief moment, I saw hints of my mother in her eyes and my father in the shape of her cheekbones. It all had the feel of a dream, until her fingers stroked my cheek, and with her warm, soft breath on my face, I knew she was real.

"Grace," I said, smiling at her. "You're here."

I struggled to sit upright, blinked away tears, and embraced my sister, folding her tightly in my arms. We held on to each other, neither one of us wanting to let go. She was my family, my only connection to my parents, and now the most important person in my life.

"Boubacar?" I asked.

And there he was, standing next to Regis at the foot of my bed, grinning at the two of us. "I did not rescue your sister. Mademoiselle Gracie rescued herself," he said, chuckling.

"She did?"

I turned back to Grace, and her eyes sparkled with pleasure and pride. "Don't look so surprised, big brother."

"But what happened? How did you—"

"When I saw Boubacar on the platform in Johannesburg I knew that I would have to get away from Determine by myself," she explained. "So before the train got to Cape Town, when it was late at night, I pretended to be asleep. When I heard Determine's snoring, I went looking for the conductor. I told him what had happened to me and how you and Boubacar had come for me at the station and how we just missed each other. He was a very nice man, and he let me stay in his room for the rest of the journey. I never saw Determine again."

"And when the train arrived at the Cape Town station," added Boubacar, "I was looking everywhere for that scoundrel until I saw a girl in a Girl Guide uniform wearing my tie. And it was Mademoiselle Gracie, getting off the train with the conductor. She ran straight to me, introduced me to her conductor friend, and voilà! Your sister completely organized her own escape."

"And Determine?" I asked. "What was he trying to do with you?"

"He said he had an auntie in Cape Town, and that after the jamboree he would take me to live with her," she answered, rolling her eyes. "He knew you were following me, Patson. After we missed each other at the Johannesburg train station, I told him that Boubacar was after him. He was very frightened of him."

"He had every reason to be," growled Boubacar. "Stupid young man."

"And just as well he ran away," said Regis. "Boubacar would have eaten him for breakfast."

It felt so good to laugh, to laugh with relief and a sense of wonder at these people standing around my bed. And then we were talking, one on top of the other, our words overflowing, sentences interrupted and completed, recounting our separate journeys to Cape Town: I reveled in Grace's exclamations of surprise at how we had crossed the river and run through the game park; Grace explaining how the Doctors Without Borders in Musina had taken Sidi and No Matter from Determine, and how frightened she was to be alone with him; Regis hilariously demonstrating to Grace his role as a fake CIO agent; Grace's troubling account of the unfriendly time she spent in Alexandra township and how she had tried to escape from the shack, but was caught by the old man; Boubacar repeatedly promising to pay every one of Regis's speeding fines that he got between Johannesburg and Cape Town; how Determine thought Grace was playing games on her cell phone; how Boubacar could have jumped on the train, but decided he couldn't leave me behind; Grace bravely walking through carriage after carriage in the middle of the night looking for the conductor; Boubacar aware of my deteriorating condition on the road trip to Cape Town, and how quickly the emergency staff at the hospital whisked me away; Regis describing how I spoke to the Wife and stood up to Commander Jesus on one leg, as steady as a rock, until he caught me.

Grace's hand never left my own as we talked and laughed together. I found myself unwilling to let her out of my sight for a moment, acutely aware of what more I could have lost.

"What are you staring at, big brother?"

"At how much you've grown up in three weeks. The last time I saw you, you were in the sheds surrounded by your toys."

"I never want to go back there. Never," she said, squeezing my hand, a frown forming on her brow.

"That part of our life is over, Grace. We will not be going back to the sheds," I said. "You will never be alone like that again."

She wrapped her arms around me and hugged me tightly. I could feel her body tremble against mine, and when she pulled away she was crying. "You sounded just like Baba then, Patson. All serious and kind."

When you go on a journey you'd like to believe that it will change your life in some way. I could never have known, when I left Bulawayo almost four months ago, how different my life would be now. I had hoped that we would arrive at a place better than the one we had left, but it was not to be. For there was no place on earth that held my father anymore. During the two weeks that I was in the hospital, the finality of my father's death finally hit home. Grace and I spoke about him constantly, recalling for each other all our separate memories of our father. The Shona believe that death is a journey, the success of which depends on the living. My father was on that journey now, and how I lived my life would be all he needed to reach his destination.

But he was not entirely gone from our lives.

One of the first things I did after I left the hospital was to take Grace and Boubacar to the mountain I could see from my hospital bed, to welcome my father back into our lives. We disembarked from the cable car that carried us swiftly over the cliffs to the top of Table Mountain and made our way along one of the many paths that lead to spectacular views of the city and sea below. And though I struggled with my crutches along the uneven path, I was determined not to let my leg be the focus of our day. I found a private place among the rocks that looked out over the gentle curve of Table Bay, and where far beyond the horizon lay the continent of Africa.

"Zimbabwe is in that direction," Boubacar said to me, pointing straight ahead. "A thousand five hundred kilometers from here, due north."

One thousand five hundred kilometers. It was hard to believe that I had traveled so far, but harder still to grasp all that had changed within me. The Patson who had begun his journey in Bulawayo was nothing like the Patson standing on this mountain above Cape Town.

"The food is ready," Grace called, and I marveled at the

confident way she served the bowl of *sadza* and meat stew she had prepared for this occasion, placing it in the center of a small cloth spread neatly over a rock.

In the last few weeks I had begun to appreciate just how much Grace's journey to Cape Town had changed her too. She seldom left my side and we spoke for hours about all that had happened to her on her journey. She told me about the abandoned children she had seen drifting through the Showground at Musina; how in Alexandra township she had felt the hatred the local people had for foreigners; and she admitted to a fear of being alone among strangers. That sparkle I had always taken for granted was gone now, and at night she often had nightmares I could only guess at. Boubacar reminded me that, just as it would take time for me to accept living with one leg, Grace would need her own time to accept all that she had lost as well.

"I didn't know your father had the habit of taking snuff," said Boubacar, handing me the tobacco and sorghum beer that were required for the *bira* ceremony.

"He didn't. These are the ingredients that are always used," I said as I solemnly placed the small packet of tobacco next to the food and then slowly poured the sorghum beer over all of it. The *bira* ceremony was a way the Shona welcomed back into the family the wandering spirit of the deceased. The ritual was always held sometime after the family member had died, to call back the ancestor's spirit to look after the children left behind. We held hands, and I did the best I could to remember the words my father had said so long ago to my mother's spirit.

"We are calling you back, Baba, to be with us. I am asking that you will guide and protect your family. Be kind to us. Remember Grace and me, for we remember you. We welcome you back into our family."

"Come back, Baba, we miss you," Grace whispered.

Then we sat together in silence, enjoying the view, until the solemnity of the moment passed. Boubacar pointed out Signal Hill to us, the place where the cannon went off every day at noon, and Robben Island, where Nelson Mandela had spent twenty-seven years in prison, and to the west the vineyards and faraway mountains of Stellenbosch. We talked about the city below, what it might be like to live here, and how different it was from Zimbabwe.

"Have you decided what you want to do, Patson? About the stones?" Boubacar's question was long overdue. On the day I left the hospital, after saying my good-byes to all the people who had taken such good care of me, I told Boubacar about the diamonds in Dr. Morris's safe and how they got there. It seemed wrong to leave them behind. I had carried them for so long they were a part of me now, and only I could take responsibility for them. I had given them to Boubacar for safekeeping, knowing that sooner or later, I would have to make a decision about them.

"Phone the Baron," I said finally. "Tell him I'm honoring our agreement. And that I have something special I want to sell."

◆ ◆ ◆

Moyo Home

Sea Point, Cape Town

5 December

Dear Baba and Amai,

My beloved parents, Joseph and Shingai Moyo,

I never understood the meaning of the
dream I had the night you came to me,
Amai. I don't know if dreams are meant
to be significant or even if one should pay
them any attention. I think perhaps they
are there to help you work out all your
thoughts of the day, or maybe they are
meant to be puzzles from the ancestors
that we are challenged to solve.

So this is how I have understood the dream
I had on my last night on the diamond
fields: The Y-shaped stick was a symbol of
me; the curling vines had to be you, Baba.
Together the goddess and baobab tree were

watching over me, your son, your creation. You both wanted a future for me that gleamed like a skyscraper soaring through the clouds.

"This is all for you," you had said, Amai, when you showed me the entrance to the many brightly lit rooms.

And so, after talking with Boubacar and Grace about the diamonds, and what they meant and what we should do with them, we decided that they were gifts from you. Look to Grace, you told me, and if I hadn't come to find her in Cape Town, Dr. Morris would never have found the stones. So I decided to walk through the doors of that skyscraper to explore all that life might bring me. The girazis may help me a lot, but only I can build the skyscraper of my life. And I promise you, Baba, I will not allow them to drive me into any tree.

The Baron came to Cape Town, inspected the stones with his loupe, and a few weeks later I became a very wealthy young man. Then a lot of things started happening all at once. I got two new prostheses, one very much like

the one Innocent showed me and the other
for general use. I'm still struggling with
my physio but I'm getting stronger and Dr.
Morris is pleased with my progress.

Boubacar has found a job as a bank
security officer, and the three of us have
moved into a flat in Sea Point overlooking
the Atlantic Ocean. Every day I exercise
along the promenade with the taste of the
sea in my mouth. Grace goes to St. Cyprian's
School for Girls and loves being in class
again. I was accepted to a school called
Bishops, and I have a whole term under my
belt. And Baba, you would approve of how
strict my teachers are.

Everything that happened in Marange is
behind us now. There's no point in going back
there. I feel sad about what is happening
in Zimbabwe, and on some days when I get a
bit homesick I feel I have lost my country
too. Who knows? Maybe one day I'll go back.

There was one thing that took me a long
time to do. I had to work up a lot of
courage before I was able to phone Sheena.
I told her the truth. About everything.

It was a long phone call, and by the end
we were laughing and I invited her and
her family to come to Cape Town for the
December holidays. I hope they come.

And so I have told you everything now,
Baba, and the story I've told is who I am
today. But when I finally came to this
page—the very last page of the diary you
gave me back in the tobacco shed—I found
a message, words scribbled in the bottom
right-hand corner, waiting for me to find
them. It seems only right that they be the
final words of my story:

Yah, Half Prince, I know you are going to make
it. Even though it looks bad now, you're going to be all
right. Did I ever lie to you? No, so believe, Patson!
And it will be good again, because the Geez are in
the Knees. That's all I'm saying and somebody as
"bright" as you should know what I'm talking about.
You're my best friend, Patson, always will be, till the
day I die. ARVES!

AUTHOR'S NOTE

This novel was written because of a red letter I received from Madolyn (yes, a real letter, on red paper, in a stamped envelope), sent all the way to Cape Town from a school in New Hampshire, USA. Madolyn had read *Now Is the Time for Running* and wanted to know more about the world I created in that novel, and asked me to write another book.

When I told Pam Gruber, my editor and publisher at Little, Brown, about Madolyn's letter and how it inspired me, she suggested that I write a companion piece to *Now Is the Time for Running*. I had never done this before, so, looking for a way in, I returned to the story of Deo and Innocent and rediscovered Patson. He was the one-legged boy who played soccer with Deo and joined them as they crossed the Limpopo River and the game park into South Africa. I couldn't remember why I wrote Patson into that novel, and I had no idea where he came from or what happened to him after he was arrested by the police. He just disappeared from the story. I do remember, however, once seeing a group of one-legged boys playing soccer, and thinking how brave they were and how difficult that must be.

In researching how Patson might have lost his leg, I discovered the Marange diamond fields in Zimbabwe, and learned that the army's Operation No Return happened at the same time as Deo and Innocent's odyssey to South Africa. After reading more about what happened in Marange, how families from all over Zimbabwe traveled to the diamond fields to find their fortunes, I realized I had found my companion story. (I also read how miners would cut their bodies with razor blades and hide small diamonds in their wounds to get them off the mines.)

In *Diamond Boy* I have brought back to life some of the characters from *Now Is the Time for Running* and discovered what Innocent contributed to Patson's journey.

So, dear reader, *Diamond Boy* exists because someone like you wrote me a letter. I hope that reading this novel will inspire not only your interest in what is happening in southern Africa, but also that a similar interest in something you read may someday inspire another author. And if you see a little of yourself in Patson's story, then that's what this reading and writing thing is all about. Thank you, Madolyn.

Michael Williams
November 2014

THE DIAMOND FIELDS OF MARANGE

"The discovery of significant alluvial diamond
deposits in the Marange area of eastern
Zimbabwe [Manicaland Province] in June 2006
should have been a means of salvation for the
virtually bankrupt country after ten years of
chaos that saw world record inflation and the
nation brought to its knees. Instead, it has led to
greed, corruption and exploitation on a grand
scale, the use of forced labour—both adults and
children—horrifying human rights abuses, brutal
killings, degradation of the environment and the
massive enrichment of a select few."*

Soon after diamonds were discovered, the ZANU-PF government declared the fields open to everyone, and so began the
Great Marange Diamond Rush. Tens of thousands of teachers,
nurses, bus drivers, goat herders, schoolchildren, and street kids
converged on eastern Zimbabwe between 2007 and 2008 to dig

---

* *The Marange Diamond Fields of Zimbabwe: An Overview*, Sokwanele
(October 2011): 6, http://www.sokwanele.com/node/2340.

for diamonds. Many of them hid in the bush during the day and burrowed under fences at night, and from dusk to dawn all of them sifted the dirt for the precious stone that might change their lives forever.

The news of the diamond rush spread around the world, and soon buyers from Belgium, Lebanon, Israel, Botswana, South Africa, and China descended on the town of Mutare. They hid in hotels and guesthouses, since, as foreigners, they were easily spotted by undercover intelligence agents. And once the country's Reserve Bank governor admitted that Zimbabwe had lost, in only nine months' time, four hundred million US dollars' worth of diamonds smuggled out of Marange, the soldiers and secret policemen were sent in to make arrests. "We must protect the nation's riches from crooks and scoundrels," one minister said.

The government launched a nationwide police operation, End to Illegal Panning, aimed at stopping the illegal mining and trade in diamonds. During the operation, police deployed some six hundred police officers, arrested about nine thousand persons in Marange, and seized gems and minerals with an estimated total value of seventy million US dollars. For the next two years, police committed numerous human rights abuses, including killings, torture, beatings, and harassment.

At the peak of the scramble for diamonds in October 2008, more than thirty-five thousand people from Zimbabwe, South Africa, Botswana, the Democratic Republic of Congo, Mozambique, Equatorial Guinea, Nigeria, Lebanon, Pakistan, the United Arab Emirates, Belgium, and India were either miners in the fields or buyers in Marange.

With the government teetering on the brink of bankruptcy, Operation No Return was launched, using the Zimbabwe National Army, Air Force, and Central Intelligence Organisation, in an attempt to both restore a degree of order and allow key army units access to the Marange riches. The attack, in daylight, was carried out by the Joint Operational Command, the country's top military commanders, using tanks, bulldozers, and helicopters to mow down the miners who ran for cover in the hills. Soldiers opened fire on defenseless miners, dogs were set loose to maul them, and some had their stomachs cut open by soldiers searching for stones. At the end of Operation No Return between two hundred and four hundred people had been killed, many of them teenagers.

Today, the diamond fields are run by the government of Robert Mugabe. In March 2013 it was reported that a 2.5-million-carat stockpile, valued at five hundred million dollars, had mysteriously disappeared before making it into the Zimbabwean treasury.

LAND MINES

One of the most deadly legacies of the twentieth century has been the use of land mines in warfare, and I was shocked to discover that the Zimbabwean army used these antipersonnel land mines to keep miners from running away from the Marange mines.

Antipersonnel land mines continue to have tragic, unintended consequences, even years after wars that employ them have ended. As time passes, their locations are often forgotten, even by those who planted them. These mines can lie dormant for decades, causing further damage, injury, and death to anyone who inadvertently steps on one.

According to One World International, there are currently more than one hundred million land mines located in seventy countries around the world. Since 1975, land mines have killed or maimed more than one million people, which has led to a worldwide effort to ban their further use and clear away existing minefields.

GLOSSARY

amai   mother

baba   father

Chimurenga   a Shona word roughly meaning "revolutionary struggle." Chimurenga songs were songs sung during the war of liberation in Zimbabwe.

CIO   Central Intelligence Organisation in Zimbabwe

ganja   slang for marijuana, which comes from the Cannabis plant intended for use as a psychoactive drug and as medicine

Ghuma -ghuma   criminal gang that preys on refugees

girazi   miners' slang for pure diamond stone

gwejana   miners' slang for child miners

madala   old man, elder

magogo/gogo   affectionate term for grandmother

MDC	Movement for Democratic Change, opposition party in Zimbabwe
muti	a term for traditional medicine, usually homeopathic, in southern Africa
Mxit	a free instant messaging application in southern Africa that runs on multiple mobile and computing platforms
ngoda	miners' slang for small, industrial diamonds
sadza	mush made from meal produced by grinding corn
sangoma	traditional healer and respected elder
shavi	ancestral spirit

ACKNOWLEDGMENTS

The writing of such a novel is possible only because of the generosity of the following people who have been willing to share with me their knowledge and skills: the witty encouragement and wholehearted support from my agent, Wendy Schmalz; the insightful commentary and literary skills of Pam Gruber, who guided me so adeptly through the editing process; my brother-in-law Dr. Marius Swart, who provided me with all the necessary medical information regarding debridement and wound care; my Zimbabwean reader, Ruvi Mubika, who ensured that all my details of Zimbabwean life were plausible and accurate; my teenage daughters and niece, Ellen-Anne, Emma, and Camilla, who taught me how to Mxit and helped me write the text messages; Miranda Madikane for giving me access to her lovely, helpful staff at the Scalabrini Centre for refugees in Cape Town; my oldest friend and critic, Amy Kaplan, for her unique ability to turn my straw prose into gold and to provide emergency support at all hours of the day; my wife, Ettie, for her words of wisdom and infinite patience with me, and the uncanny ability she has of knowing exactly what I'm trying to say when I don't.

I would also like to acknowledge the vision of seer Credo

Mutwa, for his retelling of the great Ndebele story "The Tree of Life and the Goddess," and ask his indulgence for the liberties I took with this old story. And finally I'd like to thank Madolyn Bouchard, from North Hampton School in New Hampshire, who wrote me the letter that inspired the writing of this novel.

ABOUT THE AUTHOR

Michael Williams is a writer of plays, musicals, operas and novels, and is the Managing Director of Cape Town Opera in South Africa. He is the author of several books, including *Now Is the Time for Running*, which won the 2014 UKLA Award.

ALSO BY MICHAEL WILLIAMS

On the dusty fields of Zimbabwe, Deo and Innocent are playing football. Then the soldiers arrive, looking for food and traitors – destroying the only home the boys have ever known. Now they have nothing but each other and a football stuffed with a billion worthless dollars. And so starts the journey of a lifetime, to find safety with a father they have never met. But with soldiers everywhere, they have only one chance to cross the border, one chance to escape.

Now is the time for courage.
Now is the time for running.

Winner of the 2014 UKLA Award